THE RED BIRD ALL-INDIAN TRAVELING BAND

THE RED BIRD ALL-INDIAN TRAVELING BAND

FRANCES WASHBURN

THE UNIVERSITY OF
ARIZONA PRESS

TUCSON

The University of Arizona Press
© 2014 The Arizona Board of Regents
All rights reserved

www.uapress.arizona.edu

Library of Congress Cataloging-in-Publication Data
Washburn, Frances.
The Red Bird All-Indian traveling band / Frances Washburn.
pages cm. — (Sun tracks ; v. 77) (An American Indian Literary series)
ISBN 978-0-8165-3082-3 (pbk. : alk. paper)
1. Country musicians—Fiction. 2. Indians of North America—Fiction. I. Title.
PS3623.A8673R43 2014
813'.6—dc23

                              2013034407

Publication of this book is made possible in part by the proceeds of a permanent endowment created with the assistance of a Challenge Grant from the National Endowment for the
Humanities, a federal agency.

19   18   17   16   15   14   6   5   4   3   2   1

For Misun, Billy Stratton, who listened to me tell some odd, crazy stories and said, "You should turn those into a novel." And so I have. Thank you, Soup.

THE RED BIRD ALL-INDIAN TRAVELING BAND

CHAPTER ONE

SISSY

Nobody ever sees me the way I see myself, but only the way that each person thinks I am. I met a guy from another town where a former classmate of mine had gotten a job. He'd asked her if she knew me, and what she thought of me. You know what the woman said? She said I was the smartest girl in high school and the wildest. Neither is true. People project their own weaknesses—or strengths—onto me because everyone talks to me about everything.

They tell me bad things that I don't want to know, the meannesses they've done, the evil thoughts they've had, the times when they've lain awake at night afraid that someone will find out, things they wouldn't even confess to their priest. They never realize that once they have told me, then someone knows the terrible things they did or thought. Usually, they are drunk when they tell me, but sometimes not. They give away power to me, power to harm or to help.

It's a curse I have, to be the listener, a curse that runs in our family. My mother has dozens of friends even though she is something of a recluse who rarely leaves the house except for once a year when she and my father travel to Nebraska for a few weeks to visit relatives. My dad does the grocery shopping and runs the errands that need doing while my mother stays home, cooking, cleaning, taking care of the yard, writing the checks to pay the bills. Even though there is something odd about my mother, some unformed, unnamed anxiety about being out in public here in Jackson, my dad loves her anyway. But she doesn't have to leave the house to hear about people's problems. They come to her with their troubles. She never gives advice, but they all leave apparently feeling better about whatever it was bothering them. I suspect that I've inherited this dubious gift. I tried to get out of it. I tried telling people I didn't want to hear whatever it was they felt so desperate to tell me. Like my mother, I am a human wailing wall. It would be better if they just stuck written confessions and prayers on me. Then I could burn them without ever knowing who did what to whom and why.

Now this gift or this curse has gotten me into troubles of my own, because there is an important man who thinks I know something that I don't. Someone, or several someones, have told him that everyone tells me their troubles, even more than they tell my mother, but no one so far has confessed to me that they killed Buffalo Ames at the Scenic Fourth of July Rodeo when I was singing there in the Longhorn Bar with the Red Bird All-Indian Traveling Band.

Chapter Two

THE SCENIC FOURTH OF JULY RODEO AND DANCE

Friday, July 4, 1969

Heat waves flickered across the road that became the wide, dusty main street of Scenic as the two-car convoy crossed the east–west railroad tracks driving north to Harley and Annie Ferrill's Longhorn Bar at the northern end of what Scenic called its town. Sissy rode shotgun with Clayton Red Bird driving his old Chevy Impala, the backseat crammed with guitars, a bass, microphones, leads, and all the other paraphernalia that they needed to play the gig in the Longhorn after the rodeo. Except for the big amps and Melvin's drum kit, which were in the back of Melvin's new Ford pickup behind them, padded with old raggedy blankets and tarped over against the dirt and dust and the impossibility of rain that might come through the leaky pickup camper shell. Sissy's cousin Sonny rode shotgun for Melvin, but instead of a gun, he held a can of Bud between his knees while he popped another for Melvin. Clayton disapproved. Sissy watched his face souring up as he glanced at them in his rearview mirror.

"You'd think a man like Sonny, just a few months out of seminary, wouldn't be a drunk," Clayton said.

"I don't think he should ever have been in the seminary in the first place," Sissy said. "They probably kicked him out for drinking. Whichever it is, he isn't studying for the priesthood anymore, and isn't a priest now."

"Can't you do something with him?" Clayton asked.

"I'm his cousin, not his keeper, Clayton. We've been around this pole before."

When Clayton stopped the car, Sissy jumped out to move the sawhorses that Harley had put out to reserve parking spaces for the band in front of the bar, and Melvin and Clayton backed up to the crumbling concrete steps of the Longhorn to unload the equipment. The bar and the entire town, such as it was, were already doing a brisk business to judge by the number of vehicles parked on both sides of the street and lining the two hundred yards of road out to the rodeo grounds on the north side of the Longhorn. The little faded yellow café across the street had a crush of people waiting to get in, and would have been an impossible place to expect a meal if it hadn't been that most people had brought a lunch, which they had spread out on the concrete picnic tables just north of the café. Tilted flat tin roofs over each table provided the only shade from the brassy sun hanging in mid-sky.

Vehicles full of people kept coming in from all directions on the graveled roads, mostly old beat-up pickups and cars barely held together with bubble gum and baling wire. The band members had seen several vehicles with these failed home fixes sitting alongside the road cross-country on their way up across the reservation to Scenic. Most of them had been burned. They say that the life of a stalled car on the rez is less than half an hour.

To the west, the purple teeth of the Black Hills bit the horizon, pointing at the sky, pale blue with heat. To the south, from which direction the Red Birds had driven, the Badlands simmered, a maze of shattered and upthrust limestone weathered into fantastical shapes named things like The Devil's Frying Pan, The Devil's Kitchen, or The Gates of Hell. People spoke the names as if they were capitalized like that. Farther south on the other side of the Badlands, Yellow Bear Canyon split a giant crack in the prairie, a cool haven in the blistering heat with the Cheyenne River running through it in late spring, but now a narrow sluggish stream. Low, grassy hills rolled away to the east for miles, dotted in rare places with a tiny village or town where the only businesses were the bars and gas stations and the occasional café where you took your chances on whether or not you'd get a hamburger with everything or a hamburger with everything including ptomaine. North ran more hills all the way across the rest of the state and the next state of North Dakota to the Canadian border from where the blizzards came down in the winter with nothing to hinder them but a barbed-wire fence. No such luck on this day that was already approaching a hundred degrees.

Packs of kids ran up and down the dusty street shouting and taunting each other and flinging firecrackers. The young boys had traded in their traditional Indian ponies of the past for cars, tricked out with loud mufflers and fancy paint that did not improve upon their clunker status. Old ladies sat at the picnic tables making faces at the kids, and tut-tutting most likely, if you could hear them over the noise, which you couldn't. Men gathered in clumps outside the overhanging canopy of the café across the street and in front of the Sheep Mountain Hotel on the west side of the street and south of the Longhorn, some tilting cans of beer or paper bags with a bottle inside, smoking and joking, while they waited for their womenfolk to get the food set out on the picnic tables on tailgates of pickups or underneath the tents that a few people had pitched in the sweltering heat and dust.

The bar itself looked more like it belonged in the Southwest than on the prairie. It was flat-roofed, a disadvantage for heavy winter snowfall, white stucco on the outside and covered with neatly lettered signs like *No Indians or Dogs Allowed*. That was a joke because very few people other than Indians ever came here. Other letters written in the Lakota language were more welcoming. *Pilamaya. Hoka hey*. Harley and his wife were White folks who spoke a little Lakota, but the painted words didn't make much sense, as if they had just wrote all the Indian words they knew on the side of building, or rather, their son Vincent had. He was a parolee from the state pen, in for aggravated assault and grand theft, and not supposed to go near a bar, but he had no place else to go, or so Harley had argued to the state parole board and won. As long as Vincent was out in the sticks, there wasn't much harm he could do, they thought. The signs were Vincent's handiwork, art being some of the therapy he had enjoyed in prison.

Melvin pushed past Sissy, carrying a drum in front of him that made his already big belly look twice-sized. Sweat dripped from his nose onto the Japanese Indian blanket that wrapped the drum. Sonny held the door open, leaning against it, legs crossed at the ankle, a beer in his left hand with the pinkie finger extended at a socially correct angle.

Clayton gave him a look as he passed with an armload of equipment.

Sonny smiled, showing most of the white teeth he possessed.

"Do you deliberately like to piss him off?" Sissy asked.

Sonny turned his big eyes on her. With his glasses on his big nose and his skinny frame, he looked like Jiminy Cricket. Or Mr. Peanut.

"Nope. I just like my beer. If Clayton didn't want me to start on the beer so early, he shouldn't have told us to show up eight hours before we have to play."

"I think the idea was that if he made the band show up eight hours early, he could be sure you showed up," Sissy said.

Sonny reached out and touched the ironed-in crease on her yellow-checked shirtsleeve, gasped, and flipped his hand about.

"That crease is so sharp, you can cut yourself," he said. "You got a wife to iron your shirts?"

"Shut up," she said. "I am the wife."

"Oh-ho! You're so mean you couldn't even get a woman to partner up with you."

"I only swing one way, cousin. Unlike people who are so desperate they can't even get their own gender to pay attention to them, so they have to find a captive population in a seminary."

Sonny made his eyes even bigger behind his glasses and gasped again with his hand over his mouth.

Sissy stepped up into the bar and sank into six inches of fresh sawdust on the floor, stepping back into the make-believe nineteenth century of old Western movies. The place smelled like cedar chips, stale beer, and cigarette smoke. A long and low-ceilinged room, the bar stretched all along the right side, booths on the left, while a single row of tables with cheap Japanese Indian blankets stapled on for tablecloths occupied the middle space in between the posts that supported the ceiling. Far in the back on an elevated bandstand in the corner behind the dance floor, Melvin and Clayton were setting up the instruments. A door on the opposite side of the room from the bandstand was labeled "Ladies." Another door in the back wall was labeled not "Gentlemen" but just "Men." Only the ladies room door really opened into a bathroom. The other door led out into the back alley. Sissy had discovered that a couple of years before, the first time the Red Birds had played the Longhorn, when she saw Annie Ferrill going in and out of that door and wondered what that was about. In a bold moment not unlike her, she had opened that door and seen, not a filthy broken tiled floor, pissy urinal, or rust-stained toilet, but the stars and the smell of dusty sagebrush blowing in the breeze. The Ferrills' house was just across the alley, so Annie was going back and forth to check on her supper she had slow cooking in the oven, in between helping Harley tend bar. The sign was Harley's doing.

The usual array of liquor bottles lined the back bar, arranged in stepped tiers in front of a plate-glass mirror that distorted the viewer's image like in a carnival fun house. Hand-tooled leather purses and beaded moccasins in clear plastic bags hung from hooks above the mirror, their attached price tags with large handwritten numbers big enough for a drunk to read—more products of Vincent's rehabilitation program in prison—and on a shelf at the far end stood a stuffed calf with two heads. Harley said it had been born on his own ranch a few years earlier, but Sissy suspected it was a fake, a conversation piece of his own taxidermy. A collection of business cards and odd pieces of paper with names and phone numbers written on them were adhered with yellow tape to the mirror. Racks of potato chips, jars of pickled eggs, beef jerky, and Penrose pickled sausages stood on one end of the bar, and evenly spaced along the bar were tin ashtrays that were sometimes emptied but never washed. The bar top was wood, polished by the elbows and hands of ordinary working men, of women like Annie, worn out too soon or soon to be worn out with helping men who had no luck, who were pitiful and weak and sometimes violent. Like Vincent. Or worse. Each of the supporting posts up the middle of the room boasted tacked-on notices that offered employment for someone to buck hay bales, or horses for sale, cattle for sale, notices of lost or strayed livestock (posted by the owners because no one who ever had a free animal wander into his place would ever admit to it. Finders keepers). On one of the posts was a rack with little plastic bags full of cockleburs. The tags on the bags proclaimed: *Genuine Porcupine Eggs, $3.00.* Sissy knew no one from around here would ever buy them, and so did Harley Ferrill. It was another one of his jokes.

There he stood behind the bar polishing glasses with the tail of his dirty white apron, a short rotund man, fluffy white hair topping his pleasant round pink face. The stools at the bar were occupied mostly by men—old men, young men, fancy dressed men, or men in clean but worn clothes, talking about the rodeo, about who had won the roping events that had taken place that morning and who would win the rough stock–riding events that would start in a couple of hours. The consensus for the bull riding winner was Pete Broussard, maybe because Pete had his fat ass sitting on a stool at one end of the bar, and Pete was known to be quarrelsome if he was crossed. For a fat man, he was quick with his mouth and his fists. His older brother, Howard, a more peaceable sort of man and a lot better looking, sat at the other end, so if anyone talked against Pete's chances, Howard would hear about it. A couple of women stood at the bar, too, but most of them sat in booths or at the tables, a few with their husbands or boyfriends sitting sullenly beside them when they would much rather be batting the breeze with the boys at the bar.

Howard's girlfriend, Viola Bianco, sat by herself at a table in the middle, a white initial-embroidered handkerchief wrapped around her sweating beer can. She didn't have to extend her pinkie finger to demonstrate her class; everyone knew it. Her father was a big-shot local doctor down in Jackson, and Viola was a clerk at the local clinic who did no work and didn't have to. It was said that she threw a fit when her parents moved the family from New York or some big eastern city out here to what she referred to as the armpit of the world, but Viola didn't have much earning capacity of her own so she came along. Besides, she had an illegitimate three-year-old boy that her mother held hostage. If Viola wanted mama to keep care of the kid, Viola had to move to Jackson, too. There were questions about why Dr. Bianco himself would come out to the sticks, and rumors about that, too, but nobody ever figured out any answers.

Viola looked up and nodded as Sissy walked past. They weren't friends, but never snubbed each other either. It was obvious to Sissy why Viola had picked Howard Broussard. He might be an Indian, but he was good-looking and, along with Pete and their parents, owned the biggest, most prosperous ranch for miles around. At thirty, Howard had been close to being a confirmed bachelor, but he was unlikely to escape Viola. Or her father.

And then Sissy saw Zooey Broussard, Pete's wife. She was pretty in an overripe way, if you ignored the side of her face with the puckered knife scar that ran from the base of her left nostril up to the outer corner of her eye where the scar tissue pulled the lid down slightly. She sat there with the bad girls of the rez, the ones who had illegitimate kids and no rich daddy and mama to pay the bills, girls who showed up at every rodeo, pow wow, and dance anywhere near the rez. They were probably all younger than thirty, but they looked aged and weather-beaten, and the makeup and cheap-but-new Kmart clothes didn't take off any years. Zooey had been a couple of years ahead of Sissy at Jackson High School. She married Pete Broussard the weekend after high school graduation. Everyone thought she was pregnant, but no baby ever hatched out. Gossipers said that Zooey couldn't have kids but had tricked Pete into marrying her with the "I'm pregnant" story. Pete was truly, deeply in love with Zooey, but she didn't return the favor, one of those be-careful-what-you-wish-for situations. Before she ever married Pete, Zooey had a reputation for drinking and fighting, even as a high school student, and everyone in Jackson said she should have been sent to Plankington, the state reform school. Of course that was parents' favorite threat to misbehaving teenagers. Straighten up or you'll end up in Plankington. Sissy never knew anyone who got sent to Plankington. Besides, she thought that was the boy's reformatory. She wasn't sure there was one for girls. She kept on Zooey's good side by keeping away from her, but she had a few high school friends who hadn't sense enough to do the same and had gotten beat up by Zooey for nothing or little of nothing. That was all five years ago.

Sissy wanted to go to college, but she never could figure out how to pay for it, so she waitressed at Martha's Café in Jackson, lived with her parents, and played music with Clayton Red Bird's band almost every Saturday night. Clayton's older son, Tom, begotten of a teenage marriage, had been one of Sonny's friends, but he had been killed in a car wreck some years back. Sissy used to hang out over at the Red Birds' house, and one day when Clayton had his guitar out, Sissy started singing. Clayton had liked what he heard. Sissy's parents wouldn't let her sing with the band in public until she was eighteen, but that was a few years ago. Singing was the only thing that kept her sane. Or the only thing that kept her insane, if you listened to her dad's point of view.

"Sissy! Sissy!" Clayton hollered and beckoned.

Zooey squinted her blackberry eyes and stared at Sissy when she walked past. Sissy wasn't going to the ladies room by herself that night.

The one person Sissy wanted to see, Gordon Charbonneau, wasn't there, or at least not yet. He was a friend of the Broussard brothers, a neighbor whose family had a ranch too, but never as prosperous as the Broussards'. He was some years older than Sissy, well past thirty, tall and thin with the kind of Indian good looks that you see in pictures on the backs of matchbooks with an invitation: "Draw Me." He hadn't been back on the rez long. Sissy hadn't known him before he came back, but the first time she saw him when she was on duty in the café, she had asked an older waitress, "Lynda, who is *that*?"

Lynda had grimaced.

"Bad news," she said.

"Anybody who looks like that has to have some good news," Sissy said.

"Not him," Lynda had said as she stacked plates of the lunch special up her arm.

Sissy waited until Lynda had delivered the order she was carrying and demanded more information.

"If you must know, his name is Gordon Charbonneau—you know the family, up around Porcupine. He got in trouble with drinking and carousing as a kid and got kicked out of school. His parents sent him back east before he could mess up too bad. I don't know what he did for a living, but he got in some accident that like to have killed him, and now he's back here living with his family again."

"So," Sissy said. "People can change."

Lynda shook her head as she wrung a dishcloth out of the soapy bleach water tub and started to wipe down the counter.

"He spends most Saturday nights in the American Legion Club bar, and the rumors are he doesn't do anything else. Besides, I hear he has a White wife back east and a kid."

The Red Birds never played the Legion Club. Maybe something about the name of the band—Red Bird All-Indian Traveling Band—turned off the White people who managed the place. But Sissy looked for Gordon Charbonneau wherever they played and saw him a couple of times. If he came, he sat with the Broussard brothers or by himself. Sissy never saw him falling-down drunk or out of line, even though his walk was a little off. His right leg was stiff, and when she looked closer, she saw the silver glint of a brace clamped beneath his boot sole and extending up under his pants leg.

Now, as she walked back to help with the band setup, Annie came in through the Men's Room door hand-in-hand with Julius Caesar, who promptly grabbed a handful of sawdust and threw it at Sissy with a chittering laugh. Julius Caesar was a monkey that a friend of Harley's couldn't manage anymore, and Harley and Annie had taken the beast in. Because monkeys were nonexistent in South Dakota except in zoos, Harley thought Julius might be a good customer draw. Letting go of Annie's hand, Julius ran to the bar, climbed a customer who squirmed and fought the unseen foe. On the bar top, Julius skittered from one end to the other, bumping into drinks and bottles of beer, slopping them over and scattering ashtrays while Harley slapped at him with his apron, yelling until Julius made a flying leap into Harley's arms. The customers laughed nervously.

"He's just a big old baby," Harley said. "Show him your tricks, Julius." He sat the monkey down on the bar top. The nearest customers leaned away.

"Julius. Julius Caesar! Take your picture, Julius?" Harley mimed holding a camera to his face. The monkey turned around and mooned him, turned the other way and mooned the customer whose body he had just ascended to get on the bar. The other customers laughed. Julius ran the length of the bar, grabbing a bag of potato chips from the rack as he passed. He climbed up and sat on the shelf next to the two-headed calf, ripped open the bag, scattering chips and munching the remaining ones with his mouth open, dropping crumbs.

"See?" Harley said, spreading his arms expansively. "Wouldn't harm a flea."

Annie shook her head. The customers watched the monkey warily.

When the instrument setup was done, Sissy rode with Clayton down to the rodeo arena where the rough riding was about to start. There wasn't any grandstand or bleachers to sit in; people parked their cars around the perimeter of the arena, an area about 150 yards long by 100 yards wide with the chutes and pens for the stock at the north end. People had backed their pickups in so they could sit on the tailgate, usually with an improvised shade of a blanket or a tarp. Most everyone had a beer in hand or a bottle in a bag, a handkerchief or a shirttail out to mop sweat and bat the flies that the livestock shit attracted. The fence around the arena was a six-foot-tall mesh of heavy-duty wire squares, but Sissy wondered if that would really hold a pissed-off bull. Clayton had to park at the south end because all the good spots along the long sides were already taken. Someone had put up a shade roof on the west side of the arena, where it would protect people from the afternoon sun, but it only had room for fifty or so people, and they were packed in under there so close Sissy didn't think there was enough room to sweat. Dust kicked up by the feet of horses and men in the arena wafted out over the spectators and the cars in a fine golden flour. Sonny, Sissy, and Clayton perched on the rear bumper of Clayton's car.

Sonny sneezed, wiped the dust from his beer can. He tilted it back for a long swallow, gave a big toothy grin.

"Nectar of the gods," he said.

"Future urine of the subhumans," Sissy said, taking a swallow of her own beer.

Sonny sat his beer down in the dust at his feet, reached into his pocket, and pulled out his cigarettes and lighter.

Squinting through the smoke, he said, "Sissy, why do you always have to be so negative? Don't you believe in celebrating life's small fine moments?"

"Yeah. Sure. When there are small fine moments. Of which, this ain't one."

"Ah, come on. When you are an old lady you'll be telling your grandkids about the time you went to the Scenic Fourth of July Rodeo and got to sit next to me *and* play in the band with me."

"Sonny, shut up," Clayton said. "You're getting on my nerves." He got up and walked over to Melvin's pickup parked next to his own car, sat down with a grunt on the mashed-down grass.

Sonny made big eyes behind his glasses and was about to say something else, but he stopped, looking over Sissy's shoulder and pointing with lifted chin and pursed lips.

She turned and looked.

Zooey walked between the cars and the arena fence carrying a bottle of beer by the neck, her black hair shining with blue highlights in the sun in spite of the dust in the air. As she passed each car, the men's eyes turned to follow her as if there were strings attaching their eyeballs to her butt. She didn't have to prove anything, but she kept trying anyway.

As she came even with Clayton's car, Sonny nodded at her and said, "Hey, Zooey. How's it going?"

She looked at him and smiled, showing small white teeth.

"Hey, Sonny. It's going." Her eyes slid from him to Sissy and back again to his face as she walked on, Sonny's eyes strung to her butt.

Two cars up, she stopped. Buffalo Ames and his buddies, Tim and Sol, sat back from the fence in aluminum-framed lawn chairs drinking beer. Buffalo was a big man, well over six feet with a barrel body and broad shoulders that were out of proportion to his skinny legs. Thick, unruly black hair grown long and shaggy poked out from under his white straw cowboy hat.

"Well, hellooo, Zooey," he said, jumping up and swooping off his hat in an exaggerated bow. "Please. Take my chair and let us enjoy your company."

She giggled and sat down.

"Pete ain't gonna like that," Sonny said.

"Pete's been putting up with that for a long time," Sissy said.

The Eyapaha announced the first event, saddle bronc riding, with the typical patter that accompanies rodeo events. The first man out of the chutes on the big buckskin, Casey Carter from Cheyenne River rez, was favored to win. He stuck for his full time but earned a low score. The next few riders were off before their time expired, and it looked like the favorite would take the prize in spite of his low score, because the last rider was just a kid from the west side of the rez, Joe Hiller. He had drawn a mediocre bay horse, but somebody popped a loud firecracker just as the chute opened and the horse came apart. The kid stuck like a cocklebur in a cow's tail. When the buzzer went off signaling the end of the ride, the kid swung his leg over the horse's neck and jumped to the ground, landing solidly planted on booted feet, his red and white batwing chaps flapping. He tipped his hat to the crowd as he climbed the chutes and sat on the top rail waiting for his score. He topped Casey Carter by eight points. The crowd responded with honking car horns, whistles, and yells. The kid slipped over the fence and dropped down into the area behind the chutes.

Bareback riding came next with no surprises—about half the riders got bucked off, half stuck, but only a couple got decent scores, and then came the last event, the most exciting one. Bull riding is the dessert of the rodeo, the best event, because everyone wants to see the rider get bucked off and chased by the bull, even delights in seeing a bull get a rider down even though no one admits it. It's exciting, exactly like a major wreck in a stock car race. No one goes to see who takes the checkered flag, but to see who survives the ugliest crashes. The rodeo clowns are part of the excitement of bull riding. The good ones aren't just clowning there to make the crowds gasp and laugh as they tease the bulls, but to distract the bull from a downed rider who might otherwise be gored or stomped. The Scenic rodeo hired only one clown, but he was a good one, Don Harris from over in Nebraska, a young man but a bold one who might not live to be old, some said, if he didn't quit being so bold.

Sissy saw Buffalo Ames leaning over whispering in Zooey's ear. She smiled widely as she slapped him on the shoulder.

The first bull was an old Charolais Brahma cross with a broken horn who gave the rider a good solid straight-ahead bucking pattern with no whirls or reverses. The rider stuck, earning a respectable score, and the bull trotted easily to the exit gate without a challenge to the clown. The next two riders were off before the buzzer with no score. One of the bulls gave a half-hearted scoop with his horns at the clown but couldn't be enticed into an interesting contest.

Everyone was waiting for Pete Broussard to ride. Some of the spectators wanted to see him win, and the others secretly hoped he'd get bucked off or worse, but no one wanted to be near him afterward. He came out of the chute on a brindle Brahma that ducked back, slamming Pete's leg against the closing chute gate, turned back to the arena and went into a spin. Pete leaned into the well, one hand held high as the bull went round and round like a dangerous dog chasing its tail. Suddenly, the bull planted its feet, gave a half-turn the other way and a little up-and-down jerking buck. Pete's balance hand wavered, he slipped to one side—the wrong side when the bull turned again—and Pete went off head first. For a moment his hand hung up in the rigging, and as the bull plunged down the arena, Pete was dragged a few feet before dropping into a puddle of soupy green cow shit. He rolled onto his back before he came up to a sitting position. Don Harris, the clown, in baggy pants and big shoes and a goofy porkpie hat tied on with a yellow scarf, held his nose and faked wiping the cow shit off Pete. The bull went to the end of the arena and circled back. Pete said something to the clown that the audience couldn't hear. The clown jumped back and clapped his hands to his mouth, then shook his finger at Pete while turning his head side to side. The crowd laughed. The Eyapaha pattered on about "give the man a hand, because that's all he's gonna get here today," meaning Pete wouldn't earn any money, and the crowd clapped respectfully. The bull went from a walk to a trot, gathering speed as it ran up the center of the arena back toward the chutes, the clown, and Pete Broussard. The Eyapaha yelled, "Look out down there," and the clown turned just as the bull lowered his head. The clown stepped in front of Pete and ripped off his yellow scarf, which sent the porkpie hat flying, waved the scarf at the bull, stepped to the side, and the bull followed. The clown ducked and dodged just inches in front of the bull, managing to lead it to the fence where he gave a mighty leap, grasped the top wire with his hands, and swung his feet up just as the bull passed beneath and rammed the fence.

Pete got up and limped to the opposite side of the arena. The horse-back riders in the arena gently choused the bull, who stopped every few feet to challenge them but eventually turned and passed through the exit gate. Pete went back behind the chutes. The clown retrieved his porkpie hat, making a show of dusting his own butt with the hat and wiping his forehead with the yellow scarf.

Buffalo Ames pulled Zooey up out of the lawn chair, sat down himself and pulled her down on his lap. Neither of them paid any attention to the arena. Sol and Tim kept their eyes intently on the arena.

The last two riders were off as well, but their bulls were in a good mood, so Pete's bull was the best and only fight. While the judges figured the final scores for all the events, the Eyapaha read announcements of other rodeos coming up, of where the cowboys stood in the circuit standings to take the prizes at the end of the season, and advertisements from the Scenic Café and Harley's Longhorn Bar; the last two announcements were unnecessary advertising since there was no business competition for either the bar or the café any closer than Rapid City, fifty miles to the west, or people's own picnic baskets and private beer coolers in their own car trunks.

The crowd rumbled while they waited. A few who were more interested in eating or drinking than in hearing who won what got up and left for the café or the bar or home. A few vehicles rumbled to life and drove away before the main rush of traffic.

As the Eyapaha started announcing the winners, beginning with the morning's roping events, Pete came walking heavily down the outside fence of the arena toward the end where Sissy sat with Sonny and where Zooey sat with Buffalo Ames, Sol, and Tim. Pete looked like a mad Brahma himself, swinging his head from side to side as if looking for someone to hook.

Sissy nudged Sonny. He looked. Zooey got up off Buffalo's lap and leaned against the pickup behind her.

"Oh, oh," Sonny said. "Think we should get out of here?"

"We didn't do anything to piss him off," Sissy said. "Don't run if you're not being chased."

"That's all good and fine, but I can get run over just standing still," he said.

Down in the arena, the judges handed the calf roping winner a silver belt buckle, which he waved while the crowd cheered and horns honked.

Pete slowed when he saw Zooey, glancing from her to Buffalo to the others watching the awards ceremony. Zooey pretended surprise at seeing Pete.

"You got robbed, honey," she said.

Pete took her by the arm.

"Let's go," he said.

She jerked her arm free.

"Go where?"

He looked again at Buffalo and the other men, glanced at the arena and back at Zooey.

"Let's go get a table and eat before the café fills up."

"I don't want to eat," Zooey said. "I want to drink."

Pete shuffled his feet, looked down, looked back at her.

"I said let's go eat."

"No," she said. "I want to drink."

He stood there a minute like a spring wound too tight, ready to break and go bouncing off across the ground, then he swept off his hat and slapped his thigh, sending dust into the air.

"All *right*, god damn it. But you better be ready to go home when I say."

Zooey pouted but didn't answer.

Pete walked past them toward town and the café. As he walked away Sissy saw the green smear on his butt where he'd tried to wipe off the cow shit. She looked at Sonny, who had been looking at Pete's butt too. They laughed just a little before they caught themselves and stopped in case Pete turned around and saw them.

"Let's go," Clayton said from behind them. "I want to eat before the café fills up."

Annie ran to and fro carrying trays loaded with drinks and beer, her skinny body bent over the trays, gray hair wisping around her face. Harley stood behind the bar mixing drinks and tapping beer as sweat rings grew under his arms. Vincent, his son, was nowhere to be seen. Julius darted here and there following Annie, sometimes climbing onto the bar, or up to sit with the two-headed calf. Not yet eight o'clock, but most of the tables and booths were full, and most of the stools at the bar. The older folks had gone home; the cowboys' work was done, and now it was time for the younger people and a few of the die-hard older ones, the helpless and the hapless, to party. The Fourth of July was the biggest money-making night of the year for Harley and Annie except for New Year's Eve, which wasn't always true if a big blizzard came through right before the end of the year.

On the stage, the Red Birds had already tuned all their instruments. Melvin planted himself on his drum throne, pillows stuffed into the back of his bass drum—what for, Sissy never understood. Sonny stood with his usual casualness, leaning against the back wall, while Clayton tapped the mike, listened for feedback, made some adjustments. Sissy stood there with her old Gibson, bought out of saved tips from waitressing. This was always the hard moment for her, feeling like a racehorse in the starting gate. Singing on stage took her to another world where for a few hours she was not herself, where she was a person people listened to instead of someone expected to listen, a person who didn't have problems, or no direction, or no future. In that moment, there was no yesterday and no tomorrow, only the music.

Clayton nodded at the others, and Sonny began the repetitive bass riff that started every gig. The crowd buzz quieted.

"Welcome everyone to the Scenic Fourth of July Dance at Harley and Annie Ferrill's Longhorn Bar. There ain't no place like this place anywhere near this place so this must be the place! Annie—Harley—take a bow!"

Annie waggled the fingers of one hand distractedly over her head and almost dropped her tray. Harley waved from behind the bar. Julius grinned and hooted.

"Not you, Julius," Clayton said and got a laugh.

"We ARE the Red Bird All-Indian Traveling Band, playing the best country western music in South Dakota and maybe this entire great nation of ours, maybe even the entire world. We play places like this—we play private parties, weddings, graduations, anniversaries, birthdays, and bar mitzvahs—well, actually we never played a bar mitzvah because we don't know what that is, but if anyone wants a country band for a bar mitzvah, the Red Bird All-Indian Traveling Band is ready to go.

"Here we have, leaning against the wall, our very own, hailing from Porcupine Creek, the former almost priest, cat burglar, virgin repairman, night watchman, and all around best bass player in the world—Soooonnnnyyyy Roberts!"

While Melvin laid down a drumroll, Sonny struck a crashing chord on his bass, bent his knees, leaned back at an angle, flung both arms in the air, hopped forward on his tiptoes two steps forward, two steps back. The crowd laughed and clapped.

". . . AND right behind me, throwing his not inconsiderable weight into bashing those drums is our own, hailing from Ghost Hawk Creek over on the Rosebud rez, that biscuit tossing, goat pill flipping, cow chip pitching, cattle rustling . . ."—his voice dropped sotto voce—"I wasn't supposed to say that last one . . ."—then continued—"Mellllvinnn Conway!"

Melvin pushed back his drum throne, stood up, raising his hands holding his sticks over his head, and circled his drum three times while Sonny and Sissy played the repetitive *Ta Dum . . . Ta DUM . . . Ta DUM . . . Ta Dum . . . diddly, diddly, diddly, dee . . .* and over again.

". . . AND we have here on rhythm guitar and sometimes lead guitar when I don't feel like it, our very own, hailing from Jackson not quite Pine Ridge not quite Rosebud, hash slinging, face slapping, song warbling, best female guitar picker on this rez and many another—Sssssiiisssyyy Roberts, cousin of the great Sonnnyyyy Roberts!"

Sissy took offense to that part about the best female guitar picker, which implied that there were a whole lot of men better than her, but Clayton didn't seem to get it when she asked him to quit saying that and to quit including Cousin Sonny in her introduction. He thought he was being gallant, but Sissy raised her arms over her head anyway, stuck her left boot toe behind her right boot heel, lowered her chin a bit and dropped a deep curtsy. The crowd clapped. When she raised her eyes, she saw Zooey Broussard through the smoke sitting at a front table, right in front of the dance floor that had been swept clear of sawdust. She was not clapping while she stared at Sissy. Pete sat beside her, his sullen face shiny with sweat. Howard Broussard and Viola sat at the same table, and at the table behind them, Buffalo.

". . . AND last and most important is me, Clayton Red Bird, hailing from Mission Town over on the Rosebud rez, that metropolitan, cosmopolitan center of intellectual and social superiority because I was born there, and I am here along with Sonny, Melvin, and Sissy to give you all a good time! We are going to start with an old Hank Williams tune, so grab your lady, get up here, and hold her close while you dance the night away."

Clayton stepped back from the mike and ran through the intro. Sissy stepped up to the mike and started to sing about cheating hearts.

Oh, shit, why did Clayton pick that one? Zooey Broussard stared at Sissy like she was singing directly to her. Sissy sang to the monkey, who paid no attention whatsoever.

When that one ended, Clayton moved on to a couple of Bob Wills tunes and then one originally recorded by Ernest Tubb. Sissy didn't know if it was the words that she liked or just the way that Tubb never hit a note square but always somewhere below and then slid on up to the exact pitch. Never mind that Scenic, South Dakota, was over a thousand miles from Texas, they waltzed across it anyway.

Sissy let the music take her away, somewhere else, somewhere where people didn't know her from babyhood, didn't ask her for absolution, gave her a job that paid better than minimum wages; where she didn't have to smile at people who let their kids make messes in public that they would never let them make at home, where her dad understood what she cared about and cared that she cared, and where somebody wonderful, please god, somebody loved her.

Down in the crowded room, she caught a glimpse of her friend, Joy, who her dad called Speedy because she was little and moved like a hummingbird. Speedy flitted from table to table, sitting now with this one a while, now with that one. Sissy and Speedy had been friends since Speedy's family had moved into the house next door, when they were both in high school.

They played all the songs on Clayton's playlist for the first set, the old-time ones that were everybody's favorites, saving the newer stuff for later, while the beer flowed and cigarette ends glowed, smoke floated and people hugged each other on the dance floor and sometimes laughed and smiled. Pete danced with Zooey twice while Howard danced with Viola and then they switched. Sissy noticed that when Viola danced with Pete, she kept her monogrammed handkerchief between her hand and Pete's shoulder with six inches of space between her dress front and his shirt front. Joe Hiller, the kid who had won the saddle bronc, sat on a stool at the bar with a couple of other guys. Never mind that he wasn't twenty-one. In the Longhorn Bar, if you were too young and too short to reach the bar to get a drink, Harley would push it under, or so the saying went. Pete went out through the Men's Room door and didn't come back.

Buffalo leaned over Zooey and said something. She smiled as he led her onto the crowded dance floor. Sissy sang an old Jim Reeves love song.

If she could have held her breath and sang at the same time, she would have. Nobody else seemed to notice as Buffalo's big hand crept down Zooey's back, closing in on the top of her buttocks, because over in the corner booth by the front door somebody was shouting and somebody else was shouting back and then two bodies tumbled out of a booth onto the sawdust-covered floor and arms started flailing and a woman screamed. Clayton and Sonny and Melvin played on and Sissy sang louder. Julius ran over and screamed at the fighters, darting in and out and getting his own licks in. Harley came around the end of the bar with a Looey-ville Slugger and waded into the melee.

Over the music, which nobody was listening to by that time, Sissy heard Harley yell, "Knock it off!" Harley went to swing the bat but caught Julius up side of the head on the back swing. The monkey went down screaming and holding its head, while the downswing of the bat caught one of the fighters in the back. He didn't make a sound, but a pair of men from the bar rushed over and pulled the fighters apart. Harley stepped back.

The dancers had all stopped to watch, except Buffalo and Zooey who stood in one spot barely moving their feet, their faces less than an inch apart.

The two fighters stood facing each other, swaying and breathing hard, each one held up by one of the men from the bar.

Over the music and the din, Sissy heard Harley shout, "You two done? You gonna behave yourselves now? If the answer is no, then there's the door."

First one and then the other of the fighters stood up straighter. They looked at each other a minute longer, then the shorter man slowly reached out his arm and clapped the other one on the shoulder. The two of them hugged and walked back to their booth.

"All right then," Harley said. As he turned to go back to the bar, he saw Julius on the floor holding his head, no longer screaming, but rocking back and forth.

"Julius!" Harley yelled. "What the hell happened to you?"

The crowd tittered and then roared with laughter. Harley knelt and took Julius by the hand. Julius leaned his head against Harley's leg and pulled himself up. Harley led him back behind the bar and sat him on a stool.

Sissy finished the last line of the song just as Pete came back in through the Men's Room door, walking quickly and looking around as if he was afraid he'd missed something, which he had, but not exactly what he thought he'd missed. Buffalo and Zooey broke apart. Buffalo went out through the same door Pete had just come through, and Zooey walked unsteadily to her table and eased herself into a chair.

Clayton gave Sissy a heads-up look.

"We need a happy song," he said and turned to Melvin.

"Give us the beat."

Melvin started that familiar drumbeat that everyone associates with Indian music. BOOM boom boom boom, BOOM boom boom boom.

Clayton nodded to Sissy, who began singing Hank Williams's "Kaw-Liga."

Now, a lot of people think that song is not a good representation of Indians, that it's insulting, but Sissy only ever knew one or two Indians who didn't love it, and this crowd all loved it, joining in on the chorus. Some people liked to add loud coyote howling sounds in places, which never sounded like coyotes howling, but like drunks howling, trying to sound like coyotes.

The band took a break then, and Sonny ordered scotch and water for himself and a beer for Sissy. You could get any drink you wanted at the Longhorn as long as it was something by itself, something with a beer back, or something with water. Harley didn't know what a daiquiri was, and if any of his customers knew, they knew better than to order it in the Longhorn. Clayton walked around the bar socializing with this one and that one and trying to get someone to hire the Red Birds for a private party. Melvin said his fat was too hot, so he took his drink and stepped out the front door for some air. Sissy saw Speedy up at the bar talking and tried to catch her eye, but Speedy turned her back. Sissy was stuck at the band table with Sonny, until she saw Clayton look at her and make a circle motion with his finger in the air meaning he wanted her to circulate, but as she was about to stand up, this weedy-looking White guy sat down at the table and stuck out his hand.

"Hi, there," he said. "Andrew Godwin's the name, feed's the game."

She shook his hand and said hello.

"I came with the Broussard family," he said. "I'm out of Sioux Falls, making the rounds of ranchers in the area selling feed, feed-grade vitamins, salt and mineral blocks, and so on. Say, I sure am glad I came. You're one hell of a singer, you know that?"

"Thank you," Sissy said. "Glad you're enjoying yourself."

"Enjoying myself? Well, little lady, I haven't had this much fun since—since, well since I don't know when. You got a hell of a voice on you."

"Thank you," she repeated and wondered where this was going and knew it wasn't going anyplace she wanted to go.

Sonny stood up.

"I think I see someone I need to talk to," he said.

Sissy tried to kick him under the table but couldn't reach him. He gave her that big toothy grin and wandered toward Speedy over at the bar with his drink in his hand.

"I'd like to take you to Nashville," Andrew said. "A voice like yours could go places if you had the right person to represent you."

"And you know who that right person might be?"

"You're looking at him. I know some people who could put you in touch with the right folks to get you a record deal. Trust me, I know how these things work."

"I thought you said feed was your game."

"Well—well, it is. But I know a good voice when I hear it." He leaned toward her, lowering his voice conspiratorially. "Listen, I want to be your agent. We could take Nashville by storm."

We? *Who's this* we?, she thought. But Sissy knew he meant himself and her, and he had more in mind than helping her peddle her musical talents.

"Listen," she said, leaning back in her chair to escape his bad breath. "Do you know how many people arrive in Nashville every day thinking they are going to be stars? Dozens, probably hundreds. I can sing. But so can about ten thousand other people and—" She was just getting warmed up, but there was a racket going on at the bar. Andrew half rose from his chair.

Julius was jumping up and down and screaming. Harley tried to grab him, but the monkey danced out of his reach, ran down to the end of the bar where Joe Hiller sat with a group of the rodeo cowboys.

"Hey! Hey!" Joe yelled. "That son of a bitch stole my cigarettes!"

The crowd at the bar laughed as Julius waved the pack of cigarettes over his head, still dancing out of Harley's reach. Joe stood up on his bar stool, reaching for the monkey, lost his balance and barely saved himself from a fall, not nearly as elegant and dignified as when he made that showy leap from the bronc in the arena. The monkey danced back down the bar and snatched at Joe's Zippo, but Joe made a grab and caught the monkey by the wrist. Julius screamed. Joe yelled. The crowd roared. Joe held on, but the monkey wouldn't drop the lighter. Julius flung his head back, jerking his body from side to side, then leaned over and munched down on Joe's arm. Joe screamed; Julius screamed and dropped both lighter and cigarettes, ran back down the bar and leaped up onto the shelf with the two-headed calf, where he sat as if nothing had happened. Slowly and deliberately he turned around and mooned the room.

Joe grabbed his cigarettes and lighter and stalked out, followed by his friends.

Somebody hollered, "That monkey is losing you business, Harley!"

Somebody else yelled, "Pretty soon all you'll have is monkey business!"

Annie coaxed Julius down from his perch and took him out through the Men's Room door.

"Is it always this exciting around here?" Andrew asked as he sat back down in his chair.

"Yeah," Sissy said. "Sometimes it's even worse."

Andrew the Feed Salesman hunched lower in the chair, took a deep breath and launched back into his spiel.

"Listen, you need to get out of this. This is no life for a talented pretty girl like you. Look at you! I mean, you deserve a lot better, and I can help you get it."

"No. Thank you," Sissy said and got up to work the room. She looked around, and there was Gordon Charbonneau sitting with Pete and Zooey and Howard and Viola. She took her beer over to their table. She'd chance Zooey's irrational anger for a chance to get to know Gordon.

"Hi, how you doing?" Sissy said.

"All right," Howard said. "Good job up there," he added, motioning to the stage.

"Thanks," she said and sat down by Zooey, who was too drunk to connect with a fist even if she decided to beat up on Sissy. Her hair looked like somebody had ruffled it up with dirty hands, her white shirt had a stain on the front and the button across the middle of her chest had come undone. Her eyes fixed on Sissy's face but didn't focus.

"Say, I know you," she said, waving her drink unsteadily.

"Yup, long time now," Sissy said.

"I don't know you," Gordon said. His voice had a flat quality. Sissy couldn't decide if that meant he didn't want to know her and what the hell was she doing sitting down at the table where he was, or if that was just his natural way of speaking.

"Sissy Roberts," she said. "Guess you weren't here when Clayton introduced us all." She stuck out her hand. He took it in a loose way, not a firm grip. His hand was warm. She felt calluses on the palm. So, he did do some work on his family ranch.

"Gordon Charbonneau," he said and held her gaze for a moment. "You live around here?"

"All my life," Sissy said. "Well, I grew up and went to school in Jackson."

He nodded, stretching out his right leg with a barely audible groan as he rubbed the jeans right above his knee.

"I'm ready to go home," Viola said, her hand on Howard's sleeve. "Aren't you?"

Howard took another sip from his glass.

"Just a little bit longer," he said.

Viola quickly moved her hand off his arm, putting both hands in her lap under the table. She still looked as put together as she had before the rodeo started. Sissy wondered how she did it, if she sprayed her entire body with some preservative just before she left her house. She and Gordon might be the only stone-cold sober people in the place.

Zooey sat her drink down or tried to, but bumped Sissy's bottle of beer. It tipped sideways and foamed out with a wet gush over the Indian blanket tablecloth.

"Damn it, Zooey," Pete said, pushing his chair back to avoid the beer that did not drip off the table because the blanket soaked it up. *This place will smell mighty nice tomorrow*, Sissy thought.

"I think it's time for us to go home," Pete said, standing up.

"No," Zooey said. "I want to drink."

"I'll buy you a bottle to go."

"No. I want to hear—to hear—whatsherface here sing." She turned unfocused eyes toward Sissy. "Say, do you know that song by whatsherface—'D-I-V-O-R-C-E'?"

Pete's face went dark. He jerked Zooey up from her chair.

"I *said* it's time to go home."

She whimpered and slapped ineffectually at his arm, but he pulled her toward the front door. She sat down in the sawdust, pulled her knees up, put her hands on her knees and her head on her hands.

Howard looked at his drink, swirled the melting ice cubes.

Pete walked out of the bar.

"Do you play cribbage?" Gordon asked.

"Yeah," Sissy said. Her parents played that ubiquitous game all the time, but she hadn't played in years.

"Why don't you come out to my place next Saturday? Howard and Viola are coming. You can be my partner."

His partner. Sissy liked the sound of that, but the Red Bird was playing the next weekend at Interior after their rodeo. She was really sorry to tell Gordon that.

"I see. How about—"

Sissy hated Clayton right then. He came up behind her and tapped her on the shoulder.

"Let's go," he said.

Two songs later Sissy saw Buffalo holding Zooey up by the back door, but when she looked again they were gone. When the band had finished the last set, Sissy and Sonny repeated the riff they had played at the opening while Clayton wound it up.

"The Red Bird All-Indian Traveling Band will play at Interior after their rodeo in two weeks and we sure hope to see you all there . . ."

Sissy didn't pay attention to the rest of it. Two weeks. She had just told Gordon they played Interior next week, so she couldn't go play cards with him. She looked around. She could tell him she had made a mistake. But he was gone.

Somebody from the crowd yelled, "You aren't playing anywhere next Saturday?"

"No, not until two weeks from tomorrow tonight at Interior. I hope to see you all there."

Somebody threw a beer bottle; maybe it wasn't aimed at Clayton, but maybe it was, and then somebody else threw a beer bottle until a rain of beer bottles crashed into the stage. One bounced off Clayton's guitar with a *crack*. He cussed and ducked and pulled Sissy down beside him.

"I am not playing here again unless Harley puts some chicken wire around the stage," he said with his eyes narrowed and his teeth clenched. "And gets a bouncer. And gets rid of that god damned fucking monkey."

There was no pyrotechnic show at Scenic's Fourth of July celebration, but there had been plenty of fireworks. Just across the railroad tracks on the west side, Buffalo Ames lay curled on his side around a mostly dead clump of grass.

CHAPTER THREE

JACKSON

July 5–11

Somebody shook her.

"Leave me alone."

"Sissy. Sissy. Wake up. You're home."

She was cramped on the passenger side of Clayton's front seat while Sonny stood outside with the door open, poking a finger into her ribs. She hauled herself upright. Sonny kept poking.

"Stop it. I'm awake."

The sun, just above the horizon, shone through the tree branches that reached over the street in front of her house, lighting up the weeds that grew in most of the ditches next to the graveled street. It was too early for people to be up. She pushed her hair out of her eyes. Her head hurt. She didn't drink much when she was playing, but afterward she usually drank a couple of beers. Last night she'd had more than a couple.

"Come on, Sissy," Clayton nudged her from the other side. "I gotta get home to my kids."

"Yeah. All right. Get out of the way, Sonny."

He moved aside with one of those swooping motions of his arms like he was welcoming royalty. He had never had a hangover in his life.

Sissy opened the back door and got out her Gibson. As she started slogging up the steep driveway to the back door, Clayton yelled after her.

"Practice on Wednesday!"

She didn't look back.

The neighbor's half cocker spaniel, half everything dog leaped at the fence barking and snarling, as he had done for the past five years. Taffy hated everyone. When he was a fluffball puppy, Sissy had tried to make friends with him, but he didn't need friends, only a psychopathic need to bark and growl.

The back door to the kitchen opened with a rattle. In the yellow light reflected off the walls, she stood a minute inhaling good home smells.

Her dad sat at the kitchen table drinking coffee and smoking a cigarette while a pot of chili simmered on the stove with a big black cast-iron skillet next to it, a bowl of pancake batter on the countertop.

"Hey, Sissy," her dad said, motioning to a chair at the table. "I'm fixing breakfast."

Every Sunday morning for the thirty years her parents had been married, her father got up first and made breakfast so her mother could sleep in this one morning. Since they almost always made chili on Saturday night no matter the season, breakfast was pancakes topped with warmed-over chili. This wasn't Sunday morning, but Sissy's mom had made chili last night for the Fourth of July, even though it was only Friday.

She put her guitar in the hall next to the kitchen, poured a cup of strong coffee into a battered old blue ceramic mug and sat down.

"You look like you been shot at and missed and shit at and hit," he said with that little grin turning up the corners of his mouth. He was wearing his weekend clothes: pin-striped blue overalls over a wife beater undershirt and moccasins.

"I'm glad to know that," she said, taking short sips of the hot coffee.

"Hard night?"

She sighed. "About the usual. Pretty decent rodeo. A lot of drunks at the bar. Somebody started throwing beer bottles right at the last. Clayton says we aren't playing there anymore unless Harley puts some chicken wire around the stage." She rubbed her temples between a thumb and forefinger.

Her father got up and drew a glass of water and put the water and a bottle of aspirin on the table between them. She gave him a grateful smile.

"Thanks."

"Sissy, what are you going to do?"

She swallowed a couple of pills and followed up with half the glass of water.

Her dad turned on the heat under the skillet and gave the steaming chili a stir.

"About what?"

He raised his eyebrows and lowered his chin at her.

"About *what*?"

He held the bowl of pancake batter in the crook of his arm, beating the batter with a long-handled wooden spoon, making a womp-womp-womp sound that Sissy associated with Sunday mornings, with hot food and comfort.

"I don't know," she said.

"Sissy, I know you want to go on in school. I want you to do that. I know how to wipe the blood off a skinned knee. I can listen to you cry when you can't figure out how to do algebra even if I don't know *x* from *y*. I can read the book with you and sometimes even figure out the problems. I can teach you how to make bar chords on that old guitar, but I don't know shit about helping you figure out how to go on in school. Some things you have to figure out for yourself or get someone smarter than me to help."

She watched the hot fat pop and sizzle in the heating skillet. Her mother stirred around in their bedroom, jangling the coat hangers in the closet as she hung up her nightgown, shutting the closet door shut with a thump. Sissy waited for her dad's lecture about wasting her life playing music in crummy bars and drinking too much and coming home too late, but as always the lecture never came. Her father didn't work like that. He let her create her own lecture without any help from him. Except for the four words that poured in her ear like burning oil.

"God damn it, Sis," he said, but that was all.

Her mother sat at the end of the table and her father sat to one side while they ate, and her parents carried on that quiet conversation they had going for years that was about nothing of any matter but was the matter that held them together and gave purpose and meaning to their days.

"Harvest is going to start in a couple of weeks."

"Looks like a good year if the farmers can get it all in before a big hailstorm takes everything."

"I checked the rain gauge yesterday. Quarter of an inch. Needs to hold off now so they can get into the fields to harvest."

"Yeah."

"Bertie Michaels was over yesterday. She says her son-in-law has got her daughter all stirred up against her so bad Bertie is nervous about going over there, even to see her grandkids."

"Yeah."

"I think Bill is messing around with that Zooey Broussard."

"You tell her that?"

"No. You know Zooey. She'll move on in a few days to make trouble somewhere else. Bill will be ashamed of himself and be extra nice to Bertie and her daughter to make up for being a jerk."

"You tell her that?"

"No. I just said 'uh-huh' and 'uh-uh' in all the right places. She'll figure it out."

Sissy heard their voices continue as she went up the unpainted stairs to her hot, airless bedroom under the eaves. She opened the window to let in what little breeze there might be, which wouldn't be much, stripped off her boots and jeans and shirt and crawled into bed. She imagined them at the table drinking another cup of coffee. Faintly she heard that same discussion they had at least once a week.

"Lawrence, don't pick your teeth at the table."

"Why not?"

"It's bad manners."

"I know it. I don't do it in public."

"Why do you persist in doing it at home?"

"Lily, if a man can't pick his teeth in his own home, where can he?"

"Out in the yard. In the bathroom. Somewhere else."

Sissy heard his chair creak and knew he was leaning toward Lily, kissing her cheek.

"Do you love me anyway?"

"Yes."

Sissy dreamed of Zooey Broussard yelling with a knife in her hand. They were outside in the moonlight in a dirt parking lot full of cars. From the building behind them, she heard her own voice singing "D-I-V-O-R-C-E." Zooey turned her head at a sudden sound, and Sissy saw the moonlight catch the scar on her cheek. A scrabbling sound, like mice skittering in the distance, started up and then there was a groan and heavy breathing.

Sissy dimly remembered someone talking with a new voice downstairs, so she must have been partly awake. Clayton's daughter, Darlene, was talking to her mom, but she wasn't sure if that was part of the dream until she felt someone sit on the edge of her bed and heard the bed springs squeak.

"Sissy?"

She opened her eyes. Closed them again. Silence.

"Sissy?"

She was not waking up for anybody. The day after tomorrow she had to be at work at 6 a.m. pouring water into the big coffee maker, setting out the big pans of cinnamon rolls for the early breakfast crowd, wiping the fly specks off the glass pie case, filling the napkin holders and the salt and pepper shakers, the catsup bottles and the steel salad dressing servers, rolling sets of silverware into big paper dinner napkins, and putting the finished setups into a plastic tub under the counter ready at hand, but that would be then. Today she would sleep.

"Sissy?"

She slapped at the sharp fingers she felt poking in her ribs.

"Go away, Sonny. I'm not getting up."

"Sissy? It's me. Darlene. I need to talk to you."

Darlene. Clayton's daughter, a nice enough sixteen-year-old kid, was as persistent as a gnat, but a gnat that was tall, all big eyes and elbows. She would be pretty when she grew into her skeleton.

"Sissy?"

She pulled herself up, half-sitting against the wall. Her bed had no headboard. A little breeze came through the window along with a couple of flies that crawled in around the edge of the screen where it had torn loose from the frame.

"What?"

"Well," she said and stopped because now that she had Sissy's attention she didn't know where to begin. Sissy helped her out.

"Is this about Darrell?" Darrell was Darlene's nine-year-old brother who she looked after while her dad was out playing music and after school and during the summers while Clayton ran his small auto body and mechanic shop in partnership with Melvin on the outskirts of Jackson. From the bandstand, Clayton said he was from over on Rosebud, and he was from there. He'd been from there ever since he married his kids' mom, a pretty good singer herself, and moved to Jackson, but three years ago the woman had run off with a guitar picker from Sioux Falls. He'd probably told her he could take her to Nashville and make her a star. That's when Clayton recruited Sissy to sing with the band and her folks finally let her, seeing as how she had just turned eighteen and could pretty much do it anyway if she wanted to.

"Kinda about Darrell. And kinda about Dad."

"Okay."

Darlene gave a deep gasp, holding both hands over her face, crying.

Sissy let her go a few minutes without touching her or saying anything. When Darlene dropped her hands, snuffled and reached for the corner of Sissy's sheet, Sissy said, "Here, move so I can get up."

Darlene jumped up and stood, hands at her sides in the middle of the low-ceilinged room, her head only a few inches below the overhead light fixture, still snuffling, eyes downcast.

Sissy went to her old battered dresser with the peeling veneer top, rummaged through a drawer and found an old snagged knit top that she didn't wear anymore but hadn't yet thrown in the rag basket. There was a box of tissues downstairs in the bathroom, but she didn't want to leave Darlene alone with her sheets.

"Here. Blow."

Sissy sat down on the edge of the bed and waited for Darlene to get done sniffling. Her headache was back. Somewhere down the street, a lawn mower roared to life. Her father's old yellow tomcat, Wooly Booger, came gallumping up the stairs, stopped at the top step and said "miaow," lifted a hind leg and started cleaning his butt.

Darlene slumped on the bed, her hands clasped between her knees.

"Your dad expects you to be a housemaid and babysitter and you're tired of it."

She nodded. Sissy waited.

"You know what he did?" Darlene asked.

Sissy waited.

"Yesterday I worked all day cleaning the house while Darrell ran off to play with his friends even when I told him not to be gone all day, and he didn't come home until supper. He said he ate lunch at Jonny's house. I swept and scrubbed all the floors. I washed the dishes and dried them and put them away. I straightened up the mess that Darrell made in the living room, and I vacuumed and dusted. I washed clothes and hung them out and brought them back in and folded them and put them away, and I ironed Dad's shirts. You know how fussy he is about his shirts."

Sissy nodded.

"I cleaned the bathroom, and I even washed the curtains and ironed them and rehung them. The whole house smelled clean like pine and bleach. And I got up early this morning and had breakfast ready for Dad when he got home. And do you know what he did?"

Sissy shook her head.

"He walked in the front door, walked straight through and out the back door and stood in the middle of the yard and yelled at me. He said he told me to rake up the twigs in the back yard and that's the one thing I didn't do." She had sat up straight, her muscles stiff with indignation.

"Yes. What did you do then?"

"Cried. I was too mad to say anything."

Sissy nodded and waited.

"Dad stood by the table while he ate a couple of bites of toast, and then he went to bed. He never touched the eggs, over easy, just like he always wants them."

"Where's Darrell?"

"Still sleeping when I left. Dad's home now. He can take care of Darrell." Her lower lip stuck out a little. She gave a deep shuddering sigh, staring at Sissy's wadded up old top in her lap.

The lawn mower down the street coughed, choked, and stalled. Sissy heard someone heaving on the starter rope, heard the little two-cycle engine spin, cough, and die. Someone cussed. A fly lit on Sissy's nose but flew away before she could brush it off.

"How's your grandma and your Auntie Ruth and the kids?" Sissy asked.

Darlene didn't answer for a minute as her brain shifted gears.

"I don't know."

Ruth was Clayton's sister, a widow who ran her own small ranch over on Rosebud, taking care of her three half-raised boys and the kids' grandmother, who was Ruth and Clayton's mother.

"We were over there for Memorial Day right after school was out."

"I suppose Ruth has a big garden this year."

"Yeah. She always does. There's not much to do around the place with the cattle in the summer. She cans everything she grows in her garden."

"Lot of work, canning."

"Oh, yes," Darlene said. "But I like the way the kitchen smells while you're doing it. Especially if Auntie Ruthie is making jelly. It makes the kitchen awful hot, though."

"She still have that stock pond that everyone used to go swimming in?"

"Yeah. They got a lot of rain over there this spring, so the pond was pretty full."

"Ruthie got anyone to help her with the canning?"

"Well, just grandma, and she doesn't get around so well anymore. The boys aren't any help."

"You ever do any canning?"

"Oh, yeah. I used to help my mom . . ." Her voice trailed off. She sat a minute longer. "I'd better be going," she said, standing up and handing Sissy the snotty shirt. "Darrell will run off if Dad's not awake to stop him."

"All right," Sissy said.

She stepped around the cat and clattered halfway down the stairs, came back up two so her head showed over the rail.

"I'll see you later, Sissy."

"Yeah. Okay."

The next week at the café was routine. Few people came in for a full breakfast, just local businessmen for coffee and a roll or a piece of pie, and then more businessmen and farmers at lunch time, and of course, the courthouse biddies for coffee breaks and lunch every day. There were four of them, middle-aged women whose kids were grown and husbands were at work so they got hired at the courthouse to push the occasional paper and gossip. They always came in a pack, wearing their self-imposed uniforms of slightly better than common housedresses in flowery prints and flat shoes, hair cut and curled and sprayed into helmets on their heads that would sound like a ripe watermelon if you knocked on them with your knuckles. They dithered and dathered over the menu, changing their minds several times but inevitably choosing one of two things: a half order of the lunch special or cottage cheese and fruit, except two of the four of them would change their minds to what the other two had ordered. Once in a while, they all ordered the same thing the first time: a salad with a big slice of pie a la mode because all of them were on a permanent diet but never lost a single pound among the four of them.

For now, Sissy worked the morning shift Monday through Friday and had weekends off, a privilege that the owner, Martha, granted only to Sissy because she had worked in the café part time since high school, after school and on weekends and full time in the summers and now full time for the last few years since she graduated and didn't have any better job to go to. She'd been lucky that Martha gave her Fourth of July off because it was a Friday, but with the town putting on a free barbecue, there wouldn't be any business for the café anyway. In a couple of weeks Martha and Sissy would have their annual argument about whether or not Sissy had to work weekends when the transient harvest crews came to town and the place was open and busy seven days a week. The café seated eighty. There would be two, sometimes three or four turnovers between eleven o'clock and two, then again between five o'clock and seven or even eight if the weather was good and the crew could stay in the fields running on the lights from the big combine harvesters. The waitresses would be run off their feet, but the harvest crew bosses were cheap, so the crews ate the cheap lunch special or hamburgers and french fries—no special orders or changing their minds. They were easier to deal with than the courthouse biddies. Martha needed every waitress she could get every day and on weekends too, which interfered with whatever gig Sissy had going with the Red Birds. She'd win the argument, but Martha would be pissed for a month and the other waitresses would say it wasn't fair. Sissy wasn't about to tell Martha that she didn't have a gig this Saturday night, even though harvest wouldn't get into full swing until the following week or so. They would have their argument over the next Saturday when the Red Birds were playing at Interior.

On Friday afternoon, Sissy stood out back by the trash cans in the heat having a smoke break and listening to the roar of the exhaust fan in the wall drowning out the buzz of the flies, glad to have a weekend coming up when she wasn't waitressing or playing music.

Martha stuck her head out the back door.

"Someone is here asking to see you," she said.

"Who?" Sissy tapped her cigarette ash on the ground and took a final puff.

"I don't know. I never seen him before. Looks like a salesman."

Oh, jeezus. Probably that feed salesman from Scenic, what's his face? Andrew something.

Sissy walked back in through the steamy kitchen. In mid-afternoon, Lucille the dishwasher was just catching up from the lunch crowd. She gave Sissy a grin and a friendly splash of cold water from the sink as she passed. A few hairs had come loose from Lucille's hairnet and stuck to her cheeks. A drop of sweat clung to the end of her nose. She wiped it off with her apron tail.

A big blonde man sat at the counter stirring his iced tea. About thirty-five years old, maybe a little older or younger, he wore a crisp white shirt like the local businessmen, but he wasn't. He was the only stranger in the place. He looked like an out of uniform recruiter for the Marines.

"That's him," Martha pointed out the unnecessary.

"I'm Sissy Roberts."

He put down his teaspoon, fastening bright blue eyes on her.

"Sit down. I have some questions for you."

"The boss doesn't like me sitting down on the job," she said. He made her nervous. His voice was too serious.

"All right if I talk to you while you stand?" he asked.

"Providing you understand if a customer comes in, I have to wait on him."

"All right. You were at the Longhorn Bar in Scenic last Friday night?"

"Pretty hard to miss me since I was the one standing on the stage behind the microphone singing. Who are you, and why do you want to know?"

He took a sip of his tea.

"The only thing that quenches thirst better than iced tea is ice water. Did you know that?"

"Who are you?"

He half raised himself from the stool to get at his wallet in his back pocket, opened it and slapped it on the counter. The wallet was shiny black leather; the badge was shiny metal with letters: Federal Bureau of Investigation 5571.

"Why are you asking me questions? How did you get here so fast? Don't you have better things to do? In case you didn't know it, Al Capone never lived around here."

He didn't smile. His face looked like it should have been carved on Mount Rushmore.

"For any major felonies that can result in a prison sentence of more than three years and for any crime of property worth more than five thousand dollars committed on an Indian reservation, the FBI is required to investigate," he said.

"I know that. But Jackson isn't the reservation, or so the White people who live in this county claim. And as far as I know, it isn't a crime to sing with a country band in the Longhorn Bar at Scenic, which isn't on the reservation either. So you lose on both counts."

He put both hands flat on the countertop as if to steady himself. His fingernails were clean, pink, and square at the tips and at the base, like his creator had been practicing geometry and was tired of making circles and ovals and triangles.

"The tracks for the Union Pacific Railroad run just about one hundred yards south of the Longhorn Bar and that line marks the northern boundary of Pine Ridge Reservation."

Sissy knew the boundary was somewhere south of the Longhorn, had to be because it was illegal to sell alcohol on the rez.

"A crime committed south of those tracks is therefore on the reservation, and if it meets the other criteria I just mentioned, subject to investigation by the FBI."

"Well, it wasn't me, whatever it was. I was only near those tracks to pass over going to and from the Longhorn Bar." Probably somebody's fancy car worth more than five thousand dollars had broken down just past the tracks onto the rez and got burgled and burned.

"I know you didn't do it. Everyone I talked to says you were never alone."

Sissy had no interest in burgling a burning a car, anyway. This arrogant bastard annoyed her, dragging out information like it was holy and she had no right to know anything and every reason to be questioned like a common criminal.

"Tell me what's going on," Sissy said. "I've got work to do."

The rock face moved a little.

"Last Saturday morning the body of a well-formed mature man of about thirty years of age was found dead lying face down about ten feet south of the railroad tracks on the west side. He suffered what looks like a blow to the back of the head resulting in trauma, blood loss, and death. His driver's license identified him as Benjamin Ames, Jr., and subsequent questioning of people in Scenic said he was called Buffalo, that he was a member of the Oglala Sioux tribe and lived down in Pine Ridge. That he had been in the Longhorn Bar earlier, but no one remembers exactly when he left."

"Jeezus. You sound like a newspaper story," Sissy said. She remembered Buffalo dancing belly to belly with Zooey Broussard, Pete's foul mood after losing in the bull riding, the constant strain between Zooey and Pete. She didn't remember Buffalo and Pete being gone from the bar at the same time.

"Easier to deal with ugly situations if you put it in clinical terms."

"Or an autopsy report."

"That too." His blue eyes gazed at her.

"What would I know about it? I'm just the woman who sings in the band. Talk to somebody who might know something." She did know some things, but she wasn't going to tell the FBI, and besides, just because Zooey and Pete fought all the time and Buffalo was making eyes at Zooey didn't mean either of them had killed Buffalo.

"I'm talking to you."

"Why? I don't know anything about it. I sure as hell didn't kill Buffalo Ames."

His eyebrows shot up as he lifted his hands.

"Did I *say* you killed him?"

"Not exactly."

"You don't seem very upset about his death."

Martha peered at Sissy through the kitchen pass-through and hooked a thumb at the other end of the counter, where the salesman from the Chevrolet place waited to pay for his coffee. Sissy walked down and took his money, dinged the cash register and stuck his ticket on the spindle.

The FBI agent had drunk most of his tea and was now rattling the ice at her. Sissy refilled his glass from the big spigot jar sitting on the back counter.

"I didn't know Buffalo, except to see him around once in a while. I don't even know what he did for a living or who he went around with or anything. I can't tell you anything. Except I didn't kill him. No reason to."

He moved his head back and forth in a figure-eight shape, easing tension in his neck.

"I said I know you didn't kill him. But I've talked to a lot of people since I got here, and you know what they all say?"

"I haven't the foggiest idea. Except they all said they didn't do it."

"Right. But they all say I should talk to you."

"*Me?* Why me?"

"Because at least five of the dozen or more people I interviewed said that everybody talks to you; everybody tells you everything."

"Nobody told me they killed Buffalo Ames. Nobody told me they knew who did it. In fact, nobody even mentioned that he was dead, and the FBI was looking into it."

"Yes. I know."

"Well, if you knew that, then why are you asking me questions?"

"Because until I talked to you just now, I didn't know if anybody had talked to you, and now that I have, I believe you didn't even know the man was dead. But I also think somebody might talk to you." He took a card out of his wallet and handed it to her. "And when they do I want you to tell me all about it."

The white card had the FBI seal on it and his name: Tom Holm, Special Investigator.

"You hear me? I'm staying at the Highway Motel."

"Yeah, I hear you."

He placed a clean dollar bill on the counter, picked up his glass and drained it.

"I came down here out of the Rapid City office, which, as you know, is only forty miles from Scenic," he said. "And I don't want to be here any longer than I have to."

He stood and walked to the door. He wasn't as tall as he looked sitting on the stool, but his shoulders were about as broad as he was tall, or it seemed so. He had a rolling walk like someone who had spent years walking a ship deck. Or on horseback.

Sissy put the card in her apron pocket. People who told her things usually came back later to confess other things. They came back because she didn't tell anyone about the first things they confessed. Seal of the confessional or something like that, she supposed, but she doubted if Tom Holm would let her get away with that claim. But then, how would he find out if anybody confessed to her about the murder of Buffalo Ames? She hadn't done anything that he could use to blackmail her. The worst thing she ever did was to get picked up for minor in possession of an alcoholic beverage when she was nineteen, and that was a technicality. She had bought the beer just across the state line in Nebraska where nineteen was the legal drinking age, but made the mistake of bringing it back across the line into South Dakota where the legal drinking age was twenty-one, got stopped for a broken taillight just outside Jackson and caught with the beer. The JP was the father of a girl Sissy had gone to school with, so he let her off with a fifteen-dollar fine and a warning. Actually what Nels Nelson said was, "If you're going to drink, Sissy, do it over in Nebraska where you're of legal age and stay there until you're sober before you drive home." But he wouldn't let her pay off the entire fine all at once. She had to pay it off at fifty cents a week. He said that way she would remember longer.

She had been embarrassed and ashamed for her parents to find out. Her dad had said only, "God damn it, Sis. I thought you knew better."

She had no other sins of omission or commission for anyone to hold against her, and Tom Holm had nothing to offer as an inducement for her to tattle. If anyone ever did talk to her, that was.

CHAPTER FOUR

THE C & C ON SATURDAY NIGHT

JULY 12

Saturday, Sissy helped her mom with the laundry and cleaning while her dad piddled around with his Ford Falcon pickup, changing the oil and so on. She wished he would trade it in for a better car, but he said it got good gas mileage. It also had a sticky clutch that wouldn't pop back up after you pushed it down, so he wired it up with a bedspring, which made it hard to push down. If you didn't take your foot off just right, it would pop back fast and the metal edge of the pedal would take all the hide off your shin.

While her mother made the chili, Sissy got a shower and put on clean jeans and a white ruffled blouse and her good black boots and matching belt. She was finishing her makeup with the bathroom door open to let out the steam when her dad came by.

"You going out to the C & C?" he asked.

He knew she was going out; he could see that, and he knew that the only three places in town to go on a Saturday night were the movie theater that showed third-run B movies, or the Legion Club where the big shots went and Sissy didn't, or the C & C, which served 3.2 beer and had the latest country songs on the jukebox. He didn't want her to go out drinking, but he never said so. He just asked the obvious.

"Yeah. I'm meeting Speedy there for a little while."

Speedy had graduated a year behind Sissy but they were the same age because Speedy had flunked a year. Sissy didn't know why because Speedy was smart as a whip, always had a wisecrack or a one-liner ready, so she was usually fun to be around. She never had any big plans for the future, except to get married and have kids, so they didn't have much in common except a shared childhood history of being neighbors in a small town, waitressing at the café, and a love for music. Too bad Speedy couldn't carry a tune in a bushel basket. Sissy thought a cow had stepped on her ear. And they weren't neighbors anymore since Speedy's parents had moved to a house with cheaper rent out in the country. Two losers,

Sissy thought, years out of high school, still living with their parents and waitressing at a greasy spoon restaurant.

There was a small crowd of cars in the dirt parking lot at the C & C when Sissy got there in her old '59 Chevy. Speedy, waiting impatiently on the steps, was spending the night at Sissy's house so she wouldn't have to drive to her place out in the country when she'd been drinking.

Half the tables and booths inside were occupied. Loretta Lynn's voice came from the jukebox. A little more modern than the Longhorn up in Scenic, the wooden floors had no sawdust; there were no funny signs anywhere, no notes stuck on the mirrors, no monkey, and the table-tops were plain worn Formica with no Indian blankets stapled on. Spilled drinks got wiped up, not soaked up. They ordered draw beers at the bar, looking around while they waited for something interesting to happen.

Howard and Viola sat at the big table near the back with Sonny and Gordon Charbonneau. Sonny waved to them and motioned. They collected their beers and walked across the creaky floor to the table.

"What's going on, Cuz?" Sonny asked.

"Time and the rent," Sissy said.

He pointed at her. "Old joke, Sissy. The funny ran out a long time ago. Sit down."

She started to sit, but Speedy pushed her over one chair so she could sit by Sonny. Sissy was in the chair next to Gordon and across the table from Howard and Viola.

"I thought you were playing crib tonight at your place," Sissy said to Gordon.

"Nobody seemed interested," he said.

"I'm sorry I told you I couldn't come," Sissy said. "I got mixed up on the date we play Interior. That's next Saturday night."

"Oh, I didn't mean you." He nodded at Howard and Viola. "They didn't want to play cards tonight."

"We're celebrating," Viola said, spreading her left hand in front of Sissy's face. She had a fat diamond on her third finger.

"Congratulations," Sissy said. "When are you doing the deed?"

Viola's lips turned down at the corners. Howard leaned back in his chair wordlessly.

"He *says* this fall after the cattle are rounded up and shipped. I always wanted a summer wedding."

"We could wait until next June," Howard said.

Viola slapped him on the arm.

On Sissy's opposite side, Speedy and Sonny exchanged barbs. Speedy had a way of sticking her tongue in the side of her check so it made a little lump right after she said something she thought particularly funny. Sissy thought it was stupid, like the drumroll in a burlesque show that tells the audience when to laugh. Sonny thought it was cute.

"Did any of you hear that Buffalo Ames was murdered up at Scenic last Friday night?" Sissy asked.

"*Shhh!*" Howard said. He moved his head to the left, looking over Sissy's shoulder. Sissy turned. Tom Holm sat alone in a booth made for four by the front door. He saw her looking and raised his glass in a little salute.

"What's he doing in here?" Sissy asked.

Gordon said, "Snooping around. That's what FBI men are supposed to do. Besides, he's staying at the Highway Motel right across the street. You know there's not much to do but drink on Saturday night in Jackson."

"I suppose," Sissy said, and then in a lower voice, "Did you know about Buffalo Ames?"

Howard nodded again toward Holm.

"That guy was out at the ranch yesterday asking questions. He'd already talked to Harley and Annie. They're pretty close-mouthed about rez business, but I suppose he squeezed them into giving names of as many people in the Longhorn as they could remember."

"How do you mean?" she asked.

"You gotta know that Harley and Annie never check IDs. They serve underage kids every day if the kid has the money to pay for it. Everybody knows it; just law enforcement doesn't bother to come out to Scenic for a few underage drinkers. Too dangerous, too, with all us Indians." Everyone laughed, but there was truth in everything he had just said.

"So he threatened to have the Ferrills arrested for serving underage minors?"

"Probably," Howard said. "But worse. They'd just pay a fine for that. But if the bust was *enough* underage minors, they could damn well lose their liquor license. So, the cops—and the FBI—recruit some underage kids to go out to Scenic, get served, get busted, and you know the rest."

"I know who did it," Sonny announced solemnly.

"Who?" Viola said.

"The biggest baddest ass on the rez, the one nobody can touch, not even the FBI," he said.

"Who? Who?" Viola repeated like an owl.

"Julius," Sonny said with a pleased grin. "He hates everybody."

When the laughter died down, Sissy tried again.

"I remember seeing Buffalo there, but I saw a whole lot of people."

"I didn't see him," Gordon said. "He must've been gone by the time I got there."

Sissy thought that wasn't quite true, but she couldn't be sure, couldn't remember. Maybe Buffalo was not just gone, but dead by the time Gordon got there.

"I never noticed him arguing with anyone," Howard said. "Far as I know he never was one to fight anyway."

She didn't mention that Holm had pressured her for information. If everyone knew about that, then when and if someone was caught, people might assume she had ratted someone out. She might be glad if it just meant she didn't have to listen to people's troubles anymore, but it wouldn't stop there. She could find herself dead behind a bar some night after she'd played a gig. No one on the rez wanted to have a murderer among them, but everyone hated anyone who had anything to do with the FBI even more than they hated the FBI.

Gordon called for another round. They dropped the subject of Buffalo Ames and talked about everyday stuff while Sonny told an occasional off-color joke that he said he had heard in the seminary. After an hour, Howard invited everyone to go on the Legion Club with him and Viola.

"This beer is too thin for me," he said, standing up. "I need a scotch and water. Besides, we're supposed to meet Pete and Zooey there."

"Yeah, where are they?" Sonny asked.

"They went to eat first," Viola said.

"I thought Zooey didn't want to eat," Sissy said, and when everyone looked at her, she said, "Never mind."

Speedy glued herself to Sonny's side as he started for the door.

When Sissy didn't stand up with the others, Gordon asked, "Aren't you coming?"

She shook her head.

"I don't like that place. Too many big shots."

"We're going there. Are we big shots?" Gordon asked.

"Not that I noticed," Sissy said. "You know, the local clientele."

Gordon sat back down.

"You guys coming with us?" Howard called from the door.

Gordon waved.

"You go on. I think I'll stay here."

"Suit yourself," Howard said, and everyone but Gordon and Sissy left.

"So," Gordon said with a little grin that showed he still had all his teeth and they were very white. "What's a nice girl like you doing in a place like this?"

Sissy should've said what Sonny would have: that's an old line that has lost its funny.

"Can't find the door," she said.

Gordon talked, but not much and nothing about himself or where he had been or what happened to him or why he came back home. Sissy didn't give him much back either, so after an hour they just sat quietly listening to the jukebox and watching the few couples pushing each other around the little back dance floor to No Show Jones and Johnny Cash songs.

Gordon lightly touched her wrist with his finger.

"I have a bottle in my car, if you want something harder than beer but don't want to go to the Legion."

"Okay," Sissy said. The neon Hamm's beer sign with the clock in it read ten-thirty. *From the land of sky blue waters* flowed across the sign in blue script over the picture of the cute bears.

As they walked past Tom Holm's booth, he caught her eye, gave a little half grin and winked. Sissy ignored him. No one but the bartender had come anywhere near his booth.

Gordon drove a two-year-old maroon Riviera with black interior that still smelled new. Someone said he had bought it with the insurance money he got from the accident he was in—the accident that no one seemed to know details about. It was a nice car with a good radio tuned to KOMA Oklahoma City. That station didn't play country, but it was the only radio station they could get up in South Dakota after the sun went down.

Gordon drove west along the highway slowly like drunks do because they can't drive very well, and they're afraid if they go faster they'll weave and the cops will stop them. A couple of miles out of town he pulled off onto a narrow dirt road that wound back to the north, then into a little pull-off in front of a wire gate that led to someone's cow pasture. He switched off the lights and the engine, but left the key turned to accessory so they could listen to the radio. He moved the seat back, reached under and pulled out a fifth of Jack Daniel's.

They each had a long swallow, then lit cigarettes.

When they had put them out, he said, "I don't bite."

Sissy slid across the seat. There was no moon, only stars partly obscured by drifting horsetail clouds. Somewhere back along the highway, a truck motor whined and geared down for the long climb up the hill to the west.

"Turn around," he said, gently nudging her until she had her back to him, her legs extended on the passenger seat, her top half almost on his lap, and her arms around his neck. He smelled of Old Spice cologne and tobacco and a faint medicinal scent like liniment. He tasted like scotch and cigarettes, and she knew she did too.

"I have to go back to town," she said. "I've got to find a bathroom."

"Me, too," he said. "But I think there is a Men's Room in front of the car and a Ladies' Room in the back."

Before she had finished, she heard the car door open, and when she stood up and zipped her pants, he was standing by the opened back door on the passenger side facing away from her, hatless. A little breeze lifted strands of his black hair.

"All right?" he asked.

She hesitated, but then stepped into the backseat, shoving a jacket and a coiled rope out of the way. He slid in after her, put his arms around her, pressing her down on the seat while he unzipped his pants with the other hand. She sat up.

"Just like that?" she asked.

His face held surprise.

"What else do you want?"

"If you have to ask, you don't need to know."

He sat back up in the seat with a little gusty sigh.

Sissy got out on the opposite side, got back in the front seat, and lit a cigarette.

From the backseat, he cleared his throat and spat out the open door.

"I guess you're not that kind of a girl, huh?"

"Depends on what kind you're talking about," she said.

On the way back to town she sat way over on the passenger side while he drove. When they passed the town limits sign, he said, "Can I buy you breakfast?"

It was not quite good enough, but she accepted the apology.

The Highway Café wasn't busy yet, but it would be in a few minutes because in Jackson the bars had to close at midnight by city ordinance. Martha's Café uptown, where Sissy worked, and the Highway Café had an agreement. They didn't compete with each other on Saturday nights but alternated staying open, except when the harvesters were in town. Gordon and Sissy had their pick of the tables since the bars weren't closed yet. They ordered sausage and eggs. He grinned at her as he poured catsup on his over-easies.

"I guess I'm used to big-city girls," he said.

"I don't guess I'll ever be one of those," Sissy said.

"Do you want to be?"

"Depends on how you mean it. If you mean would I like to get out of here, the answer is yes."

"Where would you go?"

"I don't know. I just know I can't stand the thought of being here for always."

He forked eggs into his mouth and chewed.

"This place isn't that bad. You don't know what cities are like."

"I'd like to find out."

He shook his head and went on eating.

The bell over the door dingled and a group of people came in, Clayton among them.

"Hey, Sissy," he said as he sat at the table next to Sissy and Gordon. "Hey, Gordon."

"Hey. Who's with the kids? I thought you stayed home on the nights we weren't playing," Sissy said.

"I do usually. But I took them over to Ruth's place for a few weeks. Ruth can use some help with canning, and Darrell can run around with Ruth's boys." He perused the menu that he pulled from between the salt and pepper shakers and the sugar shaker.

When they had finished, Gordon drove Sissy back over to where she had parked her car at the C & C. She thanked him for breakfast, but as she started to open the car door, he touched her shoulder.

"You're all right," he said. "You have such beautiful brown eyes."

"My eyes are green," she said.

Speedy got home just before Sissy did. She saw Sonny's car going away up the street, heard Taffy next door barking like a maniac. She told him to hush, and for once he did, wagging his tail and whining. She remembered what a darling pup he had been, thought about sticking a hand through the fence to pet him, but she was worried about pulling back a stump instead of her hand.

Inside the dark house, the window fan whined and gusted; Wooly Booger rose from his bed on the rug just inside the back door. Yellow light came from under the bathroom door. Sissy rapped on it.

"Speedy?" She heard water running.

Speedy answered in a muffled voice like her nose was stuffed up.

"Yeah."

Sissy waited.

The water ran.

"Speedy?"

The lock clicked. Speedy came out, ducked past Sissy, around the corner and up the stairs. Sissy brushed her teeth and followed Speedy upstairs. She was already in bed, her face turned toward the wall.

"Speedy?"

She didn't answer.

"Sonny isn't the marrying kind," Sissy said. "You should remember that."

Chapter Five

CHICKEN CACCIATORE

July 13–18

Clouds rolling overhead like thick gray sheepskin covered the sky, insulating the ground from the sun. Thunder grumbled halfheartedly but without the follow-through of rain. Temperatures dropped, a respite for humans and animals but slowing down the ripening of grain in the fields. Farmers looked anxiously at the sky, praying it wouldn't come a long hard rain to knock down the grain stalks, shattering their seeds irretrievably or bring hail with the same outcome. The ranchers, though, sat back in comfort, knowing the cooler weather prolonged the nutrients in the grass their cattle ate, giving them heft that would translate to dollars in the fall when the spring calves were sold.

Sissy worked at the café that week, tending the daily local customers, bracing for the onslaught of work when the seasonal combiners hit town. The big combine harvesters were owned by only a few individuals who had the credit at their local banks to buy them, then to hire crews and follow the ripening grain harvest north from Texas to Oklahoma to Kansas to Nebraska, then across the state line into South Dakota and, for a few, on into North Dakota and the windswept wheat fields of Montana. Many of the local farmers in every state counted on the custom harvest crews to get their crops in. It didn't make sense for the smaller farmers to go into debt for a big combine that they would use only once a year for two or three weeks at most, so it was cheaper to hire the work done. Bigger operators owned their own harvest machinery, but if their crops looked to produce heavy, they might hire custom workers, too, in order to get the grain out of the fields and into the bins before a storm came along and wiped out all the work they had put into their fields with nothing to show but another loan signed at the bank to buy next year's seed and fertilizer.

The cool weather slowed the harvest farther south, too, so Sissy courteously waited on the courthouse biddies and the local businessmen, kicking her heels in the early afternoon when there were no customers, the side work was caught up, but the long hand on the clock was too slow in moving to two o'clock when her shift would end.

She and Speedy sat at the counter in the empty café polishing stools with their behinds when Viola came in, skirted around Speedy, and sat on the stool on the other side of Sissy.

"You're a little late for lunch," Sissy said to her. "We ran out of the special."

Viola folded the menu and fanned herself with it. She already looked cool enough in her sleeveless white blouse, her blue seersucker skirt and white flats.

"A glass of tea would be nice," she said.

"I'll get it," Speedy said.

"How come you aren't at your dad's clinic working?" Sissy asked Viola.

Viola fluttered her hand.

"Flexible schedule," she said. "I do the books, so if I say I'm caught up, nobody checks. Besides, I skipped my lunch hour on purpose. You get off work about now, don't you?"

Sissy looked up at the clock, watching the minute hand sweep upward.

"Just . . . about . . . now," she said, pulling off her apron and standing up. "See you."

Speedy set the glass of tea in front of Viola, pulled off her own apron, and grabbed her purse from under the counter. "See you tomorrow?"

"Yeah," Sissy said, fetching her own purse. "See ya."

She was almost around the counter heading for the door.

"I really need to talk to you," Viola said.

Sissy stopped in mid-step, put her foot down and turned around.

"In private."

"Okay."

Viola gathered her handbag. After the two were in Viola's new Cougar pulling away from the curb, Sissy realized that Viola hadn't taken a single sip of her tea or paid for it either.

"Are you ready for the harvesters?" Viola asked, pausing at the stop sign at the end of Main Street before turning right.

"Ready as I'll ever be," Sissy said.

"Hmm. I hear the harvest is late this year."

"Yes."

Viola drove south past the Highway Café with its empty parking lot, past the Farmer's Co-op Feed Store, past the Standard Oil station, past the fairgrounds, out toward the new subdivision on the south side of town. She lived there with her parents and her son in the biggest house on the block, a white colonial with a double car garage and a circular driveway in front with pink roses planted in the circle.

"I thought you wanted to talk to me in private," Sissy said as Viola parked in the driveway.

"Oh, I do," she said.

Her mother was home with Viola's four-year-old, Jeffrey, who ran and grasped Viola around the knees. She pulled his fingers off one by one, giving him a little push. He jumped up and down chattering in a way that reminded Sissy of Julius the monkey. Jeffrey was big for a four-year-old, with an even larger head covered in a mop of unruly brown curls.

Mrs. Bianco sat on the living room carpet surrounded by a clutter of discarded teddy bears, stuffed rabbits, wooden blocks, fanned-open cloth children's books, balls of many colors and sizes, upturned trucks and cars, a toy xylophone with a pair of mallets, and a pull-toy duck. Mrs. Bianco's hair looked like she patronized the same beauty shop as the courthouse biddies, but her dress came from a higher-scale shop, probably some expensive shop back east. It was hiked up around her knees, showing bare freckled legs with purple veins.

"Did you make chicken cacciatore?" Viola asked.

"For all the good it did me," Mrs. Bianco said, pulling herself upright by leaning on the piano bench behind her. "Your father couldn't come home for lunch. Too much work. He says."

Sissy followed Viola into the kitchen, the origin of spicy smells. Dark wood cabinets surrounded the room above and below, with appliances in the new harvest gold color.

"Hi, Sissy," Mrs. Bianco said belatedly. "Are you hungry?" She looked hopeful, so Sissy said yes. She'd never had chicken cacciatore, but it smelled almost as good as her mom's chili.

Mrs. Bianco reached into an overhead cabinet for white china plates. They had a gold rim and a bouquet of little pink flowers painted in the middle of each one. She flipped off the spotless white tablecloth, wadded it up and walked a few steps, pitching it through a door that Sissy thought was probably a laundry room. Jeffrey ran around and around the table, pulling the wooden duck that made a quacking sound as it rolled.

"My Viola is getting married," Mrs. Bianco announced, smoothing a clean white cloth on the table before she set down the plates, lining up sparkling silverware neatly alongside each plate.

"Yes, I heard," Sissy said. "I'm very happy for her. And Howard."

"Oh. Howard." Mrs. Bianco said. She opened a drawer and took out starched and pressed white napkins, folded them in fan shapes and put one by each plate. "Howard. Yes."

"I hear it's going to be in November after the Broussards' cattle are shipped," Sissy offered.

Viola tried unsuccessfully to stop the duck.

"Jeffie. Jeffie, go play in the living room," she pleaded.

Jeffrey dodged her restraining arm and resumed circling the table. As he passed behind Sissy's chair his wooden duck went astray, catching her heel with a sharp blow.

"Have you decided where to hold the wedding?" It seemed to Sissy that Mrs. Bianco would make those decisions instead of Viola.

Mrs. Bianco stopped fussing with the simmering pot on the spotless range.

"That Jennie Broussard! She keeps insisting that it has to be at Holy Rosary Church in Pine Ridge. I ask you, Pine Ridge? There isn't a paved street in the entire town. And Holy Rosary is Catholic."

Sissy didn't respond, but she didn't need to. Mrs. Bianco went on about the recalcitrance of Jennie Broussard, the dangers of organized religion that answered to a pope, I ask you, and the need to start off married life with some sense of style and class, as she poured the contents of the steaming pot into a huge china tureen that matched the plates, plunked it down in the middle of the table and sat down herself across from Viola and Sissy.

"Now," she said brightly, leaning across the table to Sissy. "What would you like for the maid of honor's dress?"

"I don't know. Don't the bridesmaids usually wear the same color dresses as the maid of honor?"

Mrs. Broussard stared at Sissy. She barked a short laugh.

"Not *you*, dear." She ladled a big helping of red soup with chicken pieces and vegetables in it onto Sissy's plate, then the same on Viola's, then her own. "I just want your advice about color and style. I haven't decided on who will be maid of honor. Certainly not Zooey!" She barked another laugh. "Denise Cannard says your dress was the most beautiful one she's ever seen at a wedding when you were maid of honor at—at— well, I can't remember whose wedding."

Sissy tried to cut a piece off the chicken leg on her plate. It rolled, splashing red soup onto the tablecloth.

"My mother made it," Sissy said.

"Oh," Mrs. Bianco said. "Well."

While Mrs. Bianco ran through the list of colors she thought appropriate for Viola's wedding, Sissy ate chicken cacciatore. It had an unfamiliar taste, maybe oregano, which Sissy had heard of, but that spice had never seen the inside of her mother's cabinet, so she didn't know. Viola got up to distract Jeffrey toward some toys in the living room.

"Winter colors don't flatter Viola," Mrs. Bianco was saying. "A summer wedding with pastels would so much better suit her skin tone, don't you think?"

Before Sissy could answer, a medium-sized yellow metal truck sailed past her ear, landing in the soup tureen, which cracked with a pop like a firecracker, flooding red soup and floating chicken parts and vegetables onto the tablecloth. Sissy pushed her chair back and stood up to escape.

Mrs. Bianco rushed into the living room, swooping Jeffrey up in her arms.

"Ohh, my little man," she cooed. "You're just such a lively little man."

Viola drove Sissy home. As they passed the fairgrounds, Sissy noticed several trucks loaded with harvesting machines and a few campers and trailers on the grounds where the harvester crews were allowed to park their equipment every year. In another week, the grounds would be so full of trucks, trailers, harvesters, and men that it would look as busy as an overturned anthill.

"What was so private about discussing your wedding?" Sissy asked Viola.

"Mother doesn't want just everyone to know," Viola said.

"That's it?"

"Well, that, and Howard says he's got to talk to you."

"About your wedding, I suppose."

"No." Viola's lips pressed together. Her hands held a tighter grip on the steering wheel. "About Buffalo Ames."

"What? Why?"

"He says you might know what to do?" Her voice went up at the end, making a question out of a statement as if she didn't agree.

"About what?"

"I don't know. He just wants to talk to you. We'll be at the Interior Rodeo and Dance on Saturday night." She was silent a minute and then she added, "He says it's important."

Sissy thought about Tom Holm. He said sooner or later someone would talk to her. She didn't want to know what Howard had to talk to her about, but she hoped it was meaningless.

As Sissy walked up the driveway to the back door, Viola called after her, "I didn't want to ask you, but Howard said I had to."

Martha took Sissy aside the next day during a slack moment after the coffee breakers had left and before the lunch crowd started coming in.

"I need you to work on Saturday. It's our turn to stay open on Saturday night, and the harvest crews are coming in. I'm going to need all the help I can get." She wiped her red roughened hands on her apron that was already stained and dirty in a line across her belly where she leaned against the kitchen counter while she worked.

"Martha, I told you the Red Birds have a gig at Interior on Saturday night. I told you that two weeks ago, and you said I could have the weekend off."

"But I didn't think the harvesters would be coming in this soon. If you're not working, we'll be run off our feet."

"What about Bessie? She could probably use some extra money." Bessie was retired from bartending at the Legion Club, a big fat woman who was slow at waiting tables, had a sagging lower lip, and smelled like she used cheap cologne instead of deodorant. But she was friendly with the customers.

Martha twisted her apron, staring out the front plate windows. A hot wind blew a discarded sheet of newspaper down the street. It floated like a low-flying hawk, hunting.

"Come on, Martha, the crews have just barely started coming in. I was by the fairgrounds yesterday. It's practically empty."

Martha turned back to the kitchen where a timer was going off.

"All right. But you work Sunday then."

Sissy started to protest. She would get in from Interior just in time to go to work in the café, if they could get out of Interior on time and didn't have to hunt up Sonny from the backseat of some willing woman's car. Maybe Speedy's.

"Two to ten shift," Martha conceded.

Not good, but she could get a few hours sleep.

Tom Holm came in on Wednesday afternoon, sitting down at the counter fifteen minutes before Sissy got off work. Speedy got his tea before leaving ten minutes early, apologizing to Sissy.

"I'm sorry, Sissy, but you have to cash him out. I got to take my mom to the doctor."

Sissy went to the other end of the counter to roll setups in napkins. Martha had gone across the street to the grocery store to turn in the meat order for the week, and Lucille the dishwasher was out back having an argument with her kids about why they couldn't take the family car. The courthouse biddies had finished their afternoon break and left. No one else came in.

"I don't have anything contagious." Holm said it in a low voice as if he was talking to himself.

Sissy paid no attention. She spread out a paper dinner napkin, placed a knife, fork, and spoon in the middle, brought one edge of the napkin to the center, then rolled the entire set into a neat package.

He lifted his tea glass to eye level and addressed it.

"I checked myself this morning when I took my shower. No scaly skin patches, nothing dripping, no open sores, no obvious physical defects."

Sissy rolled another setup. The sun shone down from a blue sky, cleared of clouds in the last hour. People moved up and down the streets, a few kids with nothing to do, several farmers in town to check with the Ag extension office about any harvest crews that had registered as looking for work, or to get parts for broken-down equipment. This time of year, all the farmers walked with a nervous step, glancing skyward often, hoping to get their harvest in before a storm came.

"I smell bad. That's why people don't talk to me. Yes, I offend."

Sissy grinned. She laughed.

Tom grinned back at her.

"That's it, huh?"

"Look," Sissy said, putting down the setup she had just rolled. "It's nothing personal. You're FBI. Nobody wants to be seen talking to you. Nobody wants anybody else to think they have told you about somebody else's relatives doing something they shouldn't have. You arrest somebody; you go away. We have to live here with the relatives of the person that got arrested, and those relatives are likely to go looking without good intentions for whoever they saw talking to you."

He looked down at his teaspoon, nodding his head.

"Yeah. Just like where I grew up."

He wanted her to ask where he grew up; she knew it. She knew he wanted to keep the conversation going. She didn't ask.

"I grew up in a little town in eastern Oklahoma. Near Tahlequah. That's Cherokee country. Not much different in a lot of ways than it is here."

Sissy rolled more setups. It was almost two o'clock, but she couldn't leave until Martha or Lucille came back.

"Lot of good people lived down around Tahlequah. But there aren't many honest ways to make a living. Took me a while to get my mind made up that I had to leave. I miss things there, but I'm glad I left."

A man in dusty work clothes and a feed store gimme cap jingled the bell on the door when he opened it. He poked his head in, looked around but didn't see who he was looking for. He pulled the door shut behind him. Tom didn't turn to look. He crunched the ice from his tea glass.

"Are you happy here, Sissy? You want to stay here all your life? I hear you graduated top of your high school class, won some big awards in whatcha call it? Scholastic contests."

Sissy didn't answer. She shoved the gray plastic tub of setups under the counter.

"What are you going to do with the rest of your life, Sissy?" he asked.

Sissy ran back through the kitchen, yanked open the back door.

"God damn it, Lucille!" she yelled at the startled woman arguing with a pair of tall, skinny boys of about sixteen. "I don't get paid past two o'clock so get the hell in here."

Tom Holm had left. He had also left a ten-dollar bill on the counter to pay for a twenty-five-cent glass of iced tea. Sissy put his change in an envelope with a note written on the back of a blank order slip: *Change for Tom Holm*, and slipped it into the cash register. Did that bastard think she would sell out that cheap?

Band practice that night did not go well either. She got to Clayton's small white house on the north side of town in plenty of time, but Sonny was late and Melvin had called earlier to say he couldn't come. By the time Sonny got there, Clayton had walked the floor for forty-five minutes, his short legs going up and down like a sewing machine needle, while Sissy tuned her guitar over and over with Clayton still insisting it wasn't exactly on pitch. But Clayton didn't say a hard word to Sonny when he came in. He never did. He sulked or took it out on Sissy, who couldn't get the intervals in "Sweet Dreams" perfect enough to please Clayton.

"Hey, Clayton, I think we need to spice things up a bit, do some more modern pop music," Sonny said.

"No, that's crap," Clayton said.

"Oh, come on. People will like it; you'll see. What about—I don't know, something by Steppenwolf."

Clayton creased his brow and, sticking out his lower jaw, said, "Steppenwolf? What the hell kind of a name is that for a band? Sounds foreign, like, like, I don't know. Where-wolf or something."

"Werewolf, not where-wolf," Sissy said. "Maybe Sonny has a point. You know, what about something by Glen Campbell. He's doing some pretty good country stuff. What about 'Galveston'? That's a good song, kind of a ballad."

"Nobody up here knows where Galveston is and nobody gives a shit," Clayton objected. He narrowed his eyes and ducked his head to see beneath the half-lowered window shade as a car went past on the street. "Wonder why Old Lady Henderson is out driving around at night? She can't see over the end of her nose."

Sonny rolled his eyes at Sissy.

"Old Lady Henderson would like some new music, I bet," he said.

Clayton stared at them.

"No. Hank Williams and Hank Snow and Patsy Cline and those guys were good enough for years and they're good enough for now," he said.

"Clayton, you're showing your age," Sonny said. "Lighten things up a little. We could do 'Crimson and Clover' or, I don't know, what about 'Hang on Sloopy'?"

"*No!*" Clayton and Sissy said together. Sonny shrugged and gave it up.

Sissy told them she was too tired to concentrate, went home and right to bed.

On Friday morning Gordon came in for coffee with the Ag extension agent. He greeted Sissy as if she was someone he didn't know at all when she brought them coffee and cinnamon rolls. Of course, he really didn't know her at all. After the Ag agent left, Gordon still sat in the booth looking out the window, so Sissy brought him a refill on the coffee.

"You have the prettiest green eyes I ever saw," he said solemnly staring at her face.

"Will that be all?" she asked.

"No. Are you still playing the Interior Rodeo on Saturday night?"

"The Red Birds are."

"Will you see me there?"

"If you go, I don't see how I could avoid seeing you," she said. But she smiled at him.

That afternoon the harvest crews hit town like a swarm of locusts. One minute there were a few of them, like the scouts of some distant horde, but within a short while pickup trucks filled all the parking slots that weren't taken up with locals. A few strangers in big hats and nice clothes mingled with the locals, but most of the newcomers were young men, clean dressed in faded jeans and shirts and lace-up work boots, young men who had just graduated from high school in Paris, Texas, or Carnegie, Oklahoma, or half a dozen towns like that, young men who had been out of school a few years, aimless. Perhaps they thought that crewing a harvest would give them a chance to see different country, have an adventure, but mostly what they saw was the amber waves of grain from the platform of a combine harvester going around and around and around a field, or the back end of the truck ahead of them as they convoyed to the next harvest town, or the crowded inside of a hot camper where they slept on sweaty sheets crammed in with half a dozen other young men who had the same dreams that would not come true. If they hadn't hired on with a cheapskate who fed them bologna sandwiches three times a day, they also saw the inside of greasy spoon cafés from

Texas to the Canadian border. And they saw local girls like the waitresses who had been warned to stay away from them, but who were unlikely to pay any attention to the warning.

During the Friday lunch rush, Speedy waited on six harvesters crammed into a booth meant for four, and one of them was nice to her. She got a bigger tip than he could afford and a plea for her to meet him back at the café at supper when she would be off work.

The waitresses called the orders through to the kitchen; they ran to take new orders, to set out glasses of water, to respond to calls for a fresh full bottle of catsup, to answer the ding from the kitchen bell and the call of "order up!" The dishwasher couldn't keep up. They substituted paper plates for crockery, paper plates that didn't contain the heat so that when Sissy removed the plates she had stacked up her arm and handed them around a table full of hungry men, she had six round circles burned on her left arm. She collided with Speedy running the opposite way and dropped a gallon jar of Thousand Island dressing with a crashing splat. She cleaned it up, but their feet slipped when they ran over the greasy spots. The bell by the cash register dinged for someone to cash out customers while the bell on the door rang constantly with people going in and out. Customers complained that the service was slow, but nobody walked out. There were only two cafés in town and both were busy.

Sissy had to stay over until three o'clock to catch up on the side work. She walked the two blocks home, wishing she had brought her car because even two blocks was too far to walk on aching feet. She took a shower and sat down with her mom who had just taken fresh cornbread out of the oven. Why her mother would insist on heating the house up with baking in the middle of the day, Sissy never could figure out. But her mother turned the window fan up another notch, put Sissy's chair in front of it and brought her iced tea.

The back door banged open as Speedy rushed in.

"Hi, hi, everybody," she said. "Sissy, I need to borrow that blue blouse of yours."

"Okay," Sissy said. "But it's dirty. You'll have to wash it."

Speedy walked around the kitchen, stopping to sniff the cornbread just out of the oven.

"I could wash it right quick," Sissy's mother volunteered.

"Do you think it would get dry?" Speedy asked.

"Depends on how soon you want to wear it," Lily said.

"What do you need it for?" Sissy asked. "How can you be hopping around like that? Aren't your feet tired too? Mine are killing me."

"What's a little pain if you got something good happening?" she said, sticking her tongue in the side of her cheek even though she hadn't said anything funny.

"All right. What do you have going?"

"I got a date tonight," she said, sitting down on the edge of a chair.

"With Sonny?" Sissy asked. Lily raised her eyebrows behind Speedy's back.

"No, a guy I just met," Speedy said.

"The only guy you could have just met would be a harvester," Lily said. "I don't know if that's a good idea."

"Oh, he's nice, he's decent. He really is."

"If you just met him, how can you tell?" Lily asked.

"You just can," Speedy said. "Look, I'll figure out something to wear. Thanks!"

She jumped up from her chair, brown ponytail wagging, banging the back door as she left.

CHAPTER SIX

INTERIOR RODEO AND DANCE

Saturday, July 19, 1969

Melvin stirred the dust under his boots walking back and forth in front of the tumbledown picket fence in front of Clayton's house. Sonny was a no-show, so either Clayton or Melvin would have to keep himself awake on his own coming home.

"He'll be there after the rodeo for the gig," Sissy said.

Clayton raised up from shoving more equipment in the backseat of his car. His oiled black hair gleamed.

"He tell you that?"

"No."

"You need to tell him he'd better straighten up. You'd think a man who'd been to the seminary would have a better sense of responsibility."

"Clayton, I'm his cousin, not his mother. Tell him whatever you want."

He slammed the car door, but it wouldn't shut. He slammed it again. It wouldn't shut. A trickle of sweat ran down the side of his face. He took out a pocketknife, fiddled with the latch on the door, then slammed it again. It shut. He dropped the knife on the ground, leaned over to pick it up.

"Clayton, if you can't get along with the way Sonny does things, why don't you get someone else to play bass? What about Rabbit? What's he doing these days?" Sissy asked.

"Maybe I will get Rabbit," Clayton said. He walked back to his house, fumbling with his door keys before opening the door and going inside.

Melvin got into his pickup, rolled down the window and drummed his thick fingers on the top of the door. Humidity curled tendrils of hair on Sissy's forehead. It would rain soon; the flies were biting, and cicadas buzzed in the trees. A few clothes hung disconsolately on a clothesline at Old Lady Henderson's house across the street.

Melvin tried to tune in to a good music station on his pickup radio, but there weren't any. He got the news and weather on KOTA out of Rapid City and left it on that station.

Claude Sauer's voice came on, saying, ". . . partly cloudy with scattered afternoon and evening thundershowers, heavy at—"

Melvin switched it off.

"Think Sonny will show up?" he said.

"Yeah. He always does. He doesn't like Clayton telling him he has to show up hours before time to start the gig."

"You mind?"

"Not if I get to see the rodeo first. But I'm not going to show up eight hours early to play a gig if there isn't anything to do until we go on."

"Yeah. Clayton's trying to be the boss," Melvin said.

"I suppose he is the boss of the Red Birds, isn't he?"

"Now he is. Marlene used to manage all that kind of stuff. You know, getting the bookings, making sure we had all the equipment, that everyone showed up on time. She said Clayton couldn't manage his way out a wet paper bag."

Sissy didn't say anything. Marlene was all right. Sissy thought she knew why Marlene left Clayton to run off with that other guitar picker if it meant getting away from this place. It wasn't that the grass was greener someplace else, it was just that she couldn't stand Clayton anymore.

"I guess she just ran out of patience," Melvin said.

Clayton came out of his house, slammed the door, tried to lock it, dropped the keys, cussed, took long steps on his short legs out to the car.

"Get in. Let's go," he said.

"Rabbit coming to take over for Sonny?" Sissy asked as Clayton cranked the car over, roared the motor, and backed out with a lurch of the transmission.

"No. He hocked his bass," Clayton said, pressing his lips together.

To get to Interior, you turn right at Kyle instead of left like you do to get to Scenic. They drove through grassland, fenced on both sides of the road with old gray twisted posts holding up rusting barb wire, here and there spliced where it had broken. The dusty road ran on like a tangled string between the fences. Black Angus cows and their half-grown calves and the necessary bulls lazily ate the fading grass, here and there reaching through the fence to get at the ungrazed taller stuff in the ditches.

You can tell a whole lot just by looking at the color of the grass up here. The celery green in the spring quickly turned emerald if it got plenty of rain or kelly green if it didn't. Around the middle of June, the seeds formed on the top of the stalks, a golden tan frosting waving in the endless wind. By the first of July, the blades faded to gray-green, reviving to kelly or emerald if the rains came, but by August the hot sun would bake the prairies and the grass to gold. The seed stalks would turn reddish brown with the first frost of September, poking up above the snow banks of winter like snorkel pipes on scuba gear above the ocean of white.

Just past Kyle heading northeast, Sissy said to Clayton, "You hear from Darlene and Darrell?"

His face brightened. He twisted his hands on the steering wheel.

"Darlene's helping with the canning. She says they put up forty-eight quarts of green beans, a dozen of beet pickles, and something like that of tomatoes. Darrell cut his foot on a beer bottle while he was swimming in the pond, but he's okay. His auntie took him into Mission IHS for a tetanus shot. Boys. I almost drowned over there in that pond as a kid." A little smile curved up the corners of his thin lips.

"They coming home soon?"

"Nah. Ruth's garden ain't half done producing, and the chokecherries will be ripe this week or next. Darlene wants to help her auntie make jelly."

Interior was a little cleaner looking than Scenic. More grass, less dirt, but the same amount of heat in midsummer. The Frontier Bar had a neon sign on the front, and the room inside was square with a low ceiling. There wasn't any bandstand, only an area in the corner marked off with chicken wire, leaving a door-sized opening back against the wall.

Clayton smiled when he saw that.

"I told them we wouldn't play here anymore without protection," he said. "At least somebody pays attention to what I say."

Melvin stared at the fenced-off area.

"How am I going to get my bass drum through that little tiny opening?" he asked.

"The question is how are you going to get your big fat belly through that little tiny opening," Sissy said. Melvin looked hurt, and Sissy regretted saying something so mean. He wasn't all that fat, and he was a nice guy.

Clayton went to look for a pair of pliers.

"What if someone lobs a bottle over the top?" Melvin asked.

The Interior rodeo grounds looked about the same as the arena at Scenic, except the shaded awning over one side was bigger and better made—poles sunk into the ground with more poles lain across the top to form rafters and cut boughs of pine lain across that. It smelled like the forest in the Black Hills after a good rain.

The Eyapaha pattered through the final roping events as Sissy, Clayton, and Melvin walked over to sit under the awning. Clayton had forgotten the lawn chairs. Melvin's jeans pulled down from his waist a little as he sat down on the ground by the Broussard brothers, Viola, and Zooey, who looked comfortable sitting in folding lawn chairs. Pete picked a long stalk of grass with a seed cluster on the end, chewed on it a minute, then stuck it in Melvin's butt crack just showing above the top back of his jeans. The grass stalk waved in the breeze like a vegetable tail. Melvin didn't notice.

Zooey sat on the other side of Pete, sober and sullen, a Coke held between her legs. Sissy sat on the cooler that held their lunch.

The last pair of team ropers came out chasing a brindle Mexican steer. The header caught both horns, flipped the steer around and led him off, and the heeler caught both heels, but he was dallying the rope instead of tying it hard and fast to the saddle horn. The heeler dropped his hand at just the wrong moment as the rope flipped itself into a little loop, catching his little finger. All eight hundred pounds of steer hit the end of the rope, popping the end of his finger off like a broken pretzel stick. He yelled and clutched his right hand with his left, but the horse paid no attention, wheeled, and the steer went down stretched between the ropes attached to both horses. The heeler slid off his horse, walked over to the far fence, leaned over and puked. The Eyapaha announced the last team as the winners in seven seconds. The heeler wiped his mouth on his shirt sleeve, walked back to his horse and slapped him on the neck with his good hand. The horse walked forward slackening the rope. His partner got off and slipped off the ropes. They coiled their ropes and walked their horses out of the arena, the horses' slow hoof-falls raising little puffs of dust. The crowd cheered. The prize was a pair of silver belt buckles for each and fifty percent of the jackpot: $250. Nothing extra for the missing finger except a round of sympathy applause.

Viola spread a red-checked tablecloth on the trampled grass and laid out the lunch she had brought along with Sissy's fried chicken, baked beans in a Tupperware bowl, and a pan of brownies. Viola set out a bowl of Jell-O that had melted, leaving banana chunks and walnuts swimming for their lives, a package of uncooked wieners, another of buns, and cupcakes with white frosting and red hot hearts. Zooey sat.

"I thought there would be a fire somewhere to roast the hot dogs," she said.

Howard said, "Never mind," and dutifully put on his china plate a raw wiener on a bun topped with sweet relish alongside a piece of fried chicken, some baked beans and a puddle of Jell-O.

Around them, families set out their own picnic food on tarps or blankets or whatever they had. Kids ran and screamed and fought, kicking up dust and bits of grass that floated in the air, settling slowly on everyone's food.

"Beans, beans, the musical fruit," Melvin said thoughtfully to his plate.

"You riding bulls today?" Clayton asked Pete.

"No," Pete said shortly. Nobody asked why.

Zooey ate a few bites, set down her plate and walked off toward the bar without a word.

"Zooey," Pete called after her. "Ain't you gonna eat?"

She kept walking.

"Well, fuck me," he said.

Everyone waited patiently through the bareback bronc event for the saddle bronc competition because the Hiller kid was riding again. Or trying to. He drew a bald-faced overo paint gelding with white eyes that came lively out of the chute, but just before the whistle blew, the horse gave a bawl, reared up and went over backward. The kid went down in a dust cloud, the horse rolled, and the crowd gasped, but the kid unwadded himself and stood up slowly, collecting his hat from where it had rolled several feet down the arena. He walked off with the Eyapaha giving his usual spiel under such circumstances: "Give that cowboy a hand, folks, 'cause that's all he's gonna get here today."

Gordon's Riviera pulled up right behind the pavilion just as the bull riding was getting under way. Gordon unfolded himself out the driver's side door, and three of Zooey's friends, Cristal, Edwinna, and Loretta, got out the passenger side and the backseat, giggling. They were all dressed more or less alike in short skirts, sleeveless tops, and high heels. Loretta, a big girl with boobs bobbing under her hot pink print top, took Gordon's arm and steered him unsteadily under the pavilion. He leaned over and said something to her in a low voice. She laughed as she tripped on a grass hummock. Gordon nodded a quiet hello to everyone, then went to stand at the fence with the women, partly blocking everyone's view.

Howard yelled, "Down in front!" and about that time an old Brahma that had ditched his rider crashed into the fence, hooking one horn and bending the wires. The women grabbed for Gordon, who almost went down under their weight.

Sissy was tired before the Red Birds even started playing.

The setting sun glowed red on the horizon when Sissy stepped out behind the building for a smoke and some quiet thought after helping Clayton and Melvin set up, Clayton fuming because Sonny hadn't shown up yet. She propped a foot behind her against the crumbling stucco, wondering where she would be next year at this time, what she would be doing, and hoping it wasn't looking forward to another summer calling orders at the pass-through at Martha's Café.

"Hey, you got a minute?" Pete Broussard stood at the corner of the building.

"Yeah. I heard Howard wanted to talk to me," Sissy said.

Pete looked over his shoulder and came around to squat on his heels by Sissy.

"Viola told him not to, so he sent me. Did you know Buffalo?" he asked.

"Just to say hi to, that's all," Sissy said.

Pete picked up a rock and tossed it from hand to hand.

"Wasn't much to know," Pete said. "He worked for us from time to time. Helped feed in the winter, round up in the fall. Sometimes he helped with haying. Can't keep hands to do that. Not for very long. It's back-breaking work tossing hundred-pound bales around."

"Yeah," she said. "I know. I was helping my granddad get in hay bales when I was twelve years old and the bales weighed more than I did."

"Too bad your granddad's dead. He was a good old man."

Sissy didn't say anything.

"Buffalo—he didn't have any enemies. Wasn't much going on upstairs, but some of the ladies liked him. I never did see why because he didn't have much of a future." Pete gave a little laugh. "Doesn't have *no* future now."

Sissy tapped the ash off her cigarette. From inside came the low rumble of voices and distant laughter.

Pete stood up and pitched the rock toward the setting sun. Bouncing across a little washout, it hit a fence post with a little pop.

"I sure wish I knew who did it. Buffalo wasn't much, but he was a decent sort of guy. I'd like to get the bastard that killed him. You got any ideas?" He squinted at her from beneath his hat brim.

"Why do you think I'd know anything about it?" Sissy asked.

"I don't know," Pete said. "Maybe you saw something from up there on the bandstand that nobody else did."

"Didn't see anything but a roomful of drunks."

Sonny appeared around the corner. He looked at Pete and then at Sissy.

"Clayton's looking for you," Sonny said.

"He's been looking for you since ten o'clock this morning," Sissy said.

"I guess he sees me now."

"How'd you know where to find me?" Sissy asked.

"You usually go around back here for a smoke before we get started," Sonny said. He slid a hand down the pressed seam on her shirt sleeve, shook his hand and made a face. "Oooh, that's a sharp crease. A man could cut himself on that."

"That's an old joke that's run out of funny."

Sonny led the way back around the building toward the lights of cars just arriving in the front parking lot, Sissy and Pete following.

Pete said, "People talk to you. Get ahold of me if you hear anything."

"I haven't heard anything," Sissy said.

Zooey stood just outside the front door with Loretta, Cristal, and Edwinna. Cristal poked Sonny in the arm as he walked past.

"Where you been?" Zooey said to Pete.

"Never mind," he said, following Sonny into the din and the dim glare. Zooey's arm blocked Sissy from the door.

"You always was a sneaky little bitch," she spat her words in Sissy's face. "What were you doing with Pete?"

"Talking, just talking," Sissy said, ducking under Zooey's arm and into the bar. Zooey grabbed for the back of Sissy's shirt and missed.

Clayton noodled scales on his guitar as Sissy stepped through the opening in the chicken-wire pen. He gave her the look. Sonny caught it and winked as Clayton went into the opening spiel.

The dance floor filled up with couples, most of them still sober for this first set. Again they played the favorite oldies first because that's what people wanted to hear, saving the newer country songs until everyone was too drunk to complain that the Red Bird versions didn't sound exactly like the ones on the radio. At the first break, the bartender plugged the jukebox in, but most of the audience listened without dancing while they drank and talked to their friends and neighbors. Jim and Lena Horn slowly waltzed to a tune that wasn't a waltz, but they were old with poor hearing. Lena wore a hat with a feather that looked like something she had worn to church for twenty-five years and probably had.

Clayton worked the room again. As they came out from the chicken pen, Sissy held onto Sonny's arm and walked to the bar to order a drink.

"When'd you get so friendly, Cuz?" he asked her.

"Since Zooey and her bunch are out to kick my ass," she said.

"What'd you do to piss her off?"

"Nothing that she thinks I did. Just sit with me, though, will you?"

"Anything for you, little cuz," he said.

Donna the bartender served them first. They were walking back to a table when Sissy felt a tug on the back of her belt. She turned expecting Zooey's fist to smash into her face, but it was Gordon grinning at her.

"How about a dance, green eyes?"

She handed her drink to Sonny, who waggled his eyebrows at her.

Gordon led her stiffly onto the dance floor, circling around Jim and Lena.

His arm around her back felt like a tree branch she could lean on but not for very long.

"Where's your girlfriend?" Sissy asked.

He leaned away from her with fake shock on his face.

"You know. Loretta. I always heard you're supposed to dance with the one that brung ya. Or you brung. Or something."

He pulled her back to him, his feet barely moving to the music. His breath gusted in her ear.

"They were at Sharp's Corner looking for a ride. I gave them one."

The music went on a little.

"Are you jealous?"

"No. Just don't want to get my ass kicked."

Gordon laughed lightly. The music stopped briefly. The jukebox clicked mechanically, the needle hissed. The jukebox played a song about a lonely man staring at the walls.

Over on the other side of the room, a scuffle ensued. Tiny Dismounts the bouncer, who was well over six feet tall, lifted a man by the back of the shirt, hustling him toward the door, which was held open by Tiny's equally big twin brother, Sleepy. Tiny gave the man a heave while Sleepy shut the door and dusted his hands.

Zooey sat with the Cristal, Edwinna, and Loretta at a table near the dance floor, staring at Sissy.

When the song ended, Sissy stepped back but didn't let go of Gordon's hand.

"Come on," she said.

Outside the back door, she gently put her arms around him and raised on tiptoes so her lips barely brushed his.

"You want something?" he said in her ear.

"Maybe I do."

He turned with his arm still around her shoulders and led her across the parking lot to his Riviera. Lightning flashed on the horizon.

Knuckles rapped on the car window.

"Sissy! Clayton's getting pissed. We're ten minutes overdue." Sonny peered through the fogged window.

Sissy untangled her legs, sat up, and opened the door.

"Quit trying to peek, Sonny, I'm fully dressed. I've not been out here long enough to get in trouble." Then to Gordon, "You got a comb?"

Back in the bar, as she leaned over to pick up her Gibson, Clayton said, "I'm changing it up. Do 'Crazy.'"

Sissy shot him a look.

"You know I can't make that interval and hit the top note square."

"Yes, you can. Just don't think about it. Sonny will help you out."

"Sonny can't help himself out," Sissy said.

"You can do it, Sis," Sonny said. Clayton was already playing the opening bars.

She hit the note square on "feeling" and went on a little stronger.

She heard Sonny singing softly behind her, unmiked. She hit the note again on "feeling," knowing she had it now.

Sonny's voice supported her to the end. It was beautiful.

Just as she finished, she looked down and there Gordon sat, just off the dance floor, looking back at her with a thoughtful expression, his hat off and a sprig of his hair sticking up from the crown of his head. She had his comb in her back pocket.

At two o'clock when the lights came up, people rushed the bar to get their take-home beer and liquor. Clayton thanked everybody for coming, reminding them that the Red Birds would play Kadoka in two weeks at the Rattlesnake Lounge in the Holiday Inn. Most of the people there at Interior wouldn't go there because even though it was right off the reservation, it was a mostly White town. No one wanted to wake up in the county jail the next day to find out that the justice of the peace wouldn't accept their money for the fine and spend the next week working it off as laborers on the Kadoka City garbage truck runs. Indian labor was cheap at the price.

Sissy and Sonny were loading equipment while Clayton had one for the road at the bar as he collected the money for the night from the owner. Melvin was helping load equipment but had gone back inside for his drums. People were loading themselves into their cars loaded drunk mostly, but a few were sober enough to drive for the others. The Broussard brothers stood outside the door talking to Jim and Lena Horn.

Lightning flashed, followed by a crack of thunder.

Zooey and her friends came across the parking lot toward Sissy and Sonny. Zooey didn't stop until she almost ran into Sissy, their faces inches apart. Sissy could smell her whiskey breath. The scar on Zooey's face shone white as lightning flashed again.

"Who the hell do you think you are?" Zooey demanded.

Sissy didn't answer. Sonny tried to pull Sissy away, but the car door was between them. Zooey crowded Sissy again, raised her hand and took a slap at Sissy's face, but Sonny's arm shot out and blocked the blow. Sissy sat back onto the car seat, her back hitting the box containing the cables and the mike.

"I'm going to beat your ass!" Zooey screamed. "You think you're so much. You ain't shit! You hear? You ain't shit, you fucking whore!" Her fists pummeled Sissy, who put up her arms to shield her face.

Sonny tried to pull Zooey off, but Cristal and Loretta batted at Sonny. Edwinna was nowhere in sight.

"I'm going to slice you up, you bitch!" Zooey yelled.

Somebody else yelled, "Hey!" and then Zooey was pulled away.

"God damn it, can't you ever behave like a decent woman!" Pete yelled and shook Zooey.

She jerked away from him and leaned back toward Sissy.

"You see this? You see this scar? I'm going to give you one worse than this. You just wait, you fucking whore!"

Pete dragged Zooey away across the parking lot.

Under the neon sign over the front door, June bugs bashed themselves against the light. Lena Horn put the tip of her tongue against the middle of her upper lip, moving her head from side to side.

"Young people never acted like that when I was growing up," she said to her husband. Then the rain came in a rush of pounding drops, thunder, and flashes of lightning.

Chapter Seven

DOG DAY NIGHTS

July 20–25

The rain that hit Interior was part of a broad front that reached all the way down to the wheat fields around Jackson. While the harvesters waited for the fields to dry out, they clogged the streets of the town, those with cars driving up and down the single main street along with the local farmers in town for repairs or groceries, the local high school kids cruising west the three blocks of Main Street, then left at the fire station, down another three blocks to the highway, east to the Standard Oil, and north back to Main Street—a big circle of vehicles whose exhaust hung heavy in the air. They jammed the town's two cafés for lunch and dinner, tracking mud onto the floor that the waitresses slipped in as they ran sweaty and harassed from table to table taking orders, bringing food, refilling coffee cups and tea glasses, clearing dishes, taking money at the cash register, and sticking tickets on the spindle beside it. In the back, Martha and the dishwasher sweated pints in the heat from the grill and the oven.

Whenever there was a break in the hustle, Speedy and Sissy took turns taking glasses of lemonade back to the kitchen workers who held the ice-cold glasses to their foreheads, rolling them back and forth in the sweat. When the last tables emptied out at closing, they locked the door, wearily swept the floor and did the side work before going home to shower and tumble into bed. Except for Speedy, who was staying in town with Sissy and her parents during the harvest season so she wouldn't have the long drive home every night. But every night she was out with her harvester boyfriend for an extra hour or two after Sissy got home.

By Wednesday the fields had started to dry out. The town population thinned out to almost nothing during the day, with the lunch crowd down to local businessmen and a few farmers. The harvest foremen bought lunch fixings at the grocery stores and carried it to the men in the fields, but they still swarmed the cafés at night for suppers that seemed to go later and later. By Saturday the harvest was more than half over. A few of the crews who had annual contracts with farmers farther north moved their crews out. They convoyed out, crowding the roads and forcing anyone stuck in a vehicle behind them to travel at less than thirty-five miles per hour up hills and around corners until they could find a place to pass.

Speedy cried to Sissy after work one night.

"You knew he was going to move on," Sissy told her.

"I know," Speedy sobbed. "But when he said good-bye, he called me Jane!"

Sissy's parents packed up the Ford Falcon and left for a month to visit Lily's sister down in Kansas. Retired from the State Highway Department two years earlier, Lawrence never went far from home for very long, and Lily never went much of anywhere, even in Jackson. Sissy tried to get her parents to spend the worst months of the winter in Texas, but Lawrence said no. He was afraid if he died down there, his soul wouldn't find its way back home. With the house empty without her parents and Speedy out somewhere with Sonny most nights, Sissy switched to evening shift at Martha's even though that meant being busier at night. At least she wouldn't be home alone in the evenings or tempted to spend those nights at the C & C watching Speedy make moon eyes at Sonny.

Toward the end of the week only a few stragglers of the harvesters still camped at the fairgrounds, which now looked like a tornado had hit a garbage dump. In spite of the city's efforts to keep trash bins stationed there and empty them regularly, wind and dogs knocked them over, people pitched things at the bins rather than in them, and the result was a morass of bottles, paper, and assorted flotsam, some half buried in mud from the rain. But the town was quieter. Floyd and Don, the city cop and his deputy, came out of hibernation to harass teenagers breaking the curfew. When the harvesters were in town, there was no way to enforce petty laws on anyone, seeing as the jail only had two cells. As long as no one committed a major crime, Floyd and Don made themselves scarce.

The night was remarkably quiet when Sissy walked the broken sidewalks home after her shift on Thursday night. Twenty years from now, would she still be walking home from a shift at the café, or would she give up and marry some local guy, hatch a couple of kids or three? Maybe she ought to think about that feed salesman's proposition, but she was convinced it wasn't a proposition that led to anything but making the salesman smile and making her cry. Maybe she could get to Nashville on her own. Or someplace else. Maybe she could save up some money and start college. Maybe she could be a music teacher. She was years into an uncertain future when a new dark blue Ford Fairlane purred up beside her, idling along at walking speed. The window rolled down. In the blue-white light of the streetlamp, Tom Holm's light hair looked incandescent.

"Sissy? Need a ride home?"

"Seeing as how I am only two blocks from home, I don't think so," she answered.

The car eased forward to keep up with her determined walk.

"We need to talk," he said.

"I don't have anything to tell you," she said, shifting her handbag higher on her tired shoulder.

"I have something to tell you," he said. "You'll be glad you listened."

She hesitated.

"Speedy will wonder where I am," she said. "She's staying with me."

"She won't wonder anything," he said. "She's with Sonny Roberts parked in his pickup at the rest area out west of town."

Maybe she was too tired to argue or maybe she wanted to hear what he had to say, but mostly she just didn't care about much anymore. She got in his car.

His hair looked slightly green in the dash lights. Driving down to the main highway, he turned right heading out of town.

"Where are we going?" she asked.

He glanced at her, jaws working a wad of gum.

"You don't want to be seen with me in town, do you?"

"No."

"All right, then."

She reached over to turn the radio on, but he put out a hand to stop her.

"I need your full attention," he said.

A mile out of town they passed the rest stop where Sonny's pickup was parked, lights out half behind the farthest picnic table.

Tom drove on. A tiny grocery store hunkered on the north side of a wide spot in the road nine miles west of Jackson where a side road led off toward Kyle and Yellow Bear Canyon. The sign on the front of the store wasn't lit up. Tom drove the Ford into the dark shadow at the side of the building where no one had mowed the grass since the beginning of summer. Tall weeds brushed the underside of the car. The motor tick-tick-ticked as it cooled. Tom spoke.

"Buffalo Ames, aged twenty-seven years old at the time of death on the night of July 4, morning of July 5. Died of massive trauma to the back of the head, probably inflicted with a heavy rock found near the body. Autopsy showed a reasonably healthy man for his age, except possible early signs of liver disease, probably from heavy drinking. Parents still living, both officials for the Sioux tribe—had been since Buffalo and his five siblings were born. The parents provided a reasonably stable home environment. Buffalo attended Holy Rosary High School where he was a marginal student at best. He played football for half of his freshman year before he quit. Played basketball all four years where he was tops on the team. There was talk about a college scholarship, but with his grade record, no college wanted to touch him. A week before he was to graduate, he was arrested in Chadron, Nebraska, for drunk and disorderly and minor in possession. It took his parents ten days to find him and bail him out, since he had no identification on him, and he wouldn't say who he was. He missed his own graduation, but it's questionable if he would have gotten a diploma anyway, with his grades."

Holm continued, "He hung around Pine Ridge for a while, doing not much of anything. Then his parents sent him to a trade school over in the eastern part of the state. Diesel mechanics. Six months later he was back in Pine Ridge living with an uncle. The uncle got him a job on the Broussard ranch. Buffalo worked on and off for ranchers from Hot Springs to Winner, never staying at any job more than a few months. He made it up with his parents, so in between jobs he stayed there or with the uncle. He had some friends he hung out with, dated a few women if you can call picking someone up in a bar dating. Well-liked by everyone, or so I hear. Funny that the ladies liked him, when he didn't seem to be going anywhere. Can you explain that to me?"

Sissy lifted a shoulder. "There isn't much to choose from around here," she said. "Any guy who is going anywhere leaves, except for the few whose parents have a farm or a ranch or a small business to pass on to the kids. There aren't many of them."

"All right. Men who graduate from high school who are going anywhere leave here. Why don't the women leave here? Why do they stay here?" He looked directly into Sissy's eyes.

"What, are you getting personal? What business is it of yours why I didn't leave here?"

"I'm not asking you personally. I'm speaking generally." When Sissy didn't answer, he added, "No offense."

"Where would a girl go? Yeah, there's a few who leave for college. The ones whose families have the money to send them. But if you don't have money or connections, what can you do? An eighteen-year-old taking off for the big city with no plan and no money and no family just isn't a good idea. A few have tried it. They get homesick and tired of being used and come home with a kid in their belly or in their arms. Why go away for that? You can end up like that right here."

Sissy lit a cigarette. Tom rolled down the window, letting in the sounds of crickets calling for mates in the high weeds.

"So, even a guy with not much of a future might be husband material. Especially since he might have prospects, what with his parents being in tight with the tribal administration. If he put himself out, he might get a job with the tribe. Right?"

Sissy exhaled a long column of blue smoke.

"Yeah. Nepotism runs amok around here."

"Buffalo had applied for a job with the tribe as cultural resource officer. I don't know what that job is, but it's a civil service job that pays a decent entry salary. Good enough for him to get married, start a family, and make a life for himself."

"Maybe he was tired of bucking hay bales at a nickel apiece and bumming off his family the rest of the time."

"Some people say that he was planning to get married."

"And? Happens every day."

"He told a couple of people that he had gotten a girl in trouble, and he wanted to marry her, but she was backing up with both feet and fending him off with both hands. Considering the shortage of husband material around here, that does sound odd."

"Damned odd," Sissy conceded. She would never find herself in that position, she told herself. Not that she was a prude about sex before marriage, but if she married somebody, she wanted it to be because she chose to and not because she had to. Love . . . well . . . how many people were lucky enough to find that or smart enough to know when it wasn't enough?

"Any single woman recently tell you that she's pregnant? Ask your advice?"

"What the hell is this? You said you had things to tell me, not things to ask me," Sissy said. She reached out to snuff her cigarette in the ashtray, but it was full of peanut shells. She pitched the butt out the window.

"I did tell you things you didn't know. Or did I?" His face had that stone-faced Mount Rushmore look again.

Sissy said, "I knew that's what the deal was when I got in this car. I don't know why I let myself think otherwise for a minute."

"I got a job to do, Sissy. I'm doing it the best way I know how."

"Do you have to enjoy it so much?"

"I like my job. I don't much care for this assignment. Don't you think I'd rather be in L.A. busting kids for marijuana and lying on the beach in my off time? Or back in Oklahoma rooting out bootleggers and petty thieves?"

"I would have thought you'd want to be in for bigger stuff. Taking down Mafia kingpins in New York City or something, not scavenging around for information about a murder on an Indian reservation."

"I'm not suicidal. Busting the small criminals is good work, too, and a lot less dangerous. You know why they sent me on this one?"

"I don't know, let's see," Sissy said. "Someone hates your ass?"

"Well, that, too. But some big belly in Washington, DC, thinks that since I'm an Indian I can get information and wrap this up better than a White guy could."

Sissy looked hard at his blonde hair.

"You're one of the funniest looking Indians I ever saw," she said.

"God damn it," Tom pursed his lips in disgust. "Look. I'm a Cherokee. Some of us are darker than a string of black billy goats at midnight because we intermarried with black slaves. Some of us have corn silk yellow hair because we intermarried with Whites going back before the Revolutionary War. But if you have Cherokees in your ancestry, you're a Cherokee. You want to see my CDIB card?"

"Not really. I never understood that certificate of Indian blood thing anyway. Who's to know who granny really did have sex with?"

"Well, right. But try to get it through some bureaucrat's head up in DC that all Indians don't look like, don't think alike—and just because I'm a Cherokee doesn't mean a Sioux is going to tell me shit about a murder."

"I'm a Sioux," Sissy said.

"And you aren't telling this Cherokee shit, are you?"

"I don't know shit to tell you! How many times do I have to say that? I didn't know Buffalo Ames, and no one has confessed to me that they killed him, or that they know anything about who might have killed him. No girl has come crying to me about being knocked up and not wanting to marry the guy that did it. I don't know anything about this! Ask somebody else."

He tapped his palm slowly on the steering wheel.

"I asked a lot of questions to a lot of people, but none of them have as much potential to give me the facts as you do."

"Even if I knew any facts, I'm not sure if I would tell you. I have to live here. You get to leave when this is done—go home to your wife and kids. You do have a wife and kids?"

He looked surprised.

"Well, yes, I have a wife. And kids."

"Is she a Cherokee, too? What would she think about you harassing another Indian woman?"

"She's not Indian. She's Jewish."

Sissy let out a laugh.

"A blonde-headed Cherokee married to a Jew. How in the hell did that happen?"

He grinned, breaking the stone of his face.

"Met her when I was in the army." His grin dropped away. "I miss her. We have two boys, and I miss them, too. I want to wrap this up and go home."

"Where's home?"

"Oklahoma City."

"I thought you came out of Rapid City, here in South Dakota."

"Assigned to OK City. I was in Rapid for a conference, so they sent me down here."

"What if you can't figure out who killed Buffalo Ames? Are they going to just leave you here?"

"No. I'll get to go home eventually, but it wouldn't look good on my record."

"So, you want me to snitch so your record will look good?"

He slammed his hand on the steering wheel.

"No, god damn it! I want to find out the truth, make an arrest, pack my bags, and go home. You're the best possible source I've got, and right now you ain't much."

"Thanks a lot. No matter which way I take 'ain't much,' it ain't good."

He started the car.

As they passed the rest stop outside of town, Sissy noticed that Sonny's pickup was still parked there. The dashboard clock read 12:48 a.m.

There were no lights on in any of the houses on Sissy's street. Tom drove the car right up into the driveway, the gravel crunching beneath the car tires.

"Sissy, there's something else. Look, you're a smart, talented young woman wasting your time in this town"—he held up a hand when she started to interrupt—"I know, I know. You can't help being stuck here. But I happen to know that you graduated at the top of your class in high school not that long ago. I figure if you had the money, you've have gone to college. The FBI has a fund to pay informants. That could be your ticket out of here."

She didn't know whether to be insulted or hopeful, but it didn't matter either way because she couldn't sell information she didn't have. The only thing she did know was that Pete Broussard wanted to get whoever had killed Buffalo Ames, but that was about a future event that might not happen if Pete didn't figure out who killed Buffalo. Indians died or got hurt in violent ways on the rez all the time from accidents, drunken fights, and what all, and sometimes someone knew who did it, but most times even the person who did the deed didn't remember doing it because they were drunk.

She got out of the car.

"Think about it, Sissy," Tom said. He backed out of the driveway, his headlights picking up a cat crossing the street as the car went away, and then the street was dark except for a pool of blue-white light beneath the streetlamp halfway down the block. Sissy stepped into the shadows by the back door, fumbling her key into the lock.

She heard them before she saw them, a rustling behind the big yellow wild rose bush at the end of the porch, then running feet. She had time to turn her head toward the sound, just, then she was hit and knocked backward off the porch, landing with both hands on the gravel of the driveway before someone else landed in the middle of her back.

"Where the hell you been, bitch? Who the hell just brought you home? Huh?" The voice was female.

A fist had her hair at the nape of her neck, raising her head and bending it backward at a painful angle. She twisted, pulling her own hair, raised her knee and pushed upward, bouncing the attacker off her onto the gravel, but she had the satisfaction of knowing that whoever this person was, they weren't attacking her because she was seen in the company of an FBI agent. They hadn't seen who had brought her home. She hoped they hadn't seen the car so they wouldn't be able to put it together later.

She started to stand up but was hit and knocked down by another person, who smashed a fist into the side of Sissy's head as she went down. Taffy barked and tore at the gate in the fence just three feet from her head.

"You think you can mess over people and get away with it? You ain't shit, you fucking bitch! You think you're hot shit standing up there in your fancy shirts pretending to play a guitar and sing." A female voice, a different one, so two women, but neither sounded like Zooey.

Sissy's head spun; her vision was blurred in the dim light.

"Who—who are you? What are you talking about?" she said, and got a kick to the ribs for her questions.

"Never mind who we are, and you know exactly what the hell we're talking about, you fucking whore! Bitch!"

"I don't know what you're talking about!" She slid away toward the fence.

"You got lucky up at Interior," the first voice said. "But your luck just ran out."

She shifted against the fence, felt Taffy's warm breath on her hand. As she moved her head, she saw two shapes dimly: Cristal and Loretta. Zooey might have put them up to it, or she might not know anything about it. No telling which. The two stood uncertainly for a minute, as if their first instinct was to knock her down and yell at her some more, but once past the first yelling and hitting, they weren't sure of the next move. Sissy knew it wouldn't take them long to get inventive. She hoped neither of them had a knife.

"I don't know why you and Zooey came after me up in Interior, either," Sissy said as calmly as she could. Her ribs hurt, and she felt blood on her palms where they had been ground into the gravel. "I didn't do a damn thing to Zooey or anybody else."

Loretta, the biggest shadow, struck out again with a foot, but Sissy jerked to the side so the blow only glanced off her calf.

"Look," Sissy said, "if she thinks I was out back of the bar messing around with Pete, she's dead wrong. I was out there having a smoke before the band went on, and he came out to talk to me, about some nonsense, I don't even remember what. There's nothing going on between me and Pete."

"You're a liar!" Cristal said. She held a long dark object in her hand, maybe a pipe or a tree branch or a baseball bat.

"I don't know what the hell you're talking about!" Sissy screamed, hoping the neighbors would wake up. Taffy continued to bark, but everyone was used to his noise.

"You know exactly what we're talking about!"

"Look, we're giving you a warning," Loretta said. "Get her."

Cristal swung the weapon just as Sissy stood up with her hand over the gate. The club caught Sissy a glancing blow on her upraised arm just as her other hand unlatched the gate and swung it open in front of her body.

Taffy rushed forward as if shot from a gun, jumping and snarling at Cristal, who dropped the club and put up her arms. Loretta kicked at the dog, who snapped at her leg, catching his teeth in her pants.

"Get the stick, get the stick!" Loretta yelled.

Cristal reached for the dropped club, but Sissy kicked it away from her. Loretta screamed as the dog's teeth finally bit into more than pants leg. She jerked free and ran limping through the backyard and out into the alley, the dog snapping at her heels, Cristal following, trying to distract the dog from Loretta without getting bit herself.

Sissy picked up the club. It wasn't a bat, but it was a stout stick. She was breathing hard, her ribs hurt, her arm hurt, her palms stung and bled. From down the alley she heard a car start, the tires squealing as it accelerated. Taffy barked on. The neighbors' windows remained dark.

Chapter Eight

MELON, JUST MELON

Kadoka sat right of the edge of the rez, too, but it was on the east side and a far different town than Scenic or Interior, because, unlike the other two, Kadoka was on the main tourist highway to the Black Hills. The town survived from the trade of local ranchers and farmers, but the gravy came from tourists passing through in their station wagons and campers from May to September, dropping money in the gas stations, local restaurants, and hotels. Most of the tourists had never seen an Indian in their life, but when they did, they wanted their picture taken with him. Or her. Ellis Old Bear and a couple of his cousins picked up some good cash standing alongside the highway dressed in pow wow costumes. The clientele that patronized the Rattlesnake Lounge in Kadoka were not there to drink away their troubles, just ordinary White people on their annual two-week vacation from the auto factory in Detroit or mid-level city workers from Cleveland or Des Moines. They arrived tired and hot and crabby in their two-year-old station wagon with the luggage rack on top, three kids fighting in the backseat, with nothing of note in scenery for three hundred miles except for the consecutive Burma Shave signs alongside the road.

Businesses were strung out along both sides of the highway like the contents of an upturned trash can, a trail of brightly colored boxy buildings, some brick, some painted in bright colors and all with signs to attract tourists: *Rattlesnake Display! World's Biggest Jack Rabbit! Get your cold drinks HERE! Hot Coffee 5 Cents No Limit Refills! Ice Cream Cones! Petrified Wood! Air Conditioned!*

Gas stations sat on the very ends of the string because each owner believed that tourists stopped at the first station going either east or west, so they hopscotched each other until gas stations stretched out on either end of town for two miles in each direction. Several small motels sat alongside the highway, but the Holiday Inn, that middle-class, middle-priced bastion of respectable accommodation, was on the north-east corner of the highway, on the only paved street that led off the highway to the residential section of town with the public school, the civic buildings, and the public park—places where tourists ventured only if they were lost or one of their kids had to pee and they couldn't find anything open.

Sonny called Sissy on Saturday morning to say he was riding up and back with Clayton, so she had to go with Melvin.

"How come?" she asked. "You looking forward to being browbeaten for two hours up there and two hours back?"

"You mean, when he starts out, 'For a guy who's been to the seminary, you sure blah blah blah'?"

"Yeah. I know how much you hate that. So what are you up to? And why couldn't you ride up with Melvin?"

"Melvin had some things to do so he won't be leaving until later."

"Okay. So, again, what are you up to?"

Silence on the other end, then he said, "More like what I'm getting away from. Fast."

She thought silently a minute longer than he had. "Oh. Speedy crowding you?"

"Something like that."

"Oh, but she's so cute when she puts her tongue in her cheek like that!"

"She's cuter when she puts her tongue someplace else, but lately she's been pushing me about putting her shoes under my bed permanently."

"I thought you were smart enough to know that. So, you aren't okay with a wife?"

"That's one thing I did learn in the seminary. No wives."

"I thought you were supposed to be celibate too."

"So I only learned half of it. Look, are you gonna trade with me or not?"

"What'll you pay me?"

"Sissy, come on. Don't do me that way."

"What way? I'm just looking out for the interest of women."

"Speedy ain't no woman. She's a vine with a mouth and claws, and she's choking me to death."

"I'll tell her how much you appreciate her. I could offer her a ride up to the gig with me and Melvin."

He groaned. "Sissy, please help me out on this one. Be a decent little cousin for a change."

"All right, all right. But you owe me one."

Clayton and Sonny were already gone when Sissy got to Clayton's place, but Melvin was waiting in his pickup parked in the driveway. He wore a charcoal gray Western suit, a white shirt, and a black string tie. He gave her a once-over look.

"What?"

"Well, first, you don't look like Sonny," he said.

"I hope not," she said, settling into the seat and dumping her handbag on the floor. "He rode up with Clayton."

"Really?" His eyes went wide with surprise.

"Yeah, I know. He wanted to leave early. He's hiding out from a girl."

"Anyone I know?"

"Speedy."

He nodded knowingly. "*That* one." But he still stared at her.

"What?"

"You're wearing jeans and a shirt and boots."

"Yeah. So? You're wearing a fancy-ass suit."

"We're playing the Holiday Inn. In Kadoka."

She slapped her forehead. "Oh, shit. I completely forgot. Dress code."

"Yeah, Clayton won't like it. The bartender might not let you in."

"Well, to hell with Clayton, and the bartender has to let me in if he wants a singer. God knows you other three can't carry a tune in a bucket. I'll give the tourists a little local color. An Indian girl dressed up like a cowboy. They'll love it. They'll probably want to take their pictures with me."

"Not without any feathers in your hair," Melvin said as he started the pickup and backed out, narrowly missing Clayton's battered trash cans.

They drove east from Jackson past fields recently harvested, the stubble already shading from gold to brown, and alfalfa fields where the last bales had been picked up, the recent rains bringing on the green crop again so that farmers might get a light third cutting of hay. Next week would be the county fair, the end of summer pow wow at Batesland where the Red Birds would play, and after that, parents and kids would swarm the local stores and make special trips to Gordon and Valentine and Rapid City to buy their kids school clothes and supplies.

Melvin hooked a thumb toward an empty field of wheat stubble.

"Be some good pheasant hunting there in a few weeks," he said. "Your dad still have that extra 12-gauge?"

Melvin liked to hunt with Sissy's dad because Lawrence owned two 12-gauge shotguns, both good bird hunting guns. He was generous in lending one or the other of them so Melvin didn't have to pay to get his own shotgun out of hock.

"Yeah. Dad says he's got a couple of places he's been watching where the hatch was good this year," she said.

A few miles east of town Melvin turned north on Highway 73, passing pastures going golden, fat black Angus or white-faced red Hereford cattle grazing in the sunshine or gathered around creaking windmills fighting flies or licking salt blocks. Past Long Valley the road dipped down and crossed a part of the Badlands that extended from west of Scenic eastward in a narrowing wedge of sandstone and limestone bluffs and rocks with here and there a wispy stand of grass and no water anywhere. She wondered how the cattle she saw out there could survive or find water.

"Sissy," Melvin started hesitantly.

"Yeah, what?"

"What's wrong with me?"

"Where do you want me to start?" she asked, but he looked so downcast that she touched his shoulder in apology.

"Melvin, there isn't anything wrong with you."

His hands gripped the steering wheel, his eyes straight ahead.

"If there's nothing wrong with me, how's come I don't have a girlfriend?"

She was surprised. She thought he had a live-in.

"What happened to . . ."—she did some quick thinking—"Carmen."

"Carmela. She left six months ago."

How was she going to offer useful advice without being hurtful? Did she say that Carmela was a pinch-faced little bitch with no brains and no sense of humor?

"She said she didn't have any future with me," he said. "She's living with Bob Red Shield over on White River in a shack with no plumbing, taking care of his five kids. If she'd rather live like that than with me, well, what does that say about me?"

"It says she's a moron," Sissy said, and then she asked, "What's this Bob Red Shield look like?"

"Just your regular kind of guy."

"Melvin, I don't know what your regular kind of guy looks like. Can you be more specific?"

"I don't know."

"Well, is he tall, short, thin, fat?"

"He's just regular."

"So he's average height, average build?"

He nodded.

"What does he do for a living? Got money?"

"No, he doesn't have a job. I hear he's got some land he inherited that he's about to sell."

"Jeezus christ, Melvin, don't you see what's going on here? Once Bob Red Shield has the money from his land sale and Carmen—or Carmela or whatever the hell her name is—she is going to live up all his money and then she'll be gone."

He glanced at Sissy as if in disbelief, but hopeful.

"You think she might come back to me then?"

"Melvin, why would you want her back?"

"Because she's the only woman that ever stayed with me for more than one night."

"Melvin, listen to me. There isn't a damned thing wrong with you. Look at yourself, all decked out in that fancy suit. You look good!"

He looked down at his shirt front, brushed off imaginary crumbs or dust.

"You think so? I mean, I'm kind of getting a beer belly." He splayed his pudgy hands on the steering wheel. "And I can't get all the grease out from under my fingernails."

"That's honest dirt, Melvin. Look, you own a half interest in the auto shop, don't you? You don't drink all that much. You pay your bills. I never heard of anyone having to bail you out of jail for anything. You'd make some woman a good husband."

"Carmela didn't like it because I played in the band," he said.

"Women are always attracted to the men in the band, but once they get the man, they want him to give up the very thing that attracted them in the first place. You know why?"

"No. I never understood it myself."

"It's because they're self-centered little bitches. They want the exciting guy, but they know there are other self-centered little bitches who want the band guy, too, and they are afraid that one of them will take you away from them. And besides that, they want all the attention. For christ sakes, those women are even jealous of the guy's guitar—or drums or whatever."

"Yeah. I remember Carmela got mad every time I had to go to practice."

Sissy remembered Carmela coming along to the gigs, sitting alone at a table in front of the bandstand and glaring at any woman who she thought might be eyeing up Melvin—not that many did, but there were a few. She was sorry Melvin missed her, but she knew he would be even more miserable if he still had her.

"So, how come we never went out together? You and me?" Melvin asked.

Sissy thought fast. Melvin was fat, not grossly obese, but solid, big. He was a nice man. Maybe somewhere in his late thirties, she thought. It was true that he would make some woman a good husband. He'd be loyal and faithful; he'd bring home his paycheck every Friday night. He would take out the trash, and if there were kids, he'd help them with their homework with a pencil whose point he licked before he tried writing on a Big Chief tablet. But he would never read a book that wasn't a manual for rebuilding a transmission. He'd never listen to the news or wonder about what went on in South America or think seriously about who to vote for. He'd never vote. His one talent besides repairing transmissions was playing drums, and he was happy playing with the Red Birds every other weekend. He was nowhere close to what Sissy wanted.

"Melvin, I like you, but you're like a brother to me," she said, knowing full well that no man likes to hear that. She tried to do better. "I'm not sure I'm the marrying kind, Melvin, and you deserve a woman who wants to be a wife and mother. That's not me. I don't know what I want, but I know being a waitress and playing with the Red Birds on weekends is not what I want to do for the rest of my life. I want to see the world. After I've done that, I might decide there isn't anyplace better than right here. If I do, then I'll look you up."

"Really?" He took his eyes off the road and looked at her for a long time.

"How old are you, Melvin?"

"Thirty-nine."

"Jack Benny thirty-nine, or really thirty-nine?"

"Huh?"

"Never mind. Here's a deal. Twenty years from now when I come back from wherever I'm going, if you still aren't married, which you will be, I'll look you up. Or I'll look up you and your wife and kids. Okay?"

His wide smile showed slightly crooked teeth and a badly done gold crown on the right corner tooth, compliments of some Indian Health Service dentist. Then the smile faded.

"Twenty years is a long time, Sissy."

"It'll go by fast. You know how time flies when you're having fun."

Even the parking lot of the Holiday Inn was upscale from the places the Red Birds usually played. This parking lot was paved with lines marking out individual parking spots where newer cars sat; a few to one side had longer spaces for cars with campers attached to the back. Even the sign was upscale—a big sign with moveable letters that would be lit up after dark, supported on a curving steel pole that reached out toward the highway in a pleasing arc. Today the sign read: *Red Bird Band in the Rattlesnake Lounge.* Sissy noticed they had left off the "All-Indian Traveling" part of the band's name. The word "Indian" would keep locals from coming, but it might have attracted the tourists. Still, the owner-managers had to live in Kadoka after the tourists went home. Melvin drove around to the side entrance to unload the equipment.

Sissy walked through the blue-carpeted, dimly lit lounge to look through into the restaurant. The room was half-filled with tourists eating an early dinner at the orange and turquoise vinyl booths. She overheard one blonde woman with two preteen children giving their order to a waitress. The neatly dressed woman wore lavender culottes and a white short-sleeved blouse, her light brown hair looking like she'd just come from an upscale salon; the two blonde and pinkly scrubbed kids held oversized shiny plastic menus. The menus in Martha's place were stiff cardboard, food-stained and grubby.

"And for dessert, we would like melon, please," the woman said.

Melon. Just melon, without specifying what kind of melon. Sissy had never had a customer in Martha's ask for "melon." They said watermelon or cantaloupe; some said muskmelon or even mushmelon. They might ask if it was sweet, but they never said just "melon." It sounded sophisticated and fancy. The waitress didn't ask what kind of melon, only collected the menus and walked away. Maybe the Holiday Inn served a mix of melon kinds carved out in those little balls like jewels instead of in slices or chunks.

Someday, Sissy vowed, she would take a vacation from wherever she ended up, come back to visit the Black Hills, stay in Holiday Inns across the country and order just "melon" in the restaurant. Then she had to laugh at herself. Was a Holiday Inn the height of her ambition? What about the Four Seasons or the Waldorf Astoria in New York City, eating fois gras or chopped liver or whatever the hell it was? No. Someday she would be rolling in money, but unpretentious. She would slum at Holiday Inns where her only concession to her wealth would be to ask for "melon" in the restaurant.

Someone touched her shoulder from behind. She turned around.

"Where is your dress?" Clayton asked.

"Hanging at home in my closet. Nice to see you too."

She left him standing there in his suit with the pissed-off look on his face while she went to help Melvin and Sonny set up.

"I see you still have both cheeks of your ass," she said to Sonny. "I thought Clayton would have chewed one of them off on the way up."

He grinned at her.

"From the looks of his face, I think he saved up his hunger to bite off your behind," he said. "How's your arm? And your hands?"

"Stiff, but I'll live. It's a good thing I don't play drums. I don't think I could manage that."

"What are you going to do about the Zooey mafia?"

"Nothing. Nothing now. Maybe I'll think of something later."

"You better watch your back. You could've called the cops."

"And tell them what? I got jumped outside my own house? What would they do about it? Have a little talk with Loretta and what's-her-bucket? That would just piss them off and make it more likely they'd do a better job next time."

"You could talk to your FBI buddy."

"He's not my buddy. And he doesn't have jurisdiction. And . . . well, there's a whole lot of reasons not to tell him anything more than I have to."

"Your funeral."

"Don't be hanging crepe just yet," Sissy said. "I'm going to get a pop. You want something?"

"CC, water back."

"I'll bring you an orange pop," she said.

The bartender was doing what all bartenders do when they aren't mixing drinks. He polished glasses, saw Sissy coming, and turned his back. She tapped on the bar.

"Could I get a Coke and an orange pop?"

The bartender reluctantly put down his towel and glass. When he handed her the two bottles of soda, he tilted his head slightly to one side and peeked over the bar.

"Ladies are not allowed in the bar wearing pants," he said.

"I'm with the band," she said, turning away.

"I have to speak to the manager about this," he said loudly.

"You do that," she said. "But I hope you know all the words to 'D-I-V-O-R-C-E,' because if I'm not singing it, you are."

Five minutes before time to start, the bar was close to full with a pretty even split between locals—men in pressed jeans, cowboy shirts, and boots, women in knee-length conservative dresses with pumps—and tourists—men in slacks, pullover knit golf shirts and loafers, women in shorter skirts or sundresses and strappy heels.

Clayton had already given them the playlist at practice earlier in the week. They would play a few modern country songs, more current popular rock songs, and a heavy dose of what Sissy thought of as vanilla pudding music—sweet but plain and bland. Sissy looked at the list. Clayton hadn't changed it much.

*   *   *

"So, let me get this straight," Sonny had said at practice as he held the sheet of notebook paper with song titles written in pencil. "No Hank Williams? No Ernest Tubb?"

Clayton shook his head. "No."

"No Jim Reeves, no Patsy Cline, no Kitty Wells?"

"No. Modern country."

Melvin got up from behind his drum kit in the corner, wended his way around the ironing board set up to one side of the arched opening into the kitchen at Clayton's house. His T-shirt tail didn't cover the two inches of butt crack showing above his jeans. He rolled into the kitchen, opened the refrigerator, and got a Bud.

Sonny squinted at the list. "Who's modern country? You think George Jones is modern?"

"He's got some new stuff out."

"And Tammy Whine-ette?" Sissy had asked.

"They're a couple," Clayton said. "We do one, we do both."

"So I have to sing like I'm like a strangled rooster."

"She's good, she's good!" Clayton said. "People like her."

"I have no idea why," Sissy said.

Clayton stood up and paced the length of the room, opened the curtain and looked out.

Sonny gave a glance at Sissy.

"All right," he said, "but why can't we do some rock-and-roll stuff? Beatles?"

"I hate the Beatles," Clayton said.

"What, no 'I Want To Hold Your Hand'?" Sonny said, nudging Sissy with his elbow. "What's wrong with that?"

Clayton grimaced. "No."

"Why not?" Sonny persisted.

Clayton slapped the back of the sofa. Dust motes rose and floated in the beam of light from the window.

You can tell Darlene has been at her aunt's for a while, Sissy thought.

"Later Beatles," Sissy said. "You know. 'Hey Jude.'"

Clayton paced back the other way.

"You get Tammy and George, and we get later Beatles," Sissy offered. "And Credence."

Clayton threw his hands out.

"All right, all right. Who runs this band, anyway? That's what I'd like to know."

The corners of Sonny's mouth turned up as he fastened his eyes on the playlist again.

"Okay, so we got modern country, some up-to-date rock, and a lot of songs that only Barbra Streisand, Frank Sinatra, and dead people ever heard of."

"Dead people! I wrote those songs down—now, do I look dead to you?"

Sissy stomped Sonny's foot hard.

Melvin went out the back door.

Sissy tapped the list. "'Night Life,'" she said. "Sonny do you know who wrote 'Night Life'?"

"Nope. No idea."

"Willie Nelson."

He leaned away with his mouth open, eyebrows raised above his glasses rims.

"You're shitting me."

"Nope. It's the truth," Sissy said. "Wrote it when he was a DJ in Austin, Texas, and sold all his rights to it for fifty dollars. It's one of the most recorded songs ever. People like Frank Sinatra and Barbra Streisand made a ton of money out of it and Willie never got another dime."

"You're shitting me."

"Nope. Willie says he has no regrets, that the fifty dollars bought a lot of groceries at the time."

Clayton winked at Sissy behind Sonny's back.

"How'd you know that?" Sonny asked.

"I read a lot," Sissy said.

"Okay, 'Night Life.' That's in. But what's 'People'? And 'Accentuate the Positive'? Jeezus."

"Those are standards," Clayton said.

"Standards for who? George Washington?"

"We've played those songs before."

Melvin looked in through the window in the back door, raised his bottle of beer in a salute to Sissy.

"God damn it, Sonny! You know these songs. They're part of what we've been practicing and playing for years. Here." He picked up a guitar and played a few bars.

"Oh, yeah," Sonny said. "Okay. Yeah. Well, suppose we put some more Willie Nelson songs in with the modern country. He's still putting out a few hits."

When practice was over, Clayton detained Sissy as she was leaving.

He pressed his lips together like he had a mouth full of vinegar that he couldn't spit out. Then he said, "Thanks for helping me out there with Sonny."

"What?"

"You know, that story about Willie Nelson writing 'Night Life.'"

"Willie Nelson did write 'Night Life,'" she said.

"You're shitting me."

Clayton struck up a more piano-bar version of their opening riff, stepped up to the mike, and said . . .

Sissy wondered if he would give the band's full name.

". . . the Red Bird All-Indian Traveling Band. I'm Clayton Red Bird and . . ."

Nobody seemed to notice. She took her bow in turn, waited for the intro to the first song, and sang not Hank Williams but Barbra Streisand, knowing her voice wasn't anywhere up to that and hating it, but the tourist crowd loved it.

At the break, Clayton said, "See, I picked the right songs, didn't I?"

"You did all right, Clayton," Sissy said, looking around the room. The crowd didn't have the enthusiasm that a crowd at the Longhorn Bar in Scenic had, but then there hadn't been fights and beer bottles flying past her head either. She saw a familiar face over in the darkest corner beyond the bar, looked again, looked away.

"What's the matter?" Clayton asked.

Sissy didn't answer but lifted her chin toward the back table. Gordon Charbonneau and Loretta sat so close you couldn't push a piece of paper between them. Gordon had his head down as he leaned toward Loretta who was whispering in his ear. Or kissing his ear. He lifted his head and laughed, white teeth showing. Loretta had a little smile.

"All I need now is for the FBI and the feed salesman to show up," Sissy said.

"Who's the feed salesman?" Clayton asked.

When the gig was over, Sissy walked past Gordon and Loretta on her way out. Loretta smiled and said hi with a lift of her chin that said more than words could have done. Sissy nodded.

Sonny rode home with Melvin, Sissy with Clayton who begged her to drive. She took the wheel while Clayton got into the backseat, wedging himself in among the equipment pieces, but he didn't sleep for the first half hour.

"I don't know why you keep chasing after Gordon Charbonneau. He's no good. A decent man, now, he would ask you to go someplace, you know, take you out to dinner. Maybe a movie or something. Go to your house and meet your parents. Where's he been these last few years? You know, he's got a kid somewhere. People say he shacked up with a

White woman back east and has a daughter. What kind of a man is that for a woman like you? You need someone dependable, stable. What's he done since he got back? Nothing. Mooches off his family up there around Porcupine, drinks on the weekends."

Sissy heard him but didn't answer. Clayton was right. Clayton was an asshole, but he was right. What was she doing? She wanted to get out of this place, go somewhere and be somebody, so why was she dangling herself after some guy who wasn't going to get her anything but a lot of misery in the same old place she'd been all her life? She ought to save up her money and go. Go where? Somewhere, some place, not here. She was tired. Physically tired tonight, tired of this place, tired of it all. Headlights in the rearview mirror stayed behind her, probably Melvin and Sonny. The road dipped down into the Badlands. She pushed the car up to eighty miles an hour. No cops out this far, almost no traffic. If she drove fast enough, maybe she could outrun this place, this life, this emptiness and endless round of the same. The car came over a little hill, green lights sparkling and shining and jostling in the midst of dark shifting shapes not a hundred yards ahead of her. What, was she hallucinating? She must be more tired than she realized. The radio played KOMA from Oklahoma City, more advertisements than music. Then the headlights picked out more distinct shapes, black, moving like dense ghosts in the night, big. She slammed on the brakes, the tires squealed, and the car passed through a herd of black Angus cattle on the road. Clayton's body slammed up against the seat, he cursed; his hand came up over the seat as his face appeared, shocked and dazed, reflected in the rearview mirror. The herd parted like the Red Sea as Clayton's car with Clayton, Sissy, and the band equipment slowed and drove right through without touching so much as one hair on one cow. Sissy pulled over and closed her eyes. She stood on the brakes so whoever was behind her would see the red taillights and slow down.

"I have to get out of this place," she said.

Chapter Nine

AUNTIE RUTH

Sissy awoke from a dream of green-eyed monsters chasing her down endless corridors with doors that were all locked. Someone was pounding on the door. Her parents were still gone. She'd have to get up.

Clayton stood on the back porch, his black hair gleaming, shirt ironed, boots polished.

"You going to a funeral?" she asked.

He stepped into the kitchen, staring at her bare legs below her dad's long shirt she wore as a nightgown.

"You're going to a—going to a—" he raised his arms and let them drop at his sides. "You're going with me. Get dressed."

Sissy held up one hand. "What, where, when, how, why?" She numbered them off on her fingers, turned, struck a match and lit the burner under the coffeepot.

He stepped from one shiny booted foot to the other, waved a hand at the coffeepot.

"We don't have time for that. Get dressed."

"You don't have time for that. I got time for that. I'm not going anywhere," she responded.

"I need you to go with me."

She held up her hand again. "What, where, when—"

"Okay, okay. Have your coffee." He turned, surveyed the room, the dirty dishes in the sink, the mail she had been piling on the countertop since her parents had been gone. He pulled out a chair and sat down at the table, drumming his fingers.

"Clayton. I am not going anywhere today. I am tired. I've not had a good night, a good week, a good month, a good year. Today is my day of rest. You are not my father or my brother, and except on the nights the band is playing, you are not my boss. Get out." She opened the back door and pointed.

He settled his butt deeper into the chair.

"Sissy, I need you to go with me. Wait—wait—" he added as she raised her splayed hand again.

"What the hell time is it, anyway?" She looked at the yellow-bordered plastic wall clock above the refrigerator. "Seven-thirty! Jeezus christ, don't you ever sleep? We just got home three hours ago."

"I've always had plenty of energy," he said. "And besides, I have to go get Darlene and Darrell."

"And you need me to go with you, why?"

"I need you to go because Darlene says she isn't coming home. She says she is staying with her auntie, and Darrell says he isn't coming home if Darlene isn't."

"Why is this any of my problem?" She said that, but a nagging voice in the back of her mind said it was her problem because she had encouraged Darlene to go stay with her aunt in the first place. *Well*, she argued with herself, *maybe both kids were better off with their aunt*. But the voice said, *yeah, and what right have you to decide that? Clayton is their father; he has a right to raise his own kids.*

"I want you to talk to Darlene. If she comes home, then Darrell will come home, too."

"You're their father, can't you make them do what you say?"

"Well, of course I can. But it's better if they come home because they want to."

"Damn it, Clayton."

The coffeepot bubbled gently, letting out steam that smelled like burned coffee beans. She turned it off, picked up a potholder and poured herself a cup. It even looked thick. She poured in some milk from the refrigerator, which promptly curdled. She poured it out, got another cup and filled it with more of the thick black liquid.

"Sissy, I know you can convince them both to come home. You can make it sound like their idea."

"Why should I? Did you ever think that they might be better off at their auntie's? A place in the country, lots of things to do so they don't get into trouble, cousins for Darrell to run around with, a motherly influence for Darlene. What is there for them here? You working late or gone off playing music, Darlene playing mother to Darrell, nothing much for them to do except watch TV and get into trouble." She sat down at the table, held the cup with both hands, and took a sip.

"I want my kids home," he said.

"I want a million dollars, a movie-star boyfriend, and a new car. You help me—I'll help you."

"Sissy, you have to come with me."

"Clayton, did you ever think that you might get more out of life if you asked instead of demanded? Did you ever think about what was best for someone else instead of being a belligerent asshole? Why do you have to make every conversation a contest of wills?"

"I don't do that. I just want what's best."

She slammed her cup down on the table.

"You want what *you* think is best for everyone. You don't listen to what anyone else wants. You don't compromise. You won't compromise. You are a bully. You bully me, Melvin, Sonny. You probably bully the people who work for you in the body shop. You bully your kids. God, I would hate to be your kid. They probably hate being your kids, and if you don't get yourself in hand, Darlene and Darrell are going to hate you, not just hate being your kids."

He went silent. He got up and looked out the window at a passing car, one with a loud muffler.

"That's not true," he said to the window.

"If it isn't now, it's going to be." She got up and poured the coffee down the drain, picked up a sour-smelling dishcloth and wiped up the coffee she'd spilled on the table.

"I ask you, Clayton, why should I convince Darlene and Darrell to come back here when I believe they're better off with their auntie?"

He sat back down at the table, put his hands on his knees and lowered his head.

"Am I really that bad?"

"You're worse. You're a lousy boss, a lousy father, and an asshole. Good thing you're a good musician. That's probably what they'll put on your tombstone: Here lies Clayton Red Bird. He was a lousy boss, a lousy father, and an . . ."

"All right, all right," he said, raising his head. "I get it. So tell me what to do to fix it."

She raised her hands to her face, one hand on each side and rubbed her eyes with her fingers. Reaching up in the cabinet, she took down a can of coffee.

"Here. Make a fresh pot of coffee while I get a shower and get dressed. Where are we going now?"

"Rosebud."

"Good, that's two hours away. I can get a good start on telling you what's wrong with you and how to fix it." First Melvin, now Clayton. Did she know any men who didn't need to be told their faults and how to fix them? How come she couldn't find a decent hardworking man like her dad? But when she thought about it, she knew that Lawrence had been perfect for Lily, but a man like him wasn't exactly what she wanted either. Weren't there men who were smart and fun and interested in the world who were also decent and hardworking? What she really wanted wasn't a man, but time and money to see what there was beyond the borders of the rez, beyond the circle of bars around it, beyond the ranches and farms and every day the same. If a man happened to drop in while she was exploring, that would be good.

By the time she had showered, toweled her hair dry, and dressed, she felt more awake, maybe because she smelled fresh-brewed coffee. Clayton sat on the edge of his chair, ready to jump up the minute she said the word, but he did have grace enough not to nag her to hurry up. With a little bit of canned condensed milk, the coffee was good.

Clayton had cleared the beer cans from the night before out of his car, cleaned the windows, even wiped the dust from the dash. Bouncy as he was with happiness or maybe just punchy from lack of sleep, Sissy resisted enumerating his faults as they drove east to Rosebud. She listened as he whistled along with the radio, tapping his fingers on the steering wheel.

Ruth's kitchen had the look of a place where useful things happened. The chipped double sink was full of soapy dishwater on one side and stacked upside-down stainless steel pots, long-handled spoons, and colanders on the other side. On the countertop by the sink, sparkling clear jars sat on a white towel, with reddish purple stains here and there from berry juice. Similar jars filled with deep red-purple jelly sat on the other side of the sink in neat rows as Ruth poured hot paraffin into the tops to seal them. The room smelled sweet but tangy, as Sissy knew the chokecherry jelly would taste on hot pancakes if she could get her dad to give up the chili for one Sunday. Another batch of dark berries boiled on the stove, steam rising into the air of the already hot kitchen. Ruth and Clayton's mother wandered in, pushing her steel walker ahead of her, took a look around and wandered back out with a rhythmic motion. Stop. Move the walker forward six inches. Stop. Move the walker.

The iced tea glasses in front of her and Clayton and Darlene sweated puddles on the faded red Formica tabletop. Darlene drew squiggles from her own puddle, her forehead furrowed, shoulders slumped beneath her stained white T-shirt.

"How was your calf crop this spring?" Clayton asked, leaning back in his chair.

Ruth carefully sat down the pot with the remaining hot paraffin, wiped the rim of a jar with a damp cloth.

"I got ninety-seven calves out of a hundred and one cows, which is pretty close to ninety-seven percent calf crop. That's as good—better, even—than the big ranchers get. One calf died when it was born in that late spring snowstorm. My fault. I didn't realize that heifer was ready to calve that early, or I could have brought the calf in the house and saved it. One calf came the wrong way and by the time I turned it, it was too late. Then I had two dry cows."

She wiped her face with the damp cloth, pitched it in the soapy water and sat down with her own glass of tea.

"That's two years in a row for those two old cows. They could benefit by a good selling, so in November they go to the auction in Winner along with the calves," she added.

"I could have told you those two were getting too old. You should've sold them a year ago," Clayton said.

Ruth shrugged.

"If it was more coming up dry than just those two, I might think it wasn't the cows at fault. Might just need a new bull in the pasture," she said.

Clayton squirmed and hitched his jeans down from his crotch.

Through the open window came the sounds of kids hollering and distant splashes.

"I think I'll go see if I can catch a blue gill or two out of that pond," Clayton said. "That is, if those damned boys haven't scared all the fish away."

"Fishing poles are on the front porch," Ruth said.

Clayton sat his tea glass down, jumped up and walked rapidly through to the living room, his boot heels clomping on the linoleum floor.

Darlene burst into tears and ran out the back door.

"Clayton means well," Ruth said as the screen door banged behind Darlene. "He just never had any tact. That girl needs a kind word now and then and a little understanding."

The minute Sissy and Clayton had walked through Ruth's front door, Clayton had looked at Darlene and said, "Go pack your stuff. Darrell's, too. You're coming home."

"Raising kids, especially a daughter, is like holding a wet bar of soap," Ruth continued. "You have to grasp it gently. If you squeeze too hard, it squirts out of your hand. Then it's likely to bounce off the shower wall and hit you in the eye. Much as I didn't get along with the kids' mother, at least she kept Clayton from coming down too hard on Darlene. No telling what's going to happen if Clayton doesn't lighten up on her."

"She's a good kid," Sissy said. "But Clayton treats her like she's Darrell's mother, and never makes Darrell do anything for himself."

"I know it," Ruth said. "Darrell doesn't get away with anything here—well, no more than Darlene and my own boys do. Darlene talks about you all the time."

"*Me?* What does she say?"

Ruth got up to stir the batch of jelly steaming on the stove.

"Oh, it's Sissy says this and Sissy says that, and she wants her clothes to look like what you wear, stuff like that."

Sissy looked down at the old worn chambray shirt of her father's that she had pulled on because she didn't have anything clean to wear, her ragged cuff jeans and battered tennis shoes, and laughed.

"Ruth, no one's called me a fashion plate lately. Darlene would be better off if she copied what Viola Bianco wears."

Ruth grimaced.

"Anyone could look nice if they had the kind of money her dad has. If Lawrence and Lily had that kind of income, you would look one hell of a lot better than Viola."

She lifted the big silver spoon, letting the cooking berry juice run off in a thick stream.

"Just right," she declared, turning off the gas burner beneath the pot. "Okay, you want to help me with this? Potholders are right there on the counter."

With Sissy grasping the handle on one side of the pot and Ruth the other, they carefully poured the deep, rich syrup into the clean jars. A few drops splashed from the last pour, landing on Ruth's white eyelet curtains.

"Sorry," Sissy said.

"Never mind," Ruth grinned. "I always liked polka dots."

"Did you hear that Viola and Howard Broussard are getting married?" Sissy asked.

"No, but I always figured she would chase him until he caught her," Ruth said. "I can't see that being a model marriage, but better than what Pete got with Zooey. Of course, I don't think Pete and Zooey getting married ruined either family. The best thing about Pete and Zooey being married is that they didn't mess up two other families by marrying other people."

"Who else would have married either one of them?" Sissy asked. She wasn't saying that to be mean; she really wondered. "I knew Zooey in high school. She had a lot of boys on the string, but not because any of them wanted to marry her. Pete, him I never knew all that well because he went to Holy Rosary High School, and besides that, he was a few years ahead of me."

"I don't know about Pete," Ruth said as she put the pot of paraffin back on the stove to melt, "but I know Zooey went around with Buffalo Ames for a while."

"Really? How come I never heard about that?" She wondered if this was something someone dreamed up after Buffalo had been killed. People always seem to remember some new pertinent information in the wake of a terrible event, like if they had only known back then they could have predicted the outcome, not necessarily to prevent it, but just to make themself sound as if they knew all along.

"It wasn't like it lasted very long. My neighbor is Jim Ames, one of Buffalo's uncles. Buffalo brought Zooey out here with him a time or two. I just happened to be over there visiting with Jim and Kay once when they were there. Didn't look like any big romance at the time, though, come to think of it. At least, not from the way Zooey acted."

"The only man Zooey ever acted like she really wanted was Pete. Until she got him. I don't know what it is with her," Sissy said.

"I'd guess she wants what every woman wants," Ruth offered.

"What do you think that is?"

"Safety. Security. But most important, I think, respect," Ruth said.

Sissy thought about that. Was that what she wanted? Partly. But first, a chance to see something of the world, and that didn't sound like Zooey, but then, what did she know? Zooey was one of the few people who had never spilled her guts to Sissy, probably never told anyone what she really wanted.

"I don't know if that's what Zooey wants," Sissy said, "but I think you nailed it for what Darlene wants."

While Ruth finished off the jars of jelly with sealing wax and cleaned up the kitchen, Sissy walked out to the cottonwood tree down over a little hill where Ruth said Darlene would be. Sissy saw her elbows showing on either side of the tree trunk as she walked up behind her and stepped around. Darlene sat with her knees pulled up, hands on knees and head on her hands, staring across the little gully to the east. Her face was puffy and red. Sissy sat down beside her.

"You ever wonder what might be over there?" Sissy said, nodding to the east where a few wispy clouds hung in the blue sky.

Darlene didn't answer.

"I do," Sissy said. "I've read about what's there. You know, in school, and then later. I know that if I could get in a car and drive, I'd come to Sioux Falls first. People here think that's a big city. What do you think?"

Darlene shrugged.

"If I got in a car and drove the other way, I'd come to Rapid City. People here think that's a big city, too. That's what people say when they're going up there to buy their kids' school clothes. Or to go to a special doctor. Or just 'cause they want to. They say they're going to 'the City.' And they say 'Sioux Falls' like it's the center of the universe. But you know what?"

Darlene didn't say anything, but Sissy hadn't expected she would. She went on.

"I got to thinking about that. If you keep driving after Sioux Falls, you come to Chicago. *That's* a big city. Then there's Philadelphia, and if you go far enough, New York City. If you go the other way past Rapid City, you cross Wyoming and then you come to Salt Lake City, and if you go far enough, there you are in San Francisco, staring out at all that ocean. But before you get to San Francisco, you go through Sacramento. Do you know there are more people in the city of Sacramento—and people there don't even think it's a city, really, more like a town—but there are more people in the city of Sacramento, California, than there are in the whole state of South Dakota. So when I hear people talk about Sioux Falls like it's some huge holy god damned special place, or calling Rapid City 'the City'—well, I think they're ignorant. But there's a difference between being ignorant and being stupid. Ignorant means you don't know something. Lots of things. But stupid means you don't have the ability to learn. Ignorant people don't have to stay that way, but stupid people will always be stupid. They can't help it. Which one are you?"

Darlene's head came up, eyes blazing.

"Why are you talking to me like that? It ain't me, it's my dad. He's the one messing everything up!"

Sissy leaned back against the cottonwood trunk.

"All right. So is Clayton stupid or ignorant?"

"What? What do you mean?"

"Mean just what I said. A while back when you had done such a good job of cleaning the house and Clayton didn't even notice, but yelled at you for the one thing you didn't do, was he being ignorant or stupid? And today, when he didn't even say hello, just ordered you to go pack your things—and Darrell's things—was he being ignorant or stupid?"

Darlene stared but didn't answer.

"I know," Sissy said. "It's a tough question. Is he acting like that and saying those things because he's stupid? Or is he just ignorant? And if he is just ignorant, can he be taught anything?"

"I don't know," Darlene mumbled, her body tension gone like a balloon with the air let out of it. "And it doesn't matter which, now does it? There ain't anything I can do about it."

"Are you sure?"

"Well, what am I supposed to do about it? If he's stupid, I can't do anything about it, and if he's ignorant, well, I can't teach him anything."

"Are you sure?" Sissy repeated.

"Stop saying that! I'm not sure about anything except he's my dad and he's supposed to—he's supposed to—" She raised her hands to the sky, then dropped them to her sides.

Sissy waited, watching a pair of hawks circling over an alfalfa field in the distance, spiraling down and down, then catching an updraft and rising again.

Darlene put her head down on her knees again.

"It's a crying shame," Sissy said, "when a sixteen-year-old has to educate a grown man, and especially so when that grown man is her father, but sometimes that's the way it is. Clayton thinks he has to be father and mother since your mom left, except he doesn't know how to be either, so he ends up doing a bad job of both. I don't like him. He's an asshole."

"My dad's not an asshole!" Darlene said, her head coming up again.

"Yeah, he is," Sissy said looking directly into Darlene's eyes.

The corners of Darlene's mouth quirked up. She giggled.

"My dad is an asshole," she said. She laughed, and then they both were laughing.

When they stopped laughing, Sissy wiped her own eyes, and said, "All right, now we've got that out of the way, the question is, is he an ignorant asshole or a stupid asshole?"

"I think . . . I think he's an ignorant asshole," Darlene said.

"Yeah, I think you're right. Remember this: everything you need to know about men, you learned in kindergarten. Boys are dumb," Sissy said, standing up and holding out her hand to pull Darlene up. "Let's go educate one of them."

Just before Clayton and Sissy left to go back to Jackson alone, Darlene took Sissy aside.

"Is that true what you said? About Sacramento? That, that there's more people there than in the whole state of South Dakota?"

"Yeah. It's true," Sissy said.

"So, how many people are there in Sacramento?"

"Last time I checked, it was a little over three hundred thousand."

"That means there's less than that in South Dakota. How did you know that?" Darlene asked.

"I read a lot," Sissy said.

Halfway back to Jackson, when Clayton finally stopped talking, Sissy thought that she didn't read as much as she used to. She couldn't remember the last time she had checked books out of the library, or even bought a cheap paperback at the drugstore. Her life was waitressing and playing music and hanging out with Speedy in the C & C. But she was so tired.

When Clayton stopped in front of her house, she reached for the door handle, but Clayton grasped her arm and held her back.

"Thanks for going over there with me," he said.

"Yeah, yeah, yeah, I'm a peach," she said.

"Well, you really are, you know. You're really good with Darrell and Darlene."

"No, I'm not," she answered. "I hardly know Darrell. He's a boy, typical I guess, always running around with his friends. Darlene, well, she's a teenage girl, and it hasn't been that long since I was one of those myself."

"You're a better mother to her than her own mother ever was. Or is," Clayton said. "You ought to have some kids of your own. You ought to have a husband and, and—" He dropped her arm and waved his hand in the air. "And all that."

"I don't think I'm the marrying kind," she said.

"What do you mean? All women are the marrying kind. You got a twat just like all women do," he said.

She closed her eyes.

"Clayton, I'm going to forget that you said something that crude and disgusting. I'm going to open the door now, go in the house and go to bed. By myself. I'm tired."

"Sissy, Sissy, I'm sorry. I guess I've just been hanging around with the men in the shop too much." He scooted across the seat toward her. In the bright moonlight, she saw his eyes, pupils dark and dilated. She put her hands up and turned with her back against the door.

"Sissy, why do you chase after guys like that Gordon What's His Name? He's no good for you. He doesn't even make a living for himself, just hangs out up there at his family's ranch, doing nothing and getting drunk every weekend. He's never going to ask you out for a real date. He's never going to walk up to your front door and take off his hat and say hello to your dad and mom. You need somebody dependable."

"Clayton, this is the same old rant I've heard before, and besides that, it's none of your damned business," Sissy said.

"Look," Clayton leaned closer. Sissy could still smell the Old Spice cologne that he must have drenched himself with that morning.

"Look," he said, "Darlene thinks the world of you, and Darrell, well, Darrell would come around. Why don't you and me—"

"*No!* No, god damn it, *no!* First Melvin, then you. What the hell is it with you guys? I know the pool of men around here isn't very damned deep, but I'm *not*, I swear to Christ, I am *not* fishing in the shallow end. I am not even fishing—*period!*"

Clayton stared at her.

"Who said anything about fishing? And what's Melvin got to do with anything?" he asked.

"Go *home*, Clayton," Sissy said as she got out and slammed the car door.

Taffy barked once as she walked up the driveway muttering, "No, not ignorant, but stupid. Stupid, stupid, stupid."

She fumbled for her house keys in her purse, found them, got them out, dropped them on the cement step with a jingle. Taffy whined again. She leaned her head against the door. God, she was so tired.

She bent and retrieved the keys, hearing a whack-whack-whack sound. Taffy's wagging tail slapped against the fence. She walked across the driveway to look over the fence. His water dish was turned over, his food bowl empty.

She unlocked the door, found some leftover meatloaf in the fridge that was beyond what she wanted to chance, ran a pitcher of water from the sink and took it out to the dog. When she had the gate open, she cautiously flipped his water bowl over with her foot, dropping the meatloaf in his food dish at the same time. Taffy went for the food while she poured the water in the dish.

"Maybe if your people took better care of you, you wouldn't be such a mean little bastard," she said. He was a cute dog with long golden-colored fur and a white stripe down his nose. She reached out to pet his head. He snarled and snapped at her hand. She went back through the gate, closing it behind her. Mean little bastard. He'd make a good weapon—an insane pissed off dog tied to a mop handle.

As she was falling asleep, she remembered that Martha had switched her shift back to mornings. She'd have to be at work at 6 a.m.

CHAPTER TEN

A REAL DATE

Monday was a rough day at work for Sissy. She had less than six hours of sleep—she was one of the unfortunate people that needed not eight, but nine hours—so she was groggy and buzzy-headed when she walked through the doors of the steak house at 6 a.m., then Speedy didn't show up, which made Martha mad and snappy about everything. The coffee-maker wasn't clean enough, the side work wasn't done, and never mind that that was the fault of the crew from the night before. Sissy wrapped setups, filled salt and pepper and sugar shakers, stuffed napkins in the holders and did a quick sweep-up under the bar stools at the counter, wondering whose backseat Speedy had fallen asleep in the night before. She was staying back at her parents' house in the country again. Sissy was as mad as Martha but didn't dare show it to the Catholics who piled in for breakfast or just coffee and rolls after the first Mass ended around seven o'clock. Then it was the early Presbyterians eating breakfast before their ten o'clock service and the Catholics eating after the second Mass at that ended at ten.

Speedy showed up at eleven o'clock, only three hours before her shift was supposed to end, looking crapulous with greasy hair, weepy red eyes, and a complexion the color of curdled milk with a little green stirred in. Sissy took pity on Speedy when she said she thought she had a case of food poisoning, took her home at shift's end and put her to bed. She had just fallen into bed herself for a nap when the phone rang and rang. She heaved herself out of bed for the trek down the stairs to the phone on the wall in the living room.

"*What!*" she yelled into the receiver.

Silence on the other end, then her dad's voice said, "Sissy? You all right?"

"Yeah," she said sitting down in the worn tweed rocker. "We were really busy in the café, and I didn't get much sleep last night."

Her dad didn't respond.

She took a deep breath, fiddling with a loose string on the edge of the cushion in the rocker.

"How's everything down there? Auntie Iris and Uncle Lee doing okay?"

"Oh, yeah. Iris and your mom made a quilt top and now they are putting the back on it and sewing it up, and your Uncle Lee and I put new brakes on his pickup a couple of days ago. He's every bit as aggravating as he always was. Won't listen to anyone. It took us four hours to do that brake job because, well, you know how he is. He wants to do it all his way, and that's almost always the wrong way. Then it has to be redone the right way. We were going to take his truck and go fishing, but by the time we finished the job it was too late to go, and he had to go to work this week."

Her Uncle Lee was a foreman in a feed mill, and not nearly as pigheaded about doing things his own way as her dad was, but she kept the peace and didn't comment about that.

"We heard they're catching some big catfish out there in Lake McConaughy, so me and your mom are going to stay another week so Lee and I can go fishing there this coming weekend. Hell, I don't know. We might go on down to the Missouri River and try our luck there."

"Well, I think you ought to," Sissy said. "Everything is fine; I'm taking care of things here." She lied easily, looking around at the clothes and magazines flung everywhere in the living room, and through the door to the kitchen counters where dishes were piled up, mail stacked on one end of the counter, cupboard doors agape—her mother's pet peeve—and the floor dirty from mud she had tracked in after the last rain. Sitting on the rag rug in front of the kitchen sink, Wooly Booger gave her the stink eye, and she was grateful that cats couldn't talk. There had been more than one time when she had forgotten to put out fresh food for him.

"When are you coming home?" she asked. She needed at least a day to clean up the place before they got home.

"Oh, another week or two," Lawrence said. "I'll call the day before we start back." He paused, then went on. "Are the harvest crews all done and moved on? Get any rain up there?"

On safer ground now, she said, "Yeah, all the fields came ripe at once. They were busier than a one-legged man at a kicking party for about ten days. Rained once in the middle of that, too, but they're done and moved on. In another couple of weeks, they'll start straggling through again on their way back south."

"How much rain did you get there at the house? Did you check the rain gauge?"

Lawrence was fussy over weather things like recording exactly how much rain they got during a year, how much snowfall and so on and arguing with the reports of Claude Sauer, the KOTA weatherman. Sissy never knew why her dad cared so much. She figured they got what they got or didn't get and measuring it exactly wasn't going to change it.

"We got six-tenths of an inch from the big rainstorm, and another inch and a tenth from a couple of other smaller storms that came through," she lied. She'd have to remember to empty the rain gauge and to record her lies on the co-op calendar that hung on the kitchen wall behind the table. "Everything greened up a little," she continued, "but I can feel fall coming on. You know how tree leaves start to look tired. Kind of off-green and dull."

"Yeah," he said. "Pheasant and grouse season will be around before you know it."

"Which reminds me. Melvin mentioned pheasant hunting the other day. He's hinting around that he wants to go with you so he can use one of your shotguns."

Lawrence chuckled a little. "That's okay. He's a cheapskate about getting his own gun out of hock, but I don't mind. He's a better shot than I am, truth be told. If I don't get my limit, and he does, he shoots enough to make up my limit, too, and gives the birds to me."

"Mom want to talk to me?"

"She ain't here right now. She and your auntie went window shopping. I think. Or some such. I'll tell her you asked about her."

After they hung up, Sissy took three steps to the sofa, laid down pulling the afghan over her bare feet and went instantly to sleep.

Speedy spent the rest of the week in town with Sissy, but she still looked peaky. Sissy asked her what on earth she had eaten to mess her up that bad, and Speedy moaned, "I don't know! There were leftovers in the fridge, and I ate them. Well, I was drunk when I got home so I don't remember exactly what it was, but I told my mom I wished she'd clean out the fridge more often."

The next Friday's morning shift at the café was light. A few country folk came in early, bought their groceries and went home without stopping in the café. The evening shift would be busier than usual because of the Catholic Church's monthly bingo night, the Masons' annual meeting, and the usual sots who always came out on Friday or Saturday night to eat at the café with the wife before going to the C & C or the Legion Club to get drunk.

Sissy and Speedy had finished all their side work and were just waiting for the clock hands to move up to two o'clock when Gordon

Charbonneau came in, hitching his left leg ever so slightly as he walked down to stand by the stool where Sissy sat.

"I'll see you at your place," Speedy said, grabbing her purse from under the counter. Lynda, one of the waitresses on the two-to-ten shift, started toward Gordon with a menu, but he waved her away.

"You doing anything tonight?" Gordon asked Sissy, leaning one hip on the stool next to her.

"Nothing special," she said. He was dressed up in a charcoal western suit with a snowy white shirt and black string tie with a turquoise bolo, black boots shining from beneath the hem of his pants. "You look nice. Going to a funeral?"

He didn't smile.

"No. An anniversary. It's my parents' forty-fifth. There's a dinner for them in the Legion Club meeting room."

"Congratulations to them," Sissy said, standing up.

He stood up, too, shoved his hat back an inch or so, shuffled his feet, and leaned on his knuckles on the bar stool top.

"I thought maybe you would go with me."

"What? To your parents' anniversary party?"

He flipped a hand.

"No, to their funeral," he said with a twist to his lips.

"You're asking me out on a date?"

"Well, not exactly."

"*Exactly* what then?"

He clamped his hat down on his head, clamped his lips shut, turned away, walking rapidly, still with that slight hitch in his leg.

"I'll go, I'll go!" she called after him.

He stopped and turned, his face relaxing.

"All right. Pick you up at eight," he said, turning back toward the door.

"You know where I live?"

"Yeah, I know."

She watched him open the door, heard the bell tinkle, saw him cross the sidewalk to his maroon Riviera, open the door, and get in, using one hand to help pull his left leg in. She got her purse from under the counter and walked out the back door into the alley, raised her fists to the sky, and screamed.

"Take *that*, Clayton! Who says he would never come to my house, never meet my family. Well, maybe that's true, but he's going to introduce me to his family!"

Her feet didn't hurt all the way home. Speedy waited just inside the back door.

"Did he ask you out? Did he ask you out?" she asked.

Sissy told her and Speedy did a little dance around the kitchen.

"All right, let's pick out something for you to wear," she said. But when they looked through Sissy's clothes, there wasn't much to choose from—jeans, shirts, T-shirts, the white uniforms she wore to work, a plain black shift she wore to funerals, and a couple of dresses from high school. She settled on a rose and white floral print sleeveless shirtdress paired with the plain white high heels she had worn to her high school graduation ceremony. She thought she still looked like a high school girl, except for a few fine lines starting to form at the corners of her eyes, but Speedy said she looked sweet. The afternoon dragged by. She was ready an hour before Gordon was due to pick her up, sitting in the kitchen, jumping up whenever a car came down the street, imagining she had to pee every fifteen minutes. Speedy had left already for the C & C, her week-long bout with food poisoning forgotten.

There was no mistaking when Gordon's car came into the driveway and he got out because Taffy started barking and wouldn't shut up. Sissy met him at the door because she didn't want him to see what a mess the house was in.

"You look . . . nice," he said.

"Thank you," she said, taking his proffered arm as she tried to get her feet to remember how to walk in high heels.

The meeting room in the Legion Club was two-thirds full, mostly with people Sissy knew on sight but not personally—several older couples, some adults in their twenties and thirties, some of whom Sissy knew to be Gordon's brothers and sisters. She knew he had several. He helped her to a seat at a table by herself while he went to the improvised bar to get them drinks.

"Hello, Sissy. What are you doing here?"

Viola and Howard had come up behind her table from the back, Viola's hand on Howard's arm. She looked as put together as she always did, like fresh peeled cucumbers in a pale green dress that Sissy bet was silk and fashionable white high-heeled sandals, a matching bag hanging from her arm.

"I'm Gordon's date," Sissy said.

Howard tilted his head back and laughed. Viola's lips curled into a semi-smile, her eyebrows raised.

"You're Gordon's *date*. Gordon doesn't have *dates*," Howard said.

Sissy flushed, feeling like the schoolgirl that she thought she looked like.

"Well, he asked me, so I guess that makes me his date," she said.

As Viola and Howard walked away, Viola turned. Looking Sissy up and down, her eyes came to rest on Sissy's white graduation heels. Her lips curved up in that little smile again.

Gordon came through the crowd carefully holding a drink in each hand. He sat down in the chair next to Sissy with a little groan, extending his leg a little. She thanked him, but then didn't know what else to say. She'd never been good at tiny talk.

He bumped her arm, nodding at the buffet of chips with dips, pigs in a blanket, and squares of cheese with fancy toothpicks stuck through them, all arranged on platters with green plastic vines twining among them.

"Want something to eat?" he asked.

She shook her head.

A tall woman with black hair down to there approached their table. She wore an apricot dress that contrasted beautifully against her dark skin.

"Hey, brother," she said, touching Gordon lightly on the shoulder. "Glad to see you. Mom and Dad will be glad you came."

Gordon's grin made him look much younger, maybe someone young enough to have a schoolgirl for a date.

"This is my little sister, Teresa," Gordon said, and to Teresa, "Sissy Roberts."

The women touched hands briefly. Teresa sat down.

"Don't you sing and play guitar for Clayton Red Bird's band?" she asked.

"That's me," Sissy said.

"I hear you're pretty good," Teresa said with a smile. "Everybody says so. There's this feed salesman who talks about you whenever he's out to the ranch. He says you sing like an angel."

Sissy grimaced.

"I've met the man," she said, "but I can't remember his name."

"I don't blame you," Teresa said with a laugh. "He's one of the most pompous men I've ever met, and I've met a few."

"Hey," Gordon said.

"Well, if the shoe fits," Teresa said, laughing again. "Mom and Dad don't like the guy much either, but we don't get to pick who the feed company sends out." She poked a finger in Gordon's side. "We don't get to pick who our relatives are either," she said.

Gordon made a shocked face.

"Come on, big brother, you know I'm kidding. But Mom and Dad are getting a bit worried about you. No girlfriend, you know."

Sissy wondered about the White woman and kids he was rumored to have back east.

"Bring her over to meet the parents," Teresa said as she got up, and then to Sissy, "Really, they don't bite."

"I like her," Sissy said as Teresa walked over to a group standing in front of the buffet table.

Gordon shrugged. "She's all right," he said. "But she doesn't have any room to talk. She's on her second divorce and not yet thirty. That made our parents pleased and proud."

"You've made them pleased and proud?" Sissy asked and could have bitten her tongue after she said it.

Gordon stood up but didn't walk away. He put out a hand, pulling her to her feet, then they danced to a slow country tune coming from a jukebox over in the corner.

"She can't sing as good as you can," Gordon said, then made a pointing gesture with his lips at the jukebox. Sissy was touched. She didn't think he paid any attention to music, that it was just background noise for drinking. He pulled her closer. Sissy felt his ribs through his suit coat and crisp white shirt, felt his breathing as it stirred the loose hair draped over her ear, caught the slightly jerky rhythm of his dancing.

When the song finished, he led her by the hand to where a couple in their mid-sixties sat enthroned in the middle of a group of chairs, mostly occupied by other older people. He stopped in front of the couple, the man's white hair moving gently in the breeze from the air conditioner, the older woman wearing a dark print dress and low-heeled black shoes, her hair obviously done at a beauty shop.

"Well, I guess this is your big day," Gordon said to them.

The dark eyes in the man's weather-beaten face squinted up at Gordon.

"It's one of many good ones," he said.

The woman smiled at him and squeezed his arm.

"Yes," she said, "and some of the others were when each of you kids was born."

Gordon made a short sweeping gesture at Sissy.

"This is Sissy Roberts," he said. "My parents, Joe and Mary Charbonneau."

Sissy nodded, taking each of their hands in turn. "Pleased to meet you," she said. She felt as if she was being scrutinized, measured up, as if she might not meet expectations. She was relieved when another couple, older people as well, stepped up. The man stuck out his hand to Joe and said something in Lakota that Sissy didn't follow. The Charbonneaus laughed.

Gordon led her away to the buffet table.

Two hours and another drink later, Gordon had introduced Sissy to two more of his sisters and a much older brother who had all given Sissy that same intense look. Zooey and Pete came in late, Zooey looking sullen and Pete grim. Pete parked Zooey at a table with a can of soda and a glass of ice in front of her and walked away, but every time someone with a drink came and sat down at the table, Zooey stole a sip from their drink. At midnight everyone stood and sang "Happy Anniversary to You" to the tune of "Happy Birthday," jamming all the syllables of "anniversary" into the same number of notes as it took to sing "birthday." Zooey stood awkwardly, weaving a bit before sitting down heavily at the end of the song.

Someone who worked for the Legion Club used a metal cart to wheel in a big cake with candles all lit. The elder Charbonneaus stood and bowed, blew out the candles, and accepted congratulations and well wishes from the crowd. As the cake was cut, Gordon cupped Sissy's elbow.

"Let's go," he said.

"Where?" Sissy asked.

"Party's over," he said.

They didn't speak as they walked up the long flight of steps from the basement private party room, or in the car as Gordon drove Sissy home. He stopped the car in the driveway, reached across and opened her door.

"Thanks for coming," he said.

"Just like that?" she asked.

"What? What else is there?"

"You really don't know," she said. "You have no fucking idea. But I do. I was just window dressing for your family. That's it. Isn't it?"

He looked straight ahead out the windshield, stroking his chin between his right thumb and forefinger as if he was considering whether he needed to shave or not.

"What is this? Your family—your parents—have been after you to settle down. So you ask me to their anniversary celebration because you think that might shut them up for a little while."

He turned to look at her, but she saw nothing there.

"No. Not exactly," he said.

"Well, *exactly* why did you ask me then?" She waited for his answer.

"I like you," he said.

"You like me. You say that like I was a well-cooked hamburger. You like me. You know what? I don't think you really care about anything. I hear you have a White wife and kids back east. Do you care about them?

Do you really have a White wife and kids back east or is that a rumor you started yourself to use as an excuse if any woman here started getting serious about you? And what about that brace you wear on your leg. Is that real? Or is that just something you put on to get sympathy and attention from women that you shut down later if they get too possessive?"

Taffy barked outside, throwing himself at the fence until it shivered.

Finally, his face registered something. It looked like shock.

"I took a fall," he said. "I was working high steel in New York."

"Really? Is that true? Or just more bullshit?"

He tapped his fingers on the steering wheel, shifting a bit in his seat.

"I was on the twenty-second floor, the highest we had built. It's just I-beams up there that high, you know. I was supposed to have a safety harness on, but I unsnapped it to reach for a hammer. I dropped it, tried to grab it." He made a grabbing motion with his hand. "My eyes followed it going down. It turned over and over, and then I went where my eyes were looking. It feels like flying, you know. It's just a couple of seconds before you hit the ground, but it feels like flying forever."

He sighed deeply.

"My parents never forgave me. They argued against me going in the first place. They didn't come to see me all the months I was in the hospital there, but they sent me a plane ticket to come home."

"So, what now? You going to keep on flying forever?" Sissy asked. The car door creaked as she opened it wider and got out.

Gordon didn't say anything. She shut the door. Taffy panted and snorted in between short barks. As Sissy unlocked the back door, the Riviera glided slowly backward out of the driveway. Inside, she flung her keys on the kitchen table with a jangle. She looked around at the mess in the kitchen, took her mom's apron from the back of a chair where it had been hanging since her parents left, and tied it on over her dress.

First, she put away the spices left out on the countertop, the big commercial-sized mayonnaise jar that her mom used to hold flour, the oddments and endments of things left out, then shut the cabinet doors. She took everything out of the sink and stacked it to one side and ran the sink full of hot water, squirting in a healthy dose of dishwashing soap. As crusty as most of the dishes were, they would have to soak a while. She dumped them into the sink, as many as it would hold.

In the living room, she picked up the scattered clothes, pitching them into a pile in the middle of the floor to carry down to the basement laundry room later, picking up the cups and glasses left here and there and carrying them into the kitchen. Wooly Booger followed her, meowing and slapping at her heels. She sorted and stacked the magazines—her dad's *Field and Stream*, her mom's *Family Circle*—shuffling the edges even, but as she put them down, she noticed the layer of dust on the coffee table.

She sat down on the sofa as the tears came. Wooly jumped up beside her, lay down and rolled over on his back, purring loudly. She was still there twenty minutes later when the back door opened.

"Sissy? You home?" Speedy called softly.

"In here," Sissy said, wiping her eyes on her mom's apron.

Speedy peeked around the door from the kitchen.

"What are you doing in here?" she asked.

"I thought I'd clean the place up a little," Sissy said.

"In the middle of the night?"

"You know," Sissy said, waving her hand at the mess. "I get to where I just can't stand it anymore, and then I have to do something about it. Even if it's the middle of the night."

Speedy came slowly into the room, perched on the edge of the worn tweed rocker.

"Sooo, I take it your date with Gordon Charbonneau didn't go very well," she said.

"You could say that," Sissy said. "And you'd be right. It was awful. I didn't know hardly anybody except just to speak to on the street. Not well. They tried to be nice, but it was uncomfortable. And Zooey was there."

"*Zooey* was there? Did she give you any crap?"

"No. Pete tried to keep her sober, but she was drinking anyway. I don't think she even noticed me."

"I'd count that as good," Speedy said.

"I'd almost rather take an ass beating from her. It would have been more interesting than the way it turned out," Sissy said.

"Gordon—so—what did he do?" Speedy asked.

"Nothing. That's most of the problem. He's like a—a—a robot or something. No feelings."

"You remember a couple of weeks ago when I went out with Sonny? And what you said to me when I came home one night? You said, he ain't the marrying kind." Speedy sat leaned over with her hands clasped between her legs.

"Yeah, I remember. But I never said I wanted to marry Gordon."

"I never said I wanted to marry Sonny, either," Speedy said.

"But you did, didn't you?"

Speedy's head lowered. She said, "Yes. If he had asked me, I would have said yes."

"Well, I'm not sure I would marry Gordon Charbonneau even if he asked," Sissy said.

"Then what do you want from him?"

"I don't know," Sissy said. "I guess I want to know I could if I wanted to."

"You're acting like Viola," Speedy said.

"No, I'm not," Sissy argued. "Viola wouldn't marry Gordon Charbonneau if he begged her on bended knee. He doesn't have enough money, or really, his family doesn't."

"Sissy, you're the smartest woman I know. You've got brains and talent. You don't have to get married to anybody. You could get out of here, go somewhere special. Not me. I don't have any brains or any talent, so I have to get married. There ain't anything else for me to do," Speedy said.

"You're starting to sound like my dad," Sissy said. "Why don't you just say 'god damn it, Sis,' like he does."

"God damn it, Sis," Speedy said, bouncing to her feet. "I think we need to get some sleep. I'll help you clean tomorrow."

CHAPTER ELEVEN

THE BARREL BULL RIDE WINNER

SATURDAY, AUGUST 16, 1969

When the region first organized itself as a county, two communities, Haysworth and Schmidt—each with no better name than that of its original founding family—vied for the honor of being county seat. Haysworth won one hundred twenty out of two hundred votes and became the county seat, but no one called the new town Haysworth. They called it Winner, and the name stuck. On the eastern edge of the Rosebud Reservation, the county filled up with immigrants—Germans, Swedes, Irish, a few Poles—who tried farming the land, but breaking up centuries of root-bound sod proved difficult. Those who managed found that the ground beneath was light stuff, blowing away in the persistent wind, so they looked to their Indian neighbors on the west, who had started cattle ranching after a long tradition of horse breeding. Within a short time, the county turned almost completely to ranching, with a few die-hard old countrymen who stubbornly refused to accept the inevitable, planting corn, barley, and wheat every year that barely yielded more than the seed it took to grow it.

Some of the White ranchers both hated and feared their Indian neighbors to the west; some Whites were indifferent, but others got on well enough to intermarry. The standing joke went like this:

> *Q. How does a White woman become a member of the Rosebud tribe?*
> *A. Get a little Indian in her.*

Because in those days, a White woman married to an Indian with mixed-blood children would be enrolled in the tribe, with all the drawbacks and benefits thereof. The drawback at the top of the list, scorn from the woman's White relatives and friends. Among the dubious benefits was the right to use the Indian Health Service, which meant putting yourself at the mercy of doctors who, because they were incompetent or drunks or insane or, rarely, just poor, could not make it in the private medical system, but were hired by the government to see to the health of Indians. The right to health care that had been written into treaties between Indians and the federal government was loosely interpreted.

Clayton was a model of tact and decorum on the ride over from Jackson to Winner with Sissy in the passenger seat. He commented on the health of the grasslands passing by the car windows as they drove, on the fatness of the cattle in the pastures, on the cleanliness of Melvin's pickup that they followed. He wondered about the fishing in Beads Lake and He Dog Lake that they passed; he spoke of the coming school year when Darrell would be entering sixth grade and Darlene would start her junior year in high school, how he hoped his kids would do well, how he wished he had tried harder when he was in school. He never mentioned Gordon Charbonneau. Not a word about Sissy's potential future as Clayton's wife, nothing at all about Sissy personally, which was better than his talk at practice on Wednesday when he had effused about Sissy's turn of phrase on a particular song, how she hit a certain note dead on, how her guitar chording was getting smoother, until she had said just three words: *Shut up, Clayton.* He had. His continual hectoring was annoying. His false praise was worse. His yammering about nothing was marginally better than the other two, so she let him run on. He was not going to wear her down.

He did drift away from his innocuous conversation a bit when they passed a herd of ten or twelve horses running and bucking out of sheer playfulness, or because the heel flies were biting.

"Fine animals, fine," Clayton said. "Look at their legs. None of those cowhocks like you see on Pine Ridge–bred horses. No soft white hoofs, either. And look at the topline, see how the hindquarters drop down in a nice line? That's some horses that could sit down and hold whatever a rider might tie onto."

"Yeah, good-looking animals," Sissy said. Since back when Pine Ridge was known as Red Cloud Agency and Rosebud as Spotted Tail, people on the two reservations had been arguing about who bred the better horses. Sissy had heard her own father going on about Pine Ridge horses just as Clayton bragged on Rosebud's. She couldn't see any real difference.

The VFW outside of Winner was usually neutral territory for everyone who lived in the area, the Indians, the Whites, and the mixed bloods. On the outskirts of the town, the square building had a small arena out back where local ranchers came for a monthly jackpot roping. There were never any rough stock riding events—these were working ranchers, not rodeo cowboys—but they had a bucking barrel event, the forerunner of the mechanical bulls that wouldn't come into popular use for years. The concept was simple: a fifty-five-gallon drum with eyebolts welded to the sides, springs attached to those, and ropes tied to the springs. The barrel, with a bull-riding rig attached for a rider to hold on to, was suspended between four poles, then four stout men pulling on each of the four ropes tried to unseat the rider on the barrel. It didn't spin and duck back like a real bull would, but it provided a reasonable practice substitute for anyone wanting to try their luck on the real animals. Inevitably at any event the VFW sponsored, men would make drunken bets about who could stay on the barrel longer.

The inside of the building was nicer than anyplace the Red Birds played except for the Holiday Inn in Kadoka. The polished dance floor was in the middle with tables arranged around that, a bar with decent stools at one end and the bandstand at the other. No chicken-wire cage surrounded it, but no one here had ever pitched a beer bottle at the band. The fights were few and all outside, usually after some drunk had lost his bet on riding the barrel bull. (*You tricked me! You started yanking on the ropes before I was settled!* I did not! *Yes, you did, you cheating son-of-a-bitch, and I'm going to kick your ass!*)

As they were setting up, Ruth came over to say hello.

"I didn't know you liked to go dancing, Ruth," Sissy said.

"I don't much," she said as she gave Sissy a hug, "but I wanted to come see if what Darlene said about you is true."

"What's she say?" Sissy asked.

"That you're better than Loretta Lynn."

Sissy was touched.

"I wouldn't say that," she said. "Loretta Lynn is damned good. I just want to be the best Sissy Roberts."

Ruth patted her on the arm and went to sit with a group of friends until the music started.

Clayton nodded at the others, and Sonny began the repetitive bass riff that always started every gig. *Te-dum Te-dum tiddly diddly dum.* The crowd buzz quieted.

"Welcome everyone to the VFW Club in the best little town in America—Winner! That's *the* Winner, folks. There ain't no place like this place anywhere near this place so this must be the place!"

Clayton ran through the usual introductions. When it came to his turn, the crowd roared and clapped. Sissy decided that since Clayton was from Rosebud, a lot more of his relatives than just Ruth must be in the audience. But there were no Broussards, no Charbonneaus. The set started with the old Hank Williams, Hank Snow, Wynn Stewart favorites, with a couple of Kitty Wells songs thrown in. The crowd was up for it; the dance floor filled, and the drinks ran freely. Here and there, good-natured laughter welled up during a quiet song. Sissy sang on autopilot, the lyrics so familiar she could let her mind go anywhere while the breath came into her lungs, back up through her throat and out, shaped by her mouth into words.

When the lights came up for the break and the jukebox came on, someone shoved a beer into her hand. She swallowed the bitter iciness gratefully, said "thanks," but the donor was gone into the crowd. She felt a tug on her sleeve, looked down into Ruth's deep brown eyes.

"Sissy, can I talk to you?"

They sat in the front seat of Ruth's Chevy, sipping their beer. Off to the side of the bar, four men tugged the ropes on the bull barrel, laughing when the rider stuck for less than a couple of seconds before tumbling in the dust. The men staggered together, slapping each other on the back, jeering at the fallen rider, then fell silent as they helped another man onto the barrel.

"You know," Ruth began, "I think Clayton really took it to heart, that talk we had with him."

"Uh huh," Sissy said.

Ruth batted at a mosquito buzzing around her face.

"I just don't know if it's going to stick, you know what I mean?"

"He hasn't really had much chance yet, has he?" Sissy asked. "The kids are still with you. The real test will be when they come home to start school in a couple of weeks."

Ruth sipped at her beer, watching as the second man went off the bull barrel.

"Men get up to such silly games," she said. "Never grow up, always little boys with their little toys."

"We women can play a few of our own," Sissy offered.

Ruth was silent, but Sissy knew there was more to come.

"See, Sissy, Darlene and Darrell don't want to go home. They want to stay with me and my boys, and I don't know if I should fight Clayton over it. He's my brother, and I love him."

"Clayton's a grown man, who ought to be able to take whatever comes. The kids are the ones that need to be considered," Sissy said.

"Yes, I know. I'd feel better if I knew there was someone there who'd look after their interests. Stand up for them. Get Clayton to see when he's messing up."

"I can do that. I do that as much as I think is right. I'm not going to go sticking my nose in too much, though. It isn't like I'm family."

Ruth fell silent again.

"No, Ruth," Sissy said. "No, no, and no."

"You don't know how much Darlene cares about you," Ruth said. "That girl talks about you all the time. It's Sissy this and Sissy that. You're already family, you just don't know it."

"*Mitakuye oyasin,*" Sissy said. We are all related. "Related, yes. Like she's my little sister. But I'm not her mother."

"You could be," Ruth said. "It would be the best thing that ever happened to those two kids."

"But that would mean I was Clayton's wife! And that would not be the best thing that ever happened to me!"

Ruth patted Sissy's arm apologetically.

"All right. Maybe you're right. But you will look after Darlene, won't you?"

Another man went off the barrel bull, ass over tin can, and the men laughed. Sissy heard Clayton's guitar strike up a series of chords. As she hurried back inside, a maroon Riviera pulled quietly into the parking lot.

Sissy was into the first song of the second set, an old Jim Reeves tune, when Pete came in, followed by Zooey, her turquoise skirt swaying, followed by Gordon and the feed salesman that she had met at the Longhorn Bar in Scenic on the Fourth of July. They hesitated a minute looking for a table, but the only empty one was across the dance floor right in front of the bandstand. She saw them move through the crowd then lost them when they sat down. Only Zooey's turquoise skirt showed between the moving legs of the dancers. When the break came, she didn't bother to get a beer but ducked out through a side door, standing in the shadows with a cigarette, watching the boys at the barrel. A crowd of a dozen or more came around the corner from the front entrance, led by Pete Broussard.

"Let me show you how it's done," he was saying. "That barrel is for pussies who think they're tough."

"You show them," Andrew the salesman said, following right at Pete's heels. Pete didn't look drunk yet; he walked a straight line, leading with his belly, and behind him the onlookers laughed, some egging Pete on, some yelling that a barrel bull was worse than a real bull because the men pulling the ropes had brains.

More people came out of the bar in a crowd until it looked like half the customers or more were outside. A couple of big Rosebud Indians clapped onto the back ropes, another onto one of the front ones, with Andrew taking the fourth. Pete climbed onto the barrel, took a good wrap around his hand with the rope attached to the barrel, clamped his hat down and raised his right hand as if it were a real bull in a real arena with prize money at stake. He nodded. The men on the ropes jerked with all their strength. The front of the barrel dipped and rose; the back dipped and jerked. Pete's legs clamped tight, a little smile frozen on his mouth.

Zooey screamed, "You show them, Pete!"

The crowd roared. The men on the ropes jerked harder. One of the men at the back end lost his footing and fell, dropping the rope, and as he fell, his opposite number jerked extra hard. The barrel did a little roll, just a little roll, slipping Pete off balance a little to the right. Then the man on the left front rope gave a mighty tug. Pete slipped farther to the right, then dropped off the barrel like a felled tree. Smack. His hat didn't come off. The crowd clapped and laughed.

"I thought only pussies couldn't ride a barrel bull!" Andrew yelled.

Pete put his hands down, pressing against the ground, pushing himself into a sitting position. No one helped him up. He got up on one knee, then the other. The Rosebud cowboys laughed, slapping their hats on their legs, shuffling their feet. When he was standing, Pete reached up and took off his hat, throwing it aside.

Andrew came over to Pete, threw his arm around Pete's shoulder.

"Better luck next time, old buddy," Andrew said.

Pete grabbed the back of Andrew's belt, pitching him away. Andrew staggered but didn't fall, a puzzled expression on his face. Pete advanced on him and the crowd hushed as Pete bunched Andrew's shirt with his left hand, pulled him close and said something too quiet to be heard. Pete didn't draw his arm back far, but his right fist hit Andrew's nose with a sound like stomping a ripe tomato. Blood flew, but Andrew didn't fall because Pete held him upright, hit him a second time, then let him drop. Andrew uttered not a word. Pete dropped to his knees beside Andrew, sat back on his butt and looked at the people in the crowd who were absolutely silent, watching. Pete brought his fist to his mouth and licked a smear of blood, let out a bellow and leaned forward, pounding his fists right-left, right-left, right-left into Andrew's face, neck, chest, the blows thumping and squelching. Andrew's arms splayed out to the sides, his hands up as if in surrender. On and on, the fists smashed down as Andrew's blood ran off into the sandy earth. Pete breathed like a racehorse at the end of the Kentucky Derby, then the blows slowed and stopped. Pete stared at the broken man, put a bloody fist on his thigh and stood slowly. He walked over and picked up his hat, settling it on his head, started walking toward the crowd that receded like a collective wave from a beach. He turned and ran back toward Andrew, kicked him, once, twice, three times in the hip, the side, the head, and each time the body rose and fell again. Pete walked off into the darkness beyond the barrel bull. The crowd muttered, shuffled, collected itself and moved back around the building.

Sissy let out her breath; her cigarette was burning her fingers.

A lone man, blonde hair gleaming in the moonlight, came trotting from the building to Andrew, took one look and yelled, "Hey, need some help over here!" A couple of men walked back, another went to the parking lot and returned with a blanket while the blonde man checked Andrew's pulse. His breathing sounded like a fat man snoring. The three men rolled Andrew onto the blanket and bore him away toward the parking lot. The blonde one looked back over his shoulder, and Sissy recognized him. Tom Holm, the FBI agent.

She lit another cigarette.

"Ain't that a hell of a deal," a voice said behind her, and she jumped like she'd been shot.

"Sonny! Damn it, don't creep up on me like that. How long have you been standing there?"

He held his hands out like claws, as he tiptoed toward her.

She slapped at him. "Stop it."

"Long enough to see what happened," Sonny said, dropping his hands to his side as he squatted down with his back against the building.

"Makes me wonder what the hell is the matter with people around here. You noticed nobody stopped him," Sissy said.

"Nobody wanted to get their own ass kicked," Sonny said. "Me neither."

"Three or four people together could've stopped him," Sissy said. "That was brutal."

"Wasn't pretty," Sonny agreed, "but shit like that happens everywhere."

"It's worse here," Sissy argued. "There's this don't-care-about-anything fog hanging over this whole place. No one tries to fix anything. Every day is more of the same and every week is like the one before and every year and nothing ever gets better." Her voice was choking.

"Aww, Cuz, you worry too much," Sonny said, but Sissy cried on.

Sonny stood up, awkwardly patting her shoulder.

"You're too sensitive. I know that's what makes you such a good singer, but it ain't a good trait for being alive."

"You're as bad as everyone else," Sissy said, her voice muffled by her shirtsleeve she was using to wipe her face.

"Don't get snot on your shirt creases," Sonny said, offering her a handkerchief from his pocket.

She blew her nose, handed the handkerchief back to Sonny.

He took it with a thumb and forefinger, said, "Eeeww!" and flung it away from himself.

"Come on," he said. "Let's go make some music."

She shook her head. "I don't hear Clayton's guitar riff yet."

"Never mind Clayton," Sonny said, taking her belt loop and pulling her behind him back into the bar.

He led her through the tables where people sat speaking in lowered voices, across the dance floor and over to the side of the bandstand.

"'House of the Rising Sun,'" he said.

"What?"

"Let's do it," Sonny said with a grin.

"Without Clayton? He'd never play that and let me sing it," she protested.

"Who needs Clayton? Come on! It'll be fun."

"You really like pissing him off, don't you?"

Sonny's grin was beatific. "Yes. Yes, I do. Come on." He went to the side of the bandstand where the jukebox sat, some mechanical gizmo inside turning and spinning blue, then pink, then green lights that looked like it had little bubbles moving through it. He pulled the plug. The crowd didn't seem to notice. No one had been on the dance floor.

She followed him up onto the stage, reaching for her guitar, but Sonny stopped her.

"Just me. I play this one. You just sing."

They didn't introduce the song. Sonny plugged in Clayton's guitar instead of his own bass, played the opening bars. Key of E minor. Sissy always liked the minor keys. The major keys sounded too sweet, too hopeful, but the minor ones—they weren't the opposite of sweet, not sour, but there was a nuance there that implied depths beyond what the major keys could express. They wept; they despaired. They asked why but gave no answers, only possibilities.

Her voice came out low and growly on the opening lines, growing stronger as she went on. The crowd hushed, watching. She sang of the whorehouse in New Orleans; she sang of poverty; she sang of youthful indiscretion leading to a lifetime of misery and shame and death. Her voice soared as she pled with god and the listeners not to do what she had done. Sonny's lone guitar wept with her, and when she had finished, her face was wet with tears again. Clayton sat at a table in front glaring, his face a black thundercloud. The crowd was silent, not so much as a tinkle of ice in a glass, only the collective breathing of the audience. Someone over in the back yelled, "yeah," someone else gave a shrill whistle, and the crowd broke into tumultuous applause that went on and on and on.

Sissy gave a little bow, turned and put her head on Sonny's shoulder.

"Thank you," she said.

"All right, Cuz. Now get your head off me, you're pissing tears on my shirt."

Clayton jumped on stage then, leaned toward them and said, "All right, you pulled a fast one on me this time. But no god damned Rolling Stones. You hear me?"

Sonny rolled his eyes.

They were packing up their instruments and equipment after the last set and a drink for the road when Tom Holm walked up to the bandstand.

"I need to talk to you, Sissy," he said. "You can ride back to Jackson with me."

"No," she said. "No."

"She's riding back with me," Clayton tried to intervene.

Holm shifted the toothpick from one side of his mouth to the other, reached into his back pocket, flipped his wallet open to his badge holding it under Clayton's nose.

Clayton waved his hand.

"All right, all right. Do what you have to." He turned to Melvin. "Make sure you pack those leads in good. Last time you had them all tangled up like a—like a—like a—you messed them up."

Sissy followed Tom out of the bar and into the warm dark parking lot where only a few cars still sat, occupants arguing or talking among themselves. The maroon Riviera was gone.

"How's that salesman guy doing?" Sissy asked as Tom started his car.

"What salesman?"

"The guy Pete beat up."

"Oh, I didn't know what he did for a living, only that he is still among the living. Preliminary exam says he's got a busted nose, busted left cheekbone, concussion, a few broken ribs, maybe a punctured lung, but he's going to live."

Tom steered the car out onto the highway, turned west, and accelerated smoothly.

"You going to arrest Pete Broussard?" Sissy asked.

"Ain't my jurisdiction," Tom said.

"You're FBI, you have jurisdiction."

"On some crimes. But I didn't see this one. I got there just as it was over, so all I saw was a beat-up guy in the dirt and a crowd walking away. I heard people talking about it, but do you think any of them is going to rat out Pete Broussard? No? I don't think so, either. I'll leave this one for the Winner cops or the Rosebud tribal police or whoever thinks they want to mess with it."

"So, what do you want to talk to me about?" Sissy asked. "You know I'm not going to file a complaint against Pete Broussard, not going to swear anything as a witness if someone else did file a complaint. So what is it? You need advice on your love life? Want a recommendation on the best brand of hemorrhoid cream? Weight loss advice? What?"

"Nope, nope, and nope."

He turned the radio on low, ran the needle across the dial but got nothing except KOMA, where a commercial for a rock-and-roll band somewhere in Kansas was on. He switched it off and relaxed back in the seat.

"Sissy, don't you ever stop making the smart-mouth remarks?"

She didn't answer.

"I've got you figured. You ain't mean. You ain't the snotty little bitch you pretend to be. You're scared."

She started to speak, but he held up a hand to stop her.

"Yeah, you are. You're scared of being stuck here in the middle of nowhere for the rest of your life. It won't do me any good to tell you things aren't any better elsewhere because you don't want to hear that, so I'm not going to try. You'll either figure out something or you won't. I can't worry about it. But I got a job to do here and I need your help."

Sissy rolled her head around on her neck.

"I don't know any more than the last time I talked to you," she said.

They rode on for a while in silence.

"I think you do," he said.

She groaned.

"I'm not saying you're withholding information. I know everyone talks to you, everyone tells you their troubles. Now, maybe no one has come right out and said they killed Buffalo Ames, but somebody has said something to you that tickled your imagination, something that's got your motor running and your thoughts ticking over. You may not even know it yet, but it's true. So, I want you to tell me about everything that's happened in the last few weeks, everyone that's talked to you about anything, even if it just seems ordinary. Tell me what you've been doing."

"Jeezus christ. I don't keep a journal, you know," she said.

"Maybe you ought to." When she didn't respond, he urged her on again.

"Come on. Talk to me. You'll feel better."

She took a deep breath and started telling him the most boring things she could think of about working at the café, about the harvest crews, about playing the gig in Kadoka, about Howard marrying Viola, about Viola's bratty kid, Jeffrey, about her parents visiting her auntie in Nebraska.

As they came into Mission Town, he stopped her from talking as he pulled over to an all-night Dairy Queen. He ordered cheeseburgers and fries and strawberry milk shakes for both of them. Sissy hadn't known how hungry she was.

She went on with her story as they drove from Mission back to Jackson through a couple of little wide spots in the road where there was a gas station or a post office, closed up and dark. She rambled in endless detail until she had bored herself so bad she had to stop, but Tom never interrupted, never told her something wasn't relevant. He listened.

She was done a mile before they got into Martin, just as they were passing the fairgrounds and the livestock auction barns.

"Now, if there's anything in any of that mess that tells you anything more than you didn't already know, I'm glad, and I hope to hell it makes you leave me alone," she said as he stopped the car in front of her house.

"I don't know yet," he said. "I'll have to think about it all."

She opened the door and stepped out of the passenger side.

"Thanks for the food," she said.

He gave a little salute with two fingers of his left hand.

The dirty dishes were still in the sink, but a scum of orange grease had formed over the water. Speedy's purse sat on the kitchen table.

CHAPTER TWELVE

THE GOLF TOURNAMENT

SUNDAY, AUGUST 17, 1969

Sissy slept late on Sunday morning, as she usually got to do, and woke feeling that something was out of whack, something missing, which she always felt when her parents were gone in the summers. Sunday mornings without the smell of chili and the smell of fresh-brewed coffee, without the sound of her dad's strong right arm whomping pancake batter always seemed empty, sad. But today there was something else. Martha was catering the country club golf tournament banquet on Sunday evening, and Sissy had promised to work. She had to be at the café at two-thirty, spend the afternoon in the hot café kitchen helping cook, then help load the food in Martha's pickup camper and get it out to the country club. After that, she would help dish it and serve. Of course, there would be the cleanup afterward. And putting up with the people who attended the banquet.

Country club, what a joke! A few years earlier, the town had applied for and gotten a government grant for small towns, which they figured out they could use to put in a community meeting building, swimming pool, and nine-hole golf course. By allowing the schools to use the pool for swimming classes, they leveraged the original grant into an education grant as well. The complex sat at the edge of town in the middle of a cow pasture. The golf course had no irrigation except what nature dropped from the skies, so most summers the rough was the rough all over; the golfers—mostly members of the commercial club and a few of the wealthier ranchers and farmers—slapped up sand on every shot and were as likely to find a rattlesnake as their golf ball lurking in the weeds.

Sissy had learned to swim in that pool, but what she remembered most was not the swimming classes themselves, but making fun of the PE teacher whose very tight swimming trunks demonstrated how poorly endowed he was. Well, that, and walking the half a mile back to town from the pool in the winter with her hair wet and freezing to the rollers that she had put in after she got out of the pool.

Speedy was already up and in the bathroom when Sissy got downstairs. The coffeepot, filled with water, sat on the sink, the coffee canister out, but no grounds put in yet. Sissy added scoops of ground coffee, put on the lid, set it on the burner, and lit the gas ring with a match. She shoved aside some clutter on the table, sat down and lit a cigarette. The lock on the bathroom door clicked. Speedy came out and sat at the table, her dark hair straggling against her stark white face.

"What's the matter with you? You look awful," Sissy said.

"I feel awful," Speedy said.

"Have you been eating leftovers out of your mom's refrigerator again?"

Speedy batted at Sissy's cigarette smoke.

"I wish you wouldn't do that," she said.

Sissy waved her cigarette in the air.

"Since when did you get to be such an anti-smoking nut?"

Speedy's face went from white to pale green. She ran back to the bathroom. Sissy heard the sound of the toilet seat lid banging against the tank, then retching. She got up and went to the door.

"Speedy? What the hell is the matter with you? I think you'd better go to the doctor. This stomach stuff has been going on too long."

No answer. The coffeepot began to gurgle and burp. Sissy turned the burner down, but not before a brown foam had risen through the spout, dribbling a bit into the burner where it hissed and steamed and burned.

The toilet flushed, then the water faucet came on.

Sissy knocked gently on the door.

"Speedy? Are you alive in there?"

She pushed the door open and went in. Speedy stood at the sink, leaning over as she scooped water onto her face.

"Speedy, this is too much. Look at you. You never were any kind of heavyweight, but it looks like you've lost fifteen pounds. You're skin and bones. I think you shouldn't wait until Monday to get to the doctor. I'll drive you out to the hospital emergency room."

Speedy turned off the faucet and stood up, still leaning on the sink with her head down.

"What the hell is it, anyway? You think you might have ulcers? Something wrong with your pancreas or your liver?"

Speedy jerked the hand towel off the rack and swabbed at her face, mumbling through the heavy terry cloth.

"Sissy, for one of the smartest people I know, you sure are stupid," she said.

"What?"

Speedy dropped the towel and shouted, "I've swallowed a watermelon seed. I've got a bun in the oven. I'm looking for a little stranger. I'm fucking pregnant! Knocked up!"

Sissy's knees went wobbly, and she held on to the edge of the sink.

"Yeah," Speedy went on. "I'm a bad girl, a bad bad bad girl. It isn't fair. Half those girls in high school were screwing their steady boyfriends every Saturday in the backseat of their cars at the mile corner. I do it one time—*one* time—and I'm knocked up."

She flipped the toilet seat down with a bang and collapsed onto it, her head in her hands. A minute later, she jumped up, whirled around, lifted the lid, and began retching into the toilet again.

It wasn't true. What Speedy said. Yes, half—or more—of the girls in high school were screwing their steadies, but at least five of those girls got pregnant and had to drop out of school to get married, that Sissy knew of. There were rumors that a couple of others who left to go stay with relatives had babies and put them up for adoption. Or had abortions. And it wasn't true that Speedy only had sex once and got pregnant, but if it made her feel better to lie to herself, well, okay.

Sissy went back to the kitchen, took a clean dishtowel out of the drawer, plopped some ice cubes in it and wadded it up. When Speedy finally came out of the bathroom, Sissy sat her down in front of the fan and handed her the ice pack.

"I'll get you some ice water, too," Sissy said. "If you sip it slow, you might be able to keep it down. You keep puking like that, you're going to get dehydrated and really have to go to the hospital."

Speedy dabbed her face with the ice pack.

"Thanks," she said. "What, no lectures from the smart girl?"

"Too late for that," Sissy said. "You know who the father is?"

Speedy slammed the ice pack down on the table, sending a couple of cubes skittering out across the table and onto the floor where they shattered and mixed with the unswept dirt.

"What do you *mean*? Sonny, of course!" Speedy said.

"Sorry, sorry, just asking," Sissy said. The coffeepot bubbled and burped. Sissy turned it off. Maybe the father was Sonny; Sissy hoped so. He wouldn't marry Speedy, but he would help support the kid. Sissy thought that Speedy would now be an enrolled member of the tribe if she had a little Indian in her. She controlled the urge to laugh. But if the father was the guy on the harvester crew or somebody else that Sissy didn't know about, Speedy would be on her own. If she decided to keep the baby.

Sissy ran a glass of water from the sink, added fresh ice cubes and set it in front of Speedy.

"What are you going to do?" Sissy asked.

Speedy had picked up the ice bag again, holding it to her face.

"My folks want me to go stay with Debbie and her husband and have the baby up there. Give it up for adoption." Debbie, Speedy's sister, lived in Montana where her husband worked in the copper mines.

"So you told them. Why haven't you told Sonny?"

"Sonny ain't the marrying kind. You told me that, and it's the truth. If I'm giving it up, why should I bother to tell him?"

She took a little sip from the glass of water. Sissy poured herself a cup of coffee, checked the refrigerator, but there was no milk and the can of condensed milk was sour. She sat down, taking out a cigarette, but got the pleading look from Speedy and tapped it back into the pack. The fan whirred in the background, riffling papers, mostly sale ads that had come in the mail and still lay on the table with the unsorted bills.

"I could be wrong, you know. About Sonny. As you pointed out so pointedly, I'm not that smart."

"He was going to be a priest," Speedy said. "They don't get married."

"They don't have sex either. Or they aren't supposed to. Sonny left the seminary, remember? I don't know why he ever went to the seminary in the first place. Of all the people I've ever known, Sonny is the least likely priest material."

Speedy didn't answer.

"Do you know when you're due?" Sissy asked.

Speedy waved the glass of water back and forth. "I don't know. I didn't count back. I guess I didn't want to think about it."

"I don't think it's going away," Sissy said. "It's not like a cold that's gone in a week or so. This is a lifetime deal. How do you feel about kids? In general, I mean."

"I never thought much about kids at all. You know I'm the youngest of us two girls. Debbie has a little boy, but she married Earl and moved off to Montana so I wasn't around her when she was pregnant, never saw the kid until it was a year old. I guess I just assumed I'd get married like she did and have kids. Someday. I never thought I'd have kids and then get married. That's ass backwards." She said "the kid" and "it." Not "the child." Not "him." Didn't say the little boy's name. Her own nephew.

At least Speedy was sitting and talking, not trying to be funny, not jumping up and down like a drop of water on a hot griddle.

"I think I'm going to go lay down," Speedy said. She started up the stairs, turned and trudged back to hug Sissy. "Thanks for not saying I told you so."

Sissy had a second cup of coffee, wondering what Sonny would do when, if, Speedy told him about the baby. What if it wasn't his baby?

How would he feel about that? She knew she was right. Sonny wasn't the marrying kind.

She looked at the mess in the kitchen that grew every day like a mutant amoeba. It would have to wait and grow some more because she was due at the café in an hour.

In the hot café kitchen, Martha stood at the back counter cutting up chickens. A mound of potatoes waited in the sink to be peeled, while eggs boiled gently on the range. One of them had broken in the water, giving the steamy kitchen a sulfur fart smell. Sissy tied on an apron and started peeling potatoes while she thought about Speedy. Getting pregnant wasn't a good way to get out of Jackson, but at least she was getting out.

Half an hour later, Lynda came in. For the next two hours, the three women cut up potatoes and eggs and onion and pickles, mixed up mayonnaise and mustard and stirred it all together to make potato salad. They chopped cabbage and carrots for coleslaw, refrigerating the salads in big stainless steel tubs. When the pies came out of the oven, they started dipping and frying the chicken. At four-thirty, Sissy left to go turn on the warming trays at the country club, set out the plates, the flatware, the napkins from the cupboards out there.

The final round of the golf tournament was finishing up just as Sissy set out the last of the plates—white china with a gold rim and *Jackson Country Club* scrolled across the middle in royal blue. Through the east-facing plate-glass windows, she could see people sitting on the cement slab that they called a patio watching men walking up to the last hole right next to the club. Several white balls stood out on the dusty grass. Sissy's dad never played golf. He said he didn't see the fun in using a stick to knock a horse turd down a gopher hole.

Mrs. Bianco sat with Viola and Mrs. Broussard, Mrs. Dale Holtz, whose husband was the mayor, and a couple of the courthouse biddies. Kids ran and screeched. Now and then one of the women yelled at them. Jeffrey had a big hot pink ball that he kicked among the watchers on the patio, crawling under the tables to retrieve it, knocking over a woman's glass of lemonade, or maybe it was something stronger. A group of men lingered outside a striped tent by the last hole, where the chairman of the commercial club, a fat man named Adams who ran the local hardware store, sat with a clipboard and a microphone in front of him. The men shuffled their feet and watched the last golfer hit his shot, which bounced up onto what they called the "green," but was really the brown. They cheered as the golfer waved his club in delight.

Adams spoke into the mike, "And that terrific shot was our leader, Dr. Bianco, who is shooting for birdie on this final hole, one under for the tournament. But right behind him is his future son-in-law—or, so we hear, ha-ha-ha—Howard Broussard at even for this round and par on the tournament. Frenchie O'Toole is at third in the standings. And we are coming up on the last hole, ladies and gentlemen. Let's give a nice round of applause for all our players!"

The people on the patio clapped politely. The kids ignored everyone.

Jeffrey kicked his hot pink ball past the patio, ran after it, accidentally kicked it again when he leaned over to pick it up. The ball took off as if it had a burning desire to escape from Jeffrey, ran up to the edge of the ninth hole green—or brown—and stopped, but Jeffrey didn't. He ran awkwardly, his too-big head propelling him now in a forward tilt, then following as his body led, then leaning from one side to the other side like a bop-em toy that had learned to run. He darted around the pimply-faced high school boy in white pants, Tim Baker, who was waiting to pull the stick out of the hole when the first golfer putted his ball. The men at the tent were watching the golfers digging through their bags for their putters; the ladies drank their lemonade or their tea, mostly with a shot of something stronger added. Tim Baker bent over to tie his shoe, and Jeffrey ran onto the brown green, stopped suddenly, staring at the white golf balls scattered here and there like Easter eggs. He bent over, picked one up, pulled out the front of his green striped polo shirt and dropped the ball into the handy holder.

"*Jeffrey!* Jeffrey, *noooo!*" Dr. Bianco dropped the putter he had just pulled from his golf bag.

Jeffrey paid no attention. He bent over, picking up another Easter egg. Another. Another. Dropped them into his shirttail bag. He liked the satisfying clack they made when they bumped up against each other.

"*Jeffrey!* Jeffrey, *noooo!*" Howard, Dr. Bianco, Frenchie O'Toole, Tim Baker, the other golfers left to play and the ones following the group, the men at the tent, the ladies on the patio—everyone except the kids froze as if a sudden January blizzard had struck, icing them immobile to the ground. The kids still screamed and ran as if the annual Jackson Country Club Golf Tournament and Jeffrey's theft of the balls was the least important thing in the world.

Mrs. Bianco turned her head toward her grandson and smiled.

Tim Baker, the first to thaw, closed his mouth, picked up his feet and ran at Jeffrey, who picked up yet another Easter egg, licked it, and stuffed it in his mouth. Tim dived for Jeffrey, intending to swoop him up and shake him down for the balls, but four feet from Jeffrey, he tripped on a hummocky bit of grass, stumbled, tried to catch himself, stumbled again and hit Jeffrey mid-body, a tackle that he had never been able to make in the three years he had played football for the Jackson High School Lions. Jeffrey and Tim went down together with Tim on top. Jeffrey did not struggle. As Tim rolled off, Jeffrey's face turned from pink to light blue, quickly darkening as a gagging sound came from his mouth, his eyes rolled up, his feet drummed the ground.

Dr. Bianco pounded up, took one look at Jeffrey, screaming, "What have you done to my Jeffrey!"

The other golfers—Howard, Frenchie, the announcer, the ladies from the patio, even the kids poured onto the golf course, surrounding them. Tim Baker's hand covered his mouth, his own eyes bulging. Dr. Bianco picked Jeffrey up but couldn't move for the crowd hemming him in.

"Get back, get back!" Bianco yelled.

"Sir, sir," Tim Baker pleaded as he pulled on Bianco's aqua knit shirt-sleeve.

Jeffrey's face went from blue to deep purple, his arm and hand movements slowing.

"Get out of the fucking way!" Bianco yelled at the crowd. A path began opening, but Tim kept following, plucking at the back of Bianco's shirt.

"Sir! Sir! I think he's choking on a golf ball!"

Bianco stopped, staring at Tim.

"I said," Tim repeated, "I think he's choking on a golf ball. He put one in his mouth just before—just before I hit him. But I didn't mean to hurt him! I tripped! It was an accident. I'm sorry!"

Bianco twirled Jeffrey like a baton, ripping off one of the kid's sandals, pounded on his back. The remaining golf balls in Jeffrey's shirttail rolled out on the ground. Nothing. He bounced Jeffrey up and down. Nothing. He knelt on the ground, holding Jeffrey upside-down, squeezing him hard around the chest. A golf ball, spit slimy, shot from Jeffrey's mouth as if propelled from a bazooka, clapped hard against Frenchie O'Toole's left ankle bone with a pop, rolled six feet and stopped two inches short of the flag on the ninth hole. The initials inked on the ball read *SB*, for Stephen Bianco.

Jeffrey sucked in wind and pushed it out in a squall of sound like an oncoming tornado. Bianco's hand went from pounding Jeffrey's back to pounding Jeffrey's butt, one-two-three-four-five. Frenchie O'Toole limped over to grab Bianco's arm.

"Stephen! Steve! Dr. Bianco!" Frenchie yelled into the hairy tuft protruding from Bianco's left ear. "Stop it! I think you've won the tournament. Your ball is in good position."

After some consultation, Howard and Frenchie and Abe Tosca took a drop at the edge of the green, agreeing to leave Dr. Bianco's ball where it lay. Howard took the first shot, putting from thirty feet. The ball humped and bumped and thumped along, tried to climb the same grassy hummock that had tripped Tim Baker into falling on Jeffrey, stopped and rolled back. Howard took another stroke to put his ball into the hole. Abe Tosca putted at the hole, passed it by fifteen feet, putted back past the hole another five feet, and put it in on his third attempt. Frenchie O'Toole gave a short sharp stroke with his putter. His ball rolled as if pulled by a string, straight for the hole, hesitated on the lip and dropped into the hole.

Bianco, calmed somewhat, picked up his marker from the edge of the green and sat his ball down two inches from the hole, drew back his putter and tapped. The ball rolled around the cup, popped out on the far side, rolled another foot. The watching crowd groaned. Bianco walked over and tapped the ball one-handed. It rolled past two inches. He tapped again, and it went in.

Sissy didn't see the end, only heard the details later. Martha had arrived with a pickup load of hot foot to be unloaded, put on the warming trays or set in bins of ice. They served chicken, scooped potato salad and coleslaw and green salad, apologized that there was no Waldorf salad, advised on which of the pies was better, scooped ice cream to top the pie, and when the food was served out, roamed the room refilling tea glasses and pouring after-dinner coffee. She was cleaning up the kitchen, loading leftovers and pans into Martha's pickup when the trophies were given out. She heard that Dr. Bianco was a gracious loser and that everyone who attended the Jackson Country Club Golf Tournament and Banquet unanimously hated Jeffrey's ever-loving guts, except, of course, for Jeffrey's grandmother. And maybe his mother, Viola, who was upset because Howard didn't win the tournament and because Howard came out to Martha's pickup to talk to Sissy while Viola sat in the main dining room holding Jeffrey when her mother went to the bathroom.

It was dark and quiet outside, except for the low rumbling of thunder in the distance from a cloud hanging off to the west but slowly creeping east, hiding the stars as it came. The humidity was coming up; tendrils of Sissy's hair had escaped the low ponytail, curling on her forehead. The air felt sticky.

"Sissy?" Howard appeared behind Martha's pickup, just as Sissy straightened up from sliding a covered pan of leftover fried chicken— mostly wings and backs and a few drumsticks—onto the back floor of the camper. The shelves fitted inside were full, the pans secured on them with bungee cords.

"Damn, Howard, you scared me," Sissy said with a start.

"Sorry," he said. "Long time no talk. You hear anything? You know, about Buffalo?"

She shook her head, then thought he might not be able to see that gesture in the dark. "No," she said. "Not a damned thing. You're not the only one who wants me to tell what I know. That FBI agent, Tom Holm, he's asking me hard."

"Yeah?"

"Yeah," she said. "I don't have any more to tell him than I do you. Wouldn't tell him, even if I did know something. You'll make that clear if anyone asks you, won't you?"

"Sure," he said. "Long as you tell me."

"Yeah," Sissy said, knowing she would never tell Howard if she ever did find out who killed Buffalo Ames. "I just want to keep it local." She hesitated a minute, then asked, "How's Pete?"

Howard kicked at the pickup tire.

"Ashamed. Sticking close to home and minding his own damned business. Trying to keep Zooey to home. Trouble with Pete is, his shame never lasts long. He hasn't always been this way, you know. Used to be . . . well, that's used to be. Back when we were kids. Back before Zooey."

"Jeffrey's going to be okay, though," Sissy added, wishing she'd asked about him before she asked about Pete.

"Unfortunately, yes," Howard said. "How's come some women come with baggage?"

"Because some men are willing to unpack it for them," Sissy said.

"How's come you and me never—"

"Howard? Howard, we're ready to leave now," Viola called from the back door of the building.

"Good night, Howard," Sissy said, watching him walk back to Viola.

She couldn't bear to turn on the kitchen light when she got home, couldn't bear to look at the mess. She brushed her teeth, took a quick shower, and went up to bed.

Speedy was in bed, breathing quietly in the dark night. Sometime in the early morning the thunderstorm hit with brilliant fireworks lightning and crashing thunder. She got up to close the windows, felt something brush against her bare legs. Wooly Booger meowed softly. She carried him back upstairs to bed with her.

CHAPTER THIRTEEN

ALLEN'S POW WOW AND CARNIVAL

SATURDAY, AUGUST 23, 1969

The Reynolds Carnival, with their usual little hardscrabble collection of rusty, run-down rides, half-dead animals, and creepy carny workers, had set up at the Allen Pow Wow every summer for fifteen years, not that the Allen community officials hadn't tried to get a decent carny company instead. All the more respectable outfits were scared to death of the Indians that made up the majority of the crowd, so every year the creepy Reynolds Carnival workers drove their gear-grinding old trucks pulling rusty sideshow setups and diseased sad-eyed animals in wired-together cages two hundred miles from the nearest sizeable town to set up on the sun-dead grass outside Allen town. The pow wow and carnival lasted only two days because neither the town proper nor the paying customers could stand any more fun time than that.

The Red Birds had played for the dance in the Allen Community Center every summer for several years with no untoward aftereffects, so they were asked back again. Melvin and Sonny, Clayton and Sissy arrived just after noon, and for once Sonny hadn't minded showing up early. He had a date, a hot one he said, blowing into his palms, then shaking them furiously while he jumped up and down. Sissy guessed that his date wasn't Speedy.

First they set up their equipment in the echoing room that doubled as a community meeting place and a basketball court for the town-sponsored team in the winter, locking it up afterward with the key provided by the pink-faced mayor, a bustling fat man who ran the local equivalent of a grocery store. The pow wow dancing had been running for an hour or more; the crowd at the arena fence had already seen the Opening Prayer, the Flag Ceremony and Prayer, the Veteran's Dance and the Men's Traditional Dance, where the long-tailed bustles of feathers sometimes held a red feather, a signifier that the dancer was a veteran who had been wounded in action. When Clayton and Sissy and Melvin gently pushed through the crowd to the fence, the Women's Traditional was in motion, ladies dipping and swaying in place, their outfits heavily beaded in red, yellow, blue—even hot pink and purple—following their motions, while the Tater Creek Singers' padded drumsticks Boom Boom Boomed.

"Look, look," Melvin nudged Sissy while pointing with his lips. "Ain't that Agnes Bear Claw? You'd think she'd be too old for this."

"Yeah, that's her," Sissy said. "She must be—what—close to ninety."

"I hear the younger women wish she'd give it up," Melvin said. "She always gets the prize. I think it's sympathy."

They watched as Agnes stood in place bending her knees to the rhythm.

"If it wasn't for the drum, we could probably hear her knees pop," Sissy said.

"Have some respect for a wise elder," Melvin said.

"Sometimes people aren't wise elders. They're just old," Sissy said.

The dance ended with Agnes walking up to take her prize, then the drum struck up an old-time dance, rarely performed, the Rabbit Dance.

Wana Wagni kte eh
Cante sica yaun sni ye-eh
Toksa kiksuya he waun kte eh
Hiya ah—hiya ah yo—oo

Sissy spoke a little Lakota—*cikal*—as her dad would say, so she followed the words of the song about a man leaving his lover and telling her not to have a sad heart. This was a couple's dance, a social dance, not competitive. Sissy wished Lawrence and Lily had gotten back in time to attend the pow wow. She walked away from the dancing over to the carnival area, through grounds already littered with soda pop bottles, discarded candy wrappers, wadded-up napkins, and here and there a beer bottle or can. The pow wow was supposed to be an alcohol-free event, but it never really was. Tinny music came from the merry-go-round where a few mothers watched their children going around and around and up and down while they glanced back over their shoulders to the dance arena. As she passed a shooting gallery with dirty stuffed toys dangling from the roof edge, she saw a carny with greasy, choppy-looking hair wearing a stained wife beater shirt leaning on the counter while he waited for customers, his eyes following her as she walked past.

She stopped at a camper with a window roughly cut into the side, a square of plywood tacked at right angles to the outside forming a little shelf under the window. The sign above it read: *Indian Tacos*. She knew the woman running it, Daisy Short Knife, so she stopped and bought a taco, a huge flat tortilla that took up an entire paper plate covered with seasoned meat, lettuce, and tomatoes. She sat in a lawn chair at a folding table eating while the grease ran down and dripped off her elbows.

"Heya, Cuz," a voice said as a hand clapped her on the back. She turned as Sonny slumped in the chair next to her, forcing a groan from the flimsy chair frame.

"You almost made me choke," she said. "Where's your girlfriend?"

"No show. I could have made her choke, too."

"You're disgusting," she said. "For a guy who spent time in the seminary . . ."

Sonny grinned, pushing his glasses back up onto his nose.

"Best jokes I ever heard were in the seminary. There ain't much else to do around there you know."

"Except praying and learning Latin. Who was she?"

"Wouldn't you like to know?"

"You talked to Speedy lately?" Sissy wiped her face and her arms with a napkin, took a sip from her soda.

"Nope, and I don't plan to."

"I think you ought to talk to her. You might find out something important."

A group of kids ran by, one little boy with an armload of toy trucks and cars running ahead. A little girl in the group following after, yelled, "If you don't start sharing, I'm going to kick you in the balls and take *all* the toys!"

"You train that one?" Sonny asked.

"No, but she's got the right idea," Sissy said. "Sounds like she's willing to share, but she ain't taking crap off anybody. That's my kind of kid."

Sonny shuddered. "I don't want any kind of kids," he said.

Sissy stared at him. He stared back. Behind his Jiminy Cricket glasses, his eyes grew big.

"No. Oh, no. Uh, uh. Speedy's pregnant, right? And she says it's my kid?"

Sissy looked down at her mostly empty plate, shoved it aside.

"I promised her I wouldn't say anything, and I'm not saying anything."

Sonny jumped up, pacing away toward the arena. He stopped, pulled off his hat and, slapping it against his leg, turned and came back.

Sissy sipped her soda. The pow wow singers drummed for the Ladies' Butterfly Dance. In the arena, women with turquoise, rose, hot orange, royal blue shawls, arms extended, swooped and stutter-stepped to the drumbeat.

Sonny grasped the back of the lawn chair across from Sissy, leaning forward, then stood tall, ran his hand through his hair so it stood up like an angry porcupine, clapped his hat on his head again and sat down.

"Sissy, can I talk to you?"

She sighed. "Why not? Everyone else does."

"Is she sure? Has she been to the doctor?"

"No, she hasn't been to the doctor, but I would guess she knows the signs. She's been puking up her guts for two weeks or more."

"How would I know if it's mine?"

"That's what most men say," Sissy said, "although, in this case you might have a valid point. There is such a thing as a paternity test."

He shook his head. "Damn, damn, damn. Can you imagine anyone calling me 'daddy'?"

"I can imagine people calling you lots of things, but never 'daddy,'" she said.

"Is she planning to keep the kid?"

"I don't think she's decided yet. Her parents want her to go out to her sister's in Montana, have the baby there and give it up for adoption."

"What do you think she's going to do?"

"I have no idea, and I don't think she does either at this point. But you know, I can't imagine her being a mother," Sissy said, "although she couldn't be any worse than Viola."

An odd look passed over Sonny's face.

"What? What did I say?" Sissy asked. She turned to see where his eyes were looking.

Zooey stood at the corner of the Taco Trailer, leaning against it while she smiled at Sonny.

Sissy turned back in time to catch the answering smile on Sonny's face. He started to stand, but she grabbed his arm.

"*Sonny! Are you fucking suicidal?*"

He shook off her hand, walked over to Zooey, who laid her own hand on his arm. As they walked around behind the camper out of sight, Sonny shot Sissy the finger.

She clapped her hand to her forehead. "Morons. I am surrounded by morons," she said.

The rest of the afternoon Sissy wandered the grounds saying hello to this one and that one, passing a bit of conversation here and there, sometimes pausing for a longer while with Melvin or Clayton, who nodded at her approvingly.

"Working the crowd, that's good," he said.

A couple of times Sissy spotted Pete working the crowd himself, peering over the heads of people and around groups, but Zooey and

Sonny stayed out of sight. The carnival music and the rumble of the crowd grew louder when the last pow wow dance ended, all the prizes were awarded, and the drum group packed up. Now more people violated the alcohol ban, meeting in groups at the trunks of cars where the cans of soda were topped up or poured out entirely and filled up with something stronger. The pink-faced mayor and a couple of men hired for security duty patrolled the grounds, carefully ignoring the drinkers while they hassled the kids who ran everywhere, now and then tossing some firecrackers left over from the Fourth of July.

The band only played until midnight, so they started at seven o'clock instead of eight. At six-thirty, Clayton started herding Melvin and Sissy toward the community center building, while looking around for Sonny, who was still nowhere to be found. The Ferris wheel turned, half the yellow lights on the spokes burned out, but people, mostly families with kids, lined up to ride. A cloud hung off along the western horizon, but a white full moon hung overhead.

The doors to the community room had been open for half an hour, allowing the older people a chance to get an early table, so the room was a third full when they stepped up on the bandstand to tune up. Fifteen minutes later, Sonny came in through a side door, his shirt rumpled and his lips swollen. After ten more minutes, Sonny was tuned up; every table in the room was full of people, most with innocent-looking bottles of soda sitting in front of them. Looking across the room, Sissy saw Gordon Charbonneau sitting at a table with Cristal, Loretta, and his sister and a man she didn't know; Howard and Viola sat with Howard's parents. Half a dozen carny folks, women and men looking thin and sad, sat in tables at the far left side, but nowhere did she see Pete or Zooey. Or Tom Holm.

Hail, hail, the gang's almost all here, she thought.

Clayton leaned over and whispered in her ear, "Remember, not 'House of the Rising Sun.' Not tonight. This is a family crowd."

The band played their opening riff, and Clayton went into his spiel.

"Ladies and gentlemen, welcome to the Allen Community Pow Wow, Carnival, *and* dance! We *are* the Red Bird All-Indian Traveling Band, playing tonight for your listening and dancing pleasure. Here we have, leaning against the wall, our very own, hailing from Porcupine Creek, the former almost-priest, cat burglar, virgin repairman, night watchman, and all-around best bass player in the world—Soooonnnnnyyyy Roberts!"

The crowd gave a cheer, not as loud as the barrooms they played, but respectable. Sonny leaned back, feet on tiptoes, hopped forward two steps, backward two steps. Then it was Melvin's introduction, then Sissy's turn, and finally Clayton's. The dance floor filled as Sissy sang "Walking After Midnight," then on to other old favorites.

At the first break, Pete came in with Zooey in tow, looking like she'd been caught doing something she shouldn't. Pete pulled her over and flung her down in a chair at the table where Gordon Charbonneau still sat with Cristal and Loretta. His sister and the other man were gone. Pete's face looked like a thundercloud. Zooey's body held a tension. Her face was sullen. Pete drank from Gordon's bottle, slammed it down on the table. Sissy looked around for Sonny but didn't see him. Zooey reached for Gordon's bottle, but Pete snatched it up and held it to his chest. Zooey subsided in her chair.

The Red Birds were well into their second set, Sissy singing that people should beware of a tall dark stranger, when a crash of thunder rocked the building, the lights flickered, the guitars zinged, and the lights went out. Some woman in the audience screamed, then the lights came back on, but the amp behind Sissy sizzled and popped like bacon grease in a hot skillet. The crowd stirred and shifted and muttered.

"I think we fried an amp," Clayton said.

Sonny and Clayton leaned over, twisting dials and strumming strings, but the sounds stayed in the instruments, dull muffled notes, while the amp uttered not so much as another buzz. From the room behind them came a crash then a louder crack. They turned. Pete advanced toward the stage carrying a chair leg, waving it like a drum major with a baton. He tripped over a lady's purse, caught his foot in a chair leg when he stumbled and tumbled old lady Short Horn from the chair into a heap on the floor. He circled another table, shoved aside chairs, kept coming, that splintered chair leg waving.

"*Sonny! Sonny Roberts, you little sawed-off son-of-a-bitch! I'm going to kill you!*" Pete bellowed.

Sonny's mouth dropped open. He stood like a statue of a Civil War soldier on a village square.

Thunder crashed again, the lights flickered off and on. Outside the wind came up with a gusty roar.

"Sonny! Sonny, get out the back door," Sissy urged, as she took his bass from his limp hands. "Go! Get out of here!"

Sonny stepped down off the bandstand, looked over his shoulder and ran. He yanked open the back door and ran through just as the chair leg in Pete's hands whistled through the air behind him. The crowd surged up from their chairs, several pressing forward and out the back door after Pete and Sonny.

Sissy set down Sonny's bass, pulled the strap of her guitar over her head and set it down too, then leaped from the stage and ran, ran around

the edge of the room, jumping over the legs of the few still-sitting customers, dodging around standing groups and out the front door just in
time to see Sonny streaking off across the grounds with Pete lumbering
along behind. Lightning flashes on Sonny's white shirt picked him out at
intervals, so the two running men looked like still shots strung together
from a movie. The wind whistled and the rain started, a few fat drops at
first.

Most of the rides were shut down, but for the Ferris wheel that turned
slowly with a few riders, then came to a stop. The riders got off, and three
more straggled up the steps and into the swinging chairs. Sonny ducked
behind the closed cotton-candy stand, but there was nowhere to go from
there. Pete stopped in front, swaying first to the left, then to the right, his
chair leg held at the ready, waiting to see which way Sonny would run
from behind the rickety stand.

Sissy caught up within fifty feet of Pete, looked around, picked up a
bottle, and pitched it at Pete, yelling, "Sonny, *run!*"

Sonny ran out from behind the stand but right into Pete's path; he
ducked, and Pete's chair leg came down, missing Sonny but crashing
through the closed window of the cotton-candy stand. The leg stuck for
a moment in the broken window with Pete tugging and bellowing over
the still-rising wind, "*Sonny Roberts! I'm going to kill you, you little sawed-
off fucking son-of-a-bitch!*"

Sissy pitched another bottle at Pete but missed as Sonny ran toward
the Ferris wheel with Pete closing on him. Sonny ran up the steps and
jumped into a swaying chair just as the wheel swept up. Pete stood on the
top step, breathing hard, shaking the chair leg.

The carny operator snapped down the door on his ticket shack. Pete
walked back down the steps, turned, and waved his stick at Sonny rising
around the wheel.

"You've got to come down sometime. And then I'm going to kill
you!"

A mighty gust of wind roared up as the rain roared down. The Ferris
wheel juddered and shook; the rusty tin roofs on the sideshows and
concession stands fluttered and flapped and the metal squealed against
the nails that barely held it down. The wind increased; the Ferris wheel
screamed like a woman in pain as it tilted slowly over five degrees. The
bottom chairs of the wheel caught on the boards of the approach, stuck,
ripped out a couple, and continued a few feet more on the upward arc before the motor growled, coughed, died. Blue smoke poured out, quickly
blown away by the wind. The riders screamed. The wind roared louder.
The wheel tilted another five degrees, but held. Then, like an ancient tree

in a primeval forest, the Ferris wheel came slowly over, crashing into the ground.

Sissy watched, helpless. The structure of the wheel crumpled, popped and cracked and was still. From the seats, someone screamed. Then Sissy saw Sonny crawling up through metal crossbars, pulling himself up and out.

"You son-of-a-bitch!" Pete yelled. "I'm going to kill you!"

As Pete started past Sissy toward the wheel, Sissy put out a foot and tripped him. He went down, started to get up but was tackled from behind.

Howard sat on Pete as he pounded his fists in the muddying earth.

"Get Sonny!" Howard yelled over the wind and the rain to Sissy. "Get him and get him the hell out of here. And get help for those folks trapped in the wheel."

Men were already running to the wheel. A couple of people drove their cars around so their headlights shone on the wreckage. Within minutes the riders were out, only scared and bruised and scraped except for one teenage boy with a broken bone poking out of his upper arm, his face so white that the multitude of pimples made his face look like a speckled turkey egg. He was hustled off in someone's car to the hospital. The ticket shack was a pile of splinters beneath a main beam of the wheel. When the wreckage was pulled away, the carny was curled up at the bottom, grinning like a maniac as blood ran from his scalp.

Sissy shoved Sonny onto the camper floor in the back of Melvin's pickup, covering him with a blanket that they used to wrap equipment.

"And stay there, you little sawed-off son-of-a-bitch. Or I'll kill you myself."

Two hours later, after everybody had been accounted for and after cups of strong black coffee hastily brewed up in the community center kitchen, the storm passed. People went out to look at the wreckage of the Ferris wheel, to marvel that nobody had been killed, and finally to get in their cars and go home. Sissy and Melvin helped Clayton pack up and load the equipment, Sissy telling them to be careful putting stuff in Melvin's camper because Sonny was balled up in a blanket on the floor.

"Lucky he ain't dead, one way or the other," Melvin said, as he and Clayton went back inside to bring out the last load.

Sissy wanted to go home and sleep for hours. As she opened Clayton's car door to get in, she was grabbed from behind and whirled around. This is getting to be a problem, she thought.

"You're a troublemaking bitch," Loretta said with a slap at Sissy's face. It connected with a pop, throwing Sissy's head back.

"Yeah, you tattletale," Sissy heard Cristal yell. "We're going to beat your ass!"

"No, you're not," another voice said.

Through her tearing eyes, Sissy saw Zooey standing behind Cristal and Loretta, who weren't saying any more.

"None of this was her fault. She didn't have anything to do with any of it, so let her alone," Zooey said.

"Well. Are you sure? I mean, she could've—"

"No. Let her alone," Zooey repeated.

Cristal and Loretta walked away slowly, as like slinking dogs as was possible.

Zooey stood there looking down at her muddied and stained jeans, her white moccasins covered in gobs of mud.

"Sissy, I'm sorry," she said.

Sissy held her hand to her burning cheek.

"Thanks," she said. "For stopping them."

"You got anything to drink?" Zooey asked.

Sissy didn't hesitate.

"There's a bottle of scotch under the seat," she said.

"I hate that shit. But if that's all you got."

They sat in the front seat of Clayton's car, Sissy on the driver's side just in case Zooey got any wild ideas about driving off. Zooey held the bottle between her legs.

"Sissy, can I talk to you?"

"Shoot."

Zooey took another swig from the bottle.

"Everybody thinks I trapped Pete into marrying me. It ain't like that."

Sissy didn't say anything.

"Pete begged me to marry him. I thought I was in love with him, too. I wasn't pregnant. I never told him I was. Six months after we got married, I still wasn't pregnant, but I wasn't doing anything to stop it, you know? And then another couple of months. And then Pete told me he couldn't have kids. He had mumps bad when he was a little kid."

Sissy didn't say anything.

Zooey took another swig from the bottle.

"I'm not like you. I'm not smart like you. I can't sing. I can't do anything right," she said. She looked at the bottle. "This is like my medicine. It takes a whole lot of it to make me believe I'm somebody else. Somebody special, like you."

Sissy took the bottle from Zooey's hands, took a drink herself. It went down like red-hot coals.

"Zooey," Sissy said. "There's all kinds of medicine, you know." She waved the bottle. "Doesn't have to be this."

"I was never cut out to be a nun," Zooey said.

"I wasn't talking about religion," Sissy said.

"Neither was I."

Zooey took the bottle back.

"You ever think about getting a divorce?" Sissy asked.

"Every god damned day," Zooey answered.

Sissy saw Melvin walking toward his pickup, veer off and come over to Clayton's car. He tapped on the window, and she rolled it down. He leaned over and looked inside at Zooey.

"Everything all right?" he asked.

"Yeah. Everything is fine. Now. Thanks, Melvin."

He stood back up, slapped the roof of the car.

"All right, then. See you at practice on Wednesday."

Zooey sat hunched over, holding the bottle with both hands. Tears gushed from her eyes and ran down her face.

"You got some relatives up at Cheyenne River, don't you?"

Zooey sniffled, wiped her nose on the back of her hand. "Yeah."

"Maybe you ought to go visit them for a couple of weeks. Take some time to think about what you want to do," Sissy said, thinking that it was the second time she had recently told a crying woman she ought to go visit her relatives. It worked out okay for Darlene, though. So far.

"Yeah. Maybe I ought to. Maybe I will," she said. She scrabbled around on the floor, found the cap for the bottle and tried to screw it on, but it kept getting cross-threaded.

"Here, I'll do it," Sissy said, taking the bottle.

Zooey opened the car door, turned back and grabbed Sissy in a hug.

"Thanks," she said. "There's one other little thing. I didn't have a damned thing to do with Buffalo Ames getting killed. I know people think it was something to do with me, that Pete might have killed him over me, but I swear, Pete didn't know anything about me and Buffalo. Wasn't much to know anyway. I never fucked him, not once. I never even paid any attention to him until that Fourth of July, well except years ago when I tried to be his friend, but he wanted more, and I didn't. He was just kind of there. And I was pissed at Pete. I'm always pissed at Pete. I was just, you know, kind of flirting with Buffalo. Something to do. And I was half-drunk. But I know I didn't kill him, and Pete didn't kill him. People get killed up here on the rez all the time over nothing, you know that. Some drunken fight over a bottle or somebody says something that pisses someone off, could be anything or nothing. It's just the way things are. You believe me, don't you?"

She said it with a plaintiveness in her voice, a need that went beyond friendship—they were never friends, still were not, and never would be—but Sissy believed her.

Back in Jackson, Clayton motioned Melvin to pull over at the Highway Café. They unrolled Sonny from the blanket in the camper where he had gone to sleep. He stepped out warily and looked around but saw nobody that looked dangerous, so they went inside and ordered breakfast.

"I got to go to Rapid next week, Melvin, so you'll be running the shop for a couple of days," Clayton said as he dumped ketchup on his hash browns.

"What for?" Melvin asked.

"Got to have a new amp, don't I? We play Batesland in two weeks."

They ate in silence for a few minutes.

"Say Sissy, where's your friend, Speedy? I thought she and Sonny were together. How come him to take up with Zooey?" Melvin asked through a mouthful of toast.

"Long story," Sissy said. "They just aren't the happy couple anymore."

Sonny mopped egg yolk with a piece of toast but didn't say anything.

Melvin swallowed. "I don't guess Pete and Zooey are either," he said.

Sonny dropped the last piece of toast on his plate, slid his chair back, and crossed his arms.

Clayton dropped Sissy at her house, and as she started up the steep driveway, she noticed something different. Lawrence and Lily's car was parked in the driveway behind Sissy's old Chevy.

"Oh, jeezus," she said. "The house is a mess, Mom's going to kill me, and Dad is going to say, 'Well, god damn it, Sis.'"

CHAPTER FOURTEEN

BASEBALL EPIPHANIES

SUNDAY, AUGUST 24, 1969

Sissy woke up to whomp-whomp-whomp as her dad beat up the pancake batter on Sunday morning, smiled, turned over and went back to sleep. She looked forward to her dad's breakfast, even without the usual chili since her mom wouldn't have had time to prepare it the night before, but not to the ass chewing she knew she had coming for not keeping the house cleaned up. When she staggered downstairs at eleven o'clock, sticky eyed and dry mouthed, the kitchen floor had been swept and mopped, the clutter was cleared from the countertops and the table, the range gleamed, and her mother stood at the sink, up to her elbows in soapy dishwater.

"Come here, sweetie and give me a hug," Lily said, blowing at a stray strand of hair that kept flopping in her face. Sissy hugged her hard, smelling the sweat on the back of her mother's neck mingled with lavender.

"I missed you so much," Sissy said.

"Honey, I had a good time but just a little too much of it this time."

Lawrence came in from the living room, barefoot and in his bib overalls, a newspaper crushed in one hand.

"Well, god damn it, Sis," he started, but Lily cut him off, waving a soapy finger.

"No, Lawrence. No. Sissy will never be much of a housekeeper, but she's got other good points. Let her alone."

"Yes, ma'am," Lawrence said. "Come here, Sissy. I missed you, little girl."

He hugged her, crushing the newspaper against her back.

"Sit down, let me get you some coffee," he offered.

"There's no milk for it," Sissy said. "The last we had went over and I forget to buy more."

"Figured that," Lily said. "We bought some at the gas station coming in last night."

Sissy sipped the hot brew—half milk—gratefully, thinking that a clean coffeepot probably made as big a difference in the taste as the milk did.

"Tell us all the stuff that's been happening while we were gone," Lawrence said. "How was the harvest? You having a good time playing music?"

Sissy told them everything that had happened while they were gone. They were shocked and dismayed by the accident with the Ferris wheel at the Allen Pow Wow, but glad there were so few injuries; they clucked their tongues at Sonny's indiscretions with Zooey and considered him lucky that Pete didn't catch him and kill him. By the time Sissy had backtracked to the part about Speedy, about the FBI agent who kept pestering her about the death of Buffalo Ames, Lily had washed and dried all the dishes and put them away and was folding the wet dishtowel to hang over the lower sink cabinet door. She poured herself a cup of coffee and sat down at the table with Lawrence and Sissy.

"I've loved Speedy like a daughter, but she's never had good judgment," Lily said. "You can lead a horse to water, but you can't make her think. What is she going to do? You think she'll keep the baby, or give it up for adoption?"

"She doesn't know. Her parents want her to go out to her sister's in Montana to have it and give it up for adoption. I think that might be for the best. I just don't think Speedy is up for motherhood, at least not yet," Sissy said.

Lawrence hadn't said much. He was old-fashioned; pregnancy and women's trouble embarrassed him, but he spoke up now, "Does she even know who the father is?"

"Lawrence!" Lily exclaimed, slapping him lightly on the shoulder.

"It's a fair question, Mom. Speedy has always been a little too free with her favors. She isn't a bad woman; she just wants to make people happy, especially men. It doesn't occur to her that she could make them just as happy if she didn't sleep with them all. She thinks it's Sonny's. That's what she keeps saying. But there was a guy on the harvest crew that I know about and I don't know—maybe some local guys, too."

"She'd better make up her mind pretty soon because that baby is going to come no matter what, and she needs a plan," Lawrence said, his face slightly red beneath his generally dark complexion.

"How far along is she?" Lily asked. "Has she seen a doctor? Does she know when she's due?"

Sissy shook her head, slapped at a buzzing fly, wondering if all the mess she had made in the house had drawn flies, decided it was probably so, but she didn't want to think about it.

"No doctor yet."

"Too bad she's White. She could use Indian Health Services if she was Indian. It isn't the best, but better than having a baby in a ditch somewhere," Lily said.

"If it's Sonny's baby, and he married her, she could go to IHS," Lawrence said.

"I don't know how far along she is," Sissy said. "Not much. Maybe a couple of months. Enough to know she's pregnant and sicker than a dog almost every morning for the past month or more."

"Really? How odd," Lily said. "Morning sickness doesn't usually hit until the second month, lasts through the third month and then you're past that. That's the way it was with you."

Lawrence cleared his throat as he spread the newspaper on the table.

"Look," he said. "The Jackson Merchants are playing Kadoka tonight. Here. Home game. Why don't we go?"

Jackson fielded their own community baseball team that played teams from other towns in the area. They had a years-long feud with Kadoka, and Kadoka had won the last three games they had played against each other.

"Says here," Lawrence said, running his fingernail along a line of print, "says here that Bill Braxton of the Jackson Merchants has been pitching better this year than ever before. And Kadoka's best batter, Dan Rousseau—you remember him, Sissy, that big stout fellow, rancher up north of Kadoka—anyway, it says that Rousseau broke his leg in a tractor accident. They've got some other good hitters, but their pitcher is only so-so. Ought to be a good game."

"What time's it start?" Lily asked.

"Seven. Or thereabouts."

"Sissy, what do you say we fix an early supper and go? Something quick and simple; sandwiches and pork and beans sound okay?"

Sissy agreed, then listened while Lawrence and Lily told her about their visit down in Nebraska, with Lawrence's interruptions to complain about the ineptness of his brother-in-law.

"Now, Lawrence, Lee is a good guy, you know that," Lily admonished.

"Yeah, he's a good guy," Lawrence said. "There just ain't much demand for his kind of good guy."

"He always asks about you, Sissy. He and Iris would love to have you come down and visit," Lily went on.

"Why don't they come visit up here? I can't afford to take off work, you know."

"I know. I wish—" Lily stopped herself. "But, you know why they don't come up here."

Sissy knew. Iris and Leroy and their kids had been in a car wreck fifteen years earlier—hit head on by a drunken driver, killing both their children, Sissy's cousins; Aaron was thirteen and Mariellen was eleven. Iris and Leroy left right after that, moved down to Nebraska and never came back even to visit. Sissy had gone with her mom and dad down to visit them several times while she had still been in school.

The air had achieved that copper quality that it takes on just before the sun sets, when the light slants just right across the land, when gnats jitter in black-netted swarms, crickets aren't quite tuned up, when the leaves on the trees turn a little in listless breezes. Lily and Lawrence and Sissy walked up the long hill behind the Dairy Queen to the bleachers at the top of the hill just as Melvin came from the opposite direction where he had parked his car along the south side of the diamond. They met on the bottom row of bleachers, climbed up a couple of steps to avoid a group of shoving kids, and sat down together.

Lily slapped the dust from the seat with her handkerchief before she sat down.

"I think we need some rain to clean off these seats," she said.

"Never say so, Miss Lily," Melvin said. "We don't want the game rained out."

"Oh, I didn't tell you," Lily said to Sissy. "We almost got to go watch some of the college baseball playoffs in Omaha. But it rained hard the afternoon of the day we planned to go, so that game was canceled, and well, we just got busy with other things and didn't get down there."

"What made you think about going?" Sissy asked. She never knew there was such a thing as college baseball, never thought of it.

"Iris and Leroy's next-door neighbor is a janitor at the branch university there in Kearney," Lily said. "They had a team in the playoffs, so he got some extra tickets. Didn't matter, that team lost their first game."

Baseball is a game made of a few moments of intense action interspersed with interminable waiting, so there is plenty of time to talk to other spectators or just to think. Sissy watched the teams warm up—the players on the field tossing balls back and forth, stretching, swinging bats—she watched Bill Braxton pitching baseballs at an improvised bull's-eye target on the sidelines and heard other people in the bleachers speculating about whether Kadoka's line-up of batters could withstand Braxton's fast ball.

She listened to Melvin telling her dad about the extraordinary number of pheasants and grouse and prairie chickens he was seeing—so many of them, they were routinely hit by cars. Why, if you happened along right after one got clipped and it wasn't too mashed, you could pluck it and dress it right there and have fried pheasant for supper. Of course, that wasn't the same as if you shot one yourself, fresh. There wasn't any sport in picking up roadkill.

Lawrence nodded. "But there isn't any sport in picking buckshot out your teeth, either," he said, but he took the hint Melvin was throwing out. "Pheasant and grouse season starts on September 20. You want to go with me? You can show me where the hunting is best, and I'll loan you one of my shotguns."

Melvin contemplated a few minutes until he was compelled by Lawrence's urging to agree.

Kadoka came to bat first. Braxton struck out the first two, walked the third, and then a skinny little guy that hadn't played for Kadoka before came to bat. Braxton had a little grin on his face, barely visible in the diminishing light before the ballpark lights switched on. The catcher gave the signal; Braxton gripped his cap brim, wound up and threw a dropping ball that started out in the strike zone but dropped fast inside and low. Ball One. The next was a strike but the little guy stood like a statue. The bat didn't lift so much as a quarter inch from his shoulders. The count came up to three and two. Braxton threw, a little high but right in the strike zone. The little guy connected with a high-flying ball that flew like a rocket over the ballpark fence, still accelerating out of sight for a home run. Braxton stuck out the next batter, but the score at the top of the first was Jackson 0, Kadoka 2.

In the second half of the first inning, Jackson eked out their own two runs, so the game stood at two and two through the second inning, the third inning, the fourth.

The audience buzzed and stretched. Lawrence and Melvin walked down the hill to the Dairy Queen and came back with strawberry malts for everyone.

A germ of an idea grew in Sissy's head. A couple of germs of ideas that had nothing to do with baseball.

The fifth inning and the sixth and the seventh passed with the score still tied at 2–2. Both teams could get a man or two on base, but the following batters couldn't hit them in. In the eighth inning, Braxton walked a man, who then tried to steal second. Braxton threw a quick lob to the first baseman. The runner, more than halfway to second, hauled his freight, but the first baseman slung the ball to second. The second baseman caught it, fumbled it, dropped it, picked it up just as the runner slid into the base. The umpire yelled, "Safe!" That was the most exciting play for the rest of the inning. Braxton struck out the next two batters. Then the Kadoka pitcher struck out the first three Jackson batters, and it was top of the ninth, bases loaded, when the skinny little guy came to bat again.

He took two called strikes, one ball, but when the fourth pitch came in right in the middle of the zone, he swung, tipped it off the end of his bat in a high-flying foul right for the crowd. They ran and ducked, dived and covered their heads like a flock of chickens with a hawk overhead. The ball came in, speeding along like a hard-hit line drive.

Sissy's two germs of ideas had started to grow. She was thinking. She barely heard the screams of the crowd but saw the ball coming at the last minute, leaned back and away, but that ball knew where it was going, knew where it was supposed to go. It changed direction. It could be said that a sudden gust of wind pushed it, but that wouldn't be true. That ball knew where it had to connect and it did. It hit Sissy directly in the left eye with a pop like a gun going off. She didn't fall. She wasn't immediately unconscious. She slowly tipped over on the seat, her legs curling up in a fetal position as if she had just gone to sleep.

Speedy said it right. For a smart girl, you are sure stupid. Not just stupid, but profoundly, deeply, wantonly stupid. Willfully obtuse. Everything you needed to know has been right in front of your eyes for weeks, maybe months; you've been walking around with your head up your uh-huh. What's the matter with you? A blind man with a wooden leg could have figured all this out.

Shut up, Sissy told the voice.

Shut up? Shut up! Is that the best you can do?

Fuck you!

Obscenities? That's it? Where's that smart mouth of yours? Where's that intellectual patter, where's the wit? Come on, you can do better than this!

I don't know what you're talking about. Who the hell are *you?*

Oh, I don't know. Call me the ghost of Christmas past. Call me Ishmael. Call me your conscience. Call me your id. Just don't call me too late for supper, hyuk, hyuk, hyuk!

This is stupid. I've been hit by a baseball. I'm unconscious. I'm hallucinating.

Are you really? I'm not real?

You're not real. You're a figment of my imagination.

If you prefer to think of it that way. Can't you guess my name?

Tom Holm?

Don't be obtuse. Try again.

Santa Claus? Wakan Tanka?

An imaginary hand flipped impatiently.

Oh, stop it. My name doesn't matter. So, god damn it, Sis, what are you going to do about it?

Dad?

No, just borrowing a figure of speech. Well. What are you going to do about it?

You've told two people they ought to go live with their relatives. You ever think maybe you were talking to yourself? Come on, moron! Figure it out.

Okay. I think I get that one now. What about the other one?

What other one?

You know.

You're on your own, kiddo.

You're the one nosing around in my subconscious. Give me something useful or get out and stop teasing me.

(Sigh.) Think. Think about everything everyone told you. I mean everyone told you. It's plain as the nose on your face. It's staring you right in the face. It's like the buffalo in the room.

The buffalo in the room? Don't you mean the elephant?

I meant what I said. That's it, genius. So long.

A flash in her eyes, brighter than an airplane landing light. A thick finger, pulling her eyelids up, another hand holding her head so she couldn't turn away. She slapped at the hands.

"She's coming around."

"You're going to be all right. Dr. Bianco says you have mild concussion."

She tried to sit up, but her head hurt. She opened her eyes. White, everywhere white, lights reflecting off a glass cabinet door, and her mother leaning over her face, brow furrowed.

"Ain't nothing mild about it," she muttered. "God, my head hurts."

"I can give you something for the headache," Dr. Bianco said. "You need to wake her every couple of hours or so, make sure she's able to speak and move her arms and legs. Watch her eyes. If her pupils are very dilated or unequal in size, or her speech becomes garbled, or you can't wake her, get her back in here."

"I have to be at work at six in the morning," Sissy said.

"*No!*" Lily and Dr. Bianco objected simultaneously.

"Twenty-four hours of bed rest," Dr. Bianco said. "Then if you have no bad signs, you can go to work."

"Home," Sissy said.

"I'd like to keep her in the hospital overnight," Bianco said.

"No. Home," Sissy insisted.

On the way home, her mouth flew open and half-digested strawberry malt gushed out, painting the floor and the back of the passenger seat. Lily cleaned her up, and Lawrence carried her upstairs to bed. At intervals throughout the night, the light in her room came on, someone tickled her feet, poked her until she said something, which inevitably started with "fuck" and continued from there. Someone made her waggle her arms, her legs, half sit up. The last time was just after sunup, when light coming through the leaves of the Chinese elm outside her window cast moving shadows and green-tinged light across her bed.

At ten o'clock her stomach grumbled. She had to pee. As she came down the stairs, one hand on the wall, her head felt like a boulder balanced on a noodle. When she refused to go back upstairs, Lily made her a bed on the sofa. Lawrence brought her tea and crackers when she wanted a hamburger and at least a pot of coffee.

"Dr. Bianco said I had to rest," she complained. "He didn't say to starve me."

Lily looked uneasily at Lawrence, but she went to the kitchen and fried up a couple of hamburgers. When Sissy had eaten most of the first one, she put it down and wiped the ketchup off her chin.

"Mom, didn't you say that Aunt Iris's next-door neighbor works at the local college? What local college? I didn't know there was a college there," Sissy asked.

"Well," Lily said, leaning her elbows on her knees, her chin in one hand, "I didn't know there was a college there either until I found out Iris's neighbor works there. He isn't a teacher you know. I think he's in charge of custodians or something like that."

"But what's the name of the college?"

Lawrence leaned around the door from the kitchen, said, "It's a branch of the University of Nebraska, I think, so wouldn't it be University of Nebraska at Kearney?"

So it had the word "university" in the name. That sounded important.

Lily's eyes widened. "Ohh," she said. "You think—oh, this might be an answer. I could call Iris and ask her what she knows about it. Would that help?"

Sissy took up her hamburger with a smile. Take *that*, Santa Claus or id or whatever your name is. And she heard in her head, *yeah, but what about the* other *thing? Figured it out yet?*

She pushed the thought away, ate her hamburger, went to the bathroom, then lay back down on the couch, her mother tucking her in just like when she was a child, but she dreamed. In her dream, she heard again all the conversations about Buffalo Ames, but the one that kept repeating was the one she'd had with Tom Holm. She heard him reciting the clinical facts of Buffalo's death, what he had uncovered about Buffalo's life before that last night at the Scenic Fourth of July Rodeo. Her thoughts circled, looked down at the center of the spiral, and saw something there she had not seen before, something she didn't want to think about because it would complicate everything. And maybe she was wrong. Maybe this was just a meaningless dream brought on by the baseball slamming into her head.

Early in the afternoon, she woke up from a doze when a heavy body sat down on the edge of the sofa.

"Sissy?" Lily's voice brought her fully awake. "Melvin and Speedy are here to see you. Clayton came by earlier, but he couldn't stay. He was going over to get Darlene and Darrell."

"Are you okay, Sissy?" Melvin's concern sounded in his voice.

"Well, hell, no, I'm not okay. My face is swelled up like a black-and-blue balloon and my left eye is almost shut. Do I look like I'm okay?"

"Sissy," Lily admonished. "Be nice."

"Yeah. All right. I'm sorry, Melvin. I've been better, but I'll be okay."

Melvin settled back, half his butt hanging off the sofa. Speedy pulled a chair over and urged Melvin into it, then sat down on the sofa herself beside Sissy.

"I worked your shift for you this morning," she said. "Martha says tell you to get better, and if you can't come in tomorrow, well, we'll manage."

"Thanks," Sissy said. "That's good of her. How you feeling?"

Speedy lifted a shoulder. She had lost that peaky cottage cheese face and the dark circles under her eyes. Sissy saw Speedy's hand reach out to the side and take Melvin's hand. Her eyes went back to Speedy, who looked defiant.

"So, did you have a good breakfast and lunch crowd?" she asked.

"The usual. Everybody's talking about the game last night. Jackson lost again."

"I suppose they're already planning how they'll win next time."

"Yeah. There was talk about getting the Bad Heart twins to play," Speedy said.

"They were pretty good in high school," Melvin said. He still wore his work clothes, grease ground into his hands and around the edges of his fingernails.

"You used to be pretty good, too, I heard," Sissy said.

"Too much water run under that old bridge," Melvin said. He gave Speedy's hand a squeeze. Sissy pretended not to see.

"Well, I gotta get on home," he said. "I just wanted to make sure you were okay."

"Yeah, thanks, Melvin. I appreciate the thought. So, unless somebody ties me down, I'll be at band practice on Wednesday."

When he had gone, Sissy said, "When did this all happen? You're moving pretty fast, aren't you?"

Speedy bit her lower lip.

"I don't think I have all that much time, you know?"

"Do you really care a fart in a whirlwind about Melvin? Or is he just convenient and gullible?" Sissy asked.

"Sissy, I've not been the most moral person, I know," Speedy started. Sissy refrained from saying "no shit." "I've went out with him before, you know, a couple of times a couple of years ago, so it ain't anything new."

"Come on, though, do you really love him?"

"No. I *like* him. And I think I can love him. He's a good person, a good man."

"Yeah, he is a good man. Do you think just liking him is enough?"

"Sissy, you can be awful god damn righteous, you know. Sometimes even loving someone more than anything in the world ain't enough."

"I know it," Sissy said, and then she said she was sorry for the second time in less than fifteen minutes.

"He knows about the baby. Everybody in town knew about it before you figured it out. Courthouse biddies, you know. They know your business before you know your business."

"So, I guess he's okay about the baby?" Sissy asked.

"You could say that. He's more excited about it than I am. Already he's planning to clear out the second bedroom at his house. For the baby. He thinks it's going to be a boy."

"You talked to Sonny?"

"No. I never said anything to him at all. I haven't seen him, but I don't think there's any point to saying anything," Speedy said.

"Not now," Sissy said, but she thought about how happy Sonny would be when he did find out about Speedy and Melvin.

"Just one thing, Speedy. We've been friends for years, you and me. But if you hurt Melvin, I swear to god, I'll beat you bloody," Sissy said.

"You'll have to catch me first. They don't call me Speedy for nothing," she said, and she stuck her tongue in the side of her cheek, making a little lumpy bulge.

Sissy was awake at four o'clock in the morning, all slept out with her headache gone. Her head looked like a purple pumpkin, but it didn't hurt unless she pressed her hand to her face in a certain spot. She got her uniform on and went to work, knowing she would have to counter relentless jokes from the customers and shocked, knowing looks from the courthouse biddies.

She was just walking out the café door to go home when Darlene came running up to her.

"Sissy! Dad sent me to get you. You've got to come!"

"What? Where? What's going on? And where's my hello and my hug?"

"Sissy, we don't have time for that!" Darlene danced from foot to foot. "Dad says you've got to come quick! Sonny's drunk and he's going to kill himself!"

"What! Where?"

"Come on! He's locked himself in his apartment, and he won't open the door. He's threatening to cut his wrists."

Sonny rented a basement room from Jerry Mills, the owner of the Texaco Station. It was small, but it had a kitchen of sorts, which Sonny rarely used because he was too lazy to cook, a bathroom that not even a blind drunk with no sense of smell would set foot in, and an outside entrance.

Clayton's car, Melvin's pickup, and a cop car with its light going round and round were all parked at the side of Jerry Mills's house where Sonny lived in the basement apartment. Down a short flight of stairs, Jerry, Clayton, Melvin, and the two city cops, Floyd and Don, jostled each other in the narrow space at the bottom, Clayton pounding on the door.

"Sonny! Sonny, don't do it. There ain't anything worth killing yourself over," Clayton yelled.

Nothing from within.

"Sonny. Sonny! If you do this, I'm going to fire your ass. You'll never play for another band again," Clayton yelled.

"God damn it, Sonny, don't you dare get blood all over my apartment," Jerry hollered.

From the top of the stairs, Sissy called down, "Get out of the way, and let me give it a try."

Jerry came up the stairs first, shaking his finger under Sissy's nose.

"You'd better get that cousin of yours under control," he said.

Floyd grabbed his arm and pulled him out of the way.

"Clayton, Melvin. Get out of the way."

Clayton gave the door a final kick before following Melvin up the stairs.

"Sonny? Sonny, it's Sissy. Open the door. I got some really good news for you. You'd be stupid to kill yourself now."

Silence from within. Then Sonny's muffled voice said, "What good news? There ain't no such thing."

"I tell you, I've got something to tell you that's going to make your heart leap like a broaching whale," she said.

"You're lying. You're just trying to get me to open the shore. The blore. You're trying to get me to open up."

"No, I'm not lying, Son. I'm telling the truth. I'm your cousin, and I've got no reason to lie to you. I've got great news. Wonderful news."

Silence from within.

"Sonny? You hear me, Son? Let me in, and I'll tell you," she pleaded.

"Not by the hair of my shinny shin shin," he yelled.

"Sonny, god damn it. Let me in. I'm not lying. I'm telling the fucking truth."

Silence from within, then Sonny said, "What's a breeching wheel?"

More silence. Then a click and the door opened two inches. Sissy looked up at the men and Darlene, standing with her hands over her mouth, eyes big. Clayton started toward the stairs, but she waved him back vigorously. She pushed the door open and stepped inside. It was dark, except for a lamp with a low-watt bulb lying on the floor with the shade pushed up on one side. Sonny stood up against the kitchen counter, glasses-less, shoeless, shirtless, pantsless in his tighty whities. That's tighty whities, not tidy, because there was a yellow stain on the front. His eyes gleamed like a cat's in the near dark.

The kitchen counters were piled with dishes, dirty most likely. Clothes littered the floor. The bed in the corner looked like it hadn't ever been made. Sissy felt a twinge of familiarity.

"Sonny," she said, starting toward him.

"Stay back!" he said, holding up a hand with a shiny object. "I've got a knife!"

"For chrissake, Sonny, put it down. You're acting like a ninny hammer. You're drunk!"

"Yes. Yes, I am," he said. "You think I'd be doing this if I was sober?"

"How long have you been drinking?" she asked.

"Since I got up yesterday morning," he said. "I think. What day is this?"

"It's Tuesday. I guess you didn't go to work yesterday."

The hand holding the knife dropped to his side. She started toward him again.

"No closer! No closer! I've got a knife. You stay right there, and tell me what the shoes are. What the news are."

"Sonny, listen to me. I can't talk very loud because Melvin is right outside. Listen now. You listening?"

He nodded.

She took another step closer.

"Speedy isn't going to Montana—"

Sonny brought the knife to his opposite wrist and howled.

"Sonny, stop it, stop it! She's not going to Montana because she's going to marry Melvin!"

The knife came away from his wrist.

"What?"

"Shhh. Don't say anything! Melvin knows she's pregnant, but he wants to marry her anyway," Sissy said.

Sonny looked at her, his eyes unfocused, then he yelled, "That's stupid! You're lying! You're a lying bitch! Besides that, Pete is going to kill me if he catches me."

"No, no, Sonny. It's going to be okay. Zooey is going up to Cheyenne River to her relatives, and Howard is going to keep Pete in line."

"You're not lying? You promise?"

"Sonny, it's the truth."

"No, you're lying to me. I'd rather die right here, right now! And you can't stop me!" He brought the knife down on his wrist with a sawing motion, hacking back and forth, back and forth.

Sissy rushed him. He went down in a heap, the knife clattering on the floor. She snatched it up as he grabbed for it.

"Sonny. This is a god damned butter knife," she said. She grabbed his wrist. No cuts, no blood, only a bright red mark on his left wrist.

Melvin and Clayton, Floyd and Don burst through the door, followed by Jerry, who switched on the overhead light.

Sonny squinted up at Sissy, at her black eye and swollen face.

"Jeezus, Sissy. I didn't mean to hurt you like that. I was only trying to kill myself."

"Sonny, you little sawed-off son-of-a-bitch. If you weren't my cousin, I'd have to kill you," Sissy said.

RED POWER

On Wednesday afternoon when Sissy got home from her shift, she threw a load of her sheets into the washer. Her mom and dad had cleaned the downstairs rooms, but upstairs was her responsibility, something her dad reminded her of the night before when he had walked up the stairs just far enough to see over the stair rail and into her room, and said, "Looks like a hog wallow up here," turned around and clumped back down. She had just dumped in the soap when she heard car tires crunching on the gravel in the driveway.

She was climbing the outside basement steps just as Sonny stepped out of his blue Pinto, walked up and gave her a hug, stepped back and looked at the left side of her face. Taffy barked maniacally from the neighbor's yard.

"Oooo," he said, "looks like that would hurt."

She grabbed his left arm, shoved his shirtsleeve up and looked at his wrist, where there wasn't so much as a thin line of bruise.

"Oooo," she said, "looks like that would hurt."

He snatched his arm back.

"Never mind. I had a momentary mental aberration."

"Momentary?" she asked, "Don't look now, but I think it's become a permanent condition."

"You hurt me, Sissy. You cut me to the quick, and this might be the last time you ever see me," he said, putting his hand over his left shirt front. She looked around him at the Pinto, at the backseat piled to the roof with full bags and boxes, at the clothes hanging on a rod stretched across the back.

"Jerry kicked you out, huh? So, you're planning to move into Uncle Lawrence's basement?"

He feigned deeper hurt.

"I would never, I repeat, never take advantage of a relative like that!"

"Really? So what's changed, then?" Sissy asked, one arm on her hip.

"Actually, Jerry did kick me out," he said, putting his arm around her and leading her to the back door. "But, he's doing me a favor. It's time I moved on to bigger and better things."

"Back to the seminary, then?" she asked as she opened the back screen door.

"I said moving on, not back," he said to her, and to Lily, who was folding clothes on the table, "Hi, Aunt Lily. Where's Unc?"

Lily gave him a hug and sat him down at the table.

"He's down at the gas station playing dominoes with his buddies. Want some iced tea?"

"Don't encourage him, Mom. If you feed him, he'll think he lives here," Sissy said.

"Don't be silly, Sissy," Lily said. "Sonny is always welcome."

Sissy shot Sonny a disgusted look and sat down.

"I came to say good-bye, Auntie Lily," Sonny said as she poured tea from the pitcher for the three of them, added ice cubes from the bin in the freezer. "I'm going east to work the high steel."

"Sonny, no! That's so dangerous," Lily exclaimed.

Sonny chuckled.

"No, I'm not. That's so dangerous. I'm moving up to Rapid City, stay with friends for a few days. One of them promised me he could get me on working out at the air base."

"Well, that might be a good idea," Lily said. "A lot of people made good careers out of doing civilian work out at Ellsworth."

"I figure it might be a good opportunity for me," Sonny said.

"Oh, hold on a minute," Lily said, "I have to move the sprinkler in the backyard. I'll be right back."

When she had gone out the door, Sissy said, "So, you're running like a scared rabbit with your tail between your legs?"

Sonny choked on his tea, splattering his shirt front and laughing.

"A scared *rabbit*? How does a rabbit tuck that little puff ball of a tail between its legs to run?" he asked.

"Shut up, Son, you know what I mean."

"What can I say? I'm a lover, not a fighter."

"Sonny, you are not a lover. Look how bad you messed up that career option. You're a runner not a fighter, and you sure as hell aren't any good at the priesting profession, either," she said.

Sonny sat his tea down on the table hard, slopping half of it on the table.

"So, I'm no good at anything, is that what you're saying? What you? What are you good at? Serving *tea* to the ladies from the house, and coffee to the businessmen and the farmers while you dodge their grabby hands? Singing every other Saturday night with a half-assed band run by a moronic megalomaniac who thinks he's Johnny Cash? What are *you* doing with your life?" His lower lip stuck out belligerently as he leaned forward in his chair.

"I got some more news for you," Sissy said as she mopped up the spilled tea from the floor and the table and tossed the dirty dishcloth into the sink. "I happen to have a new plan."

"Oh, yeah?"

"Yeah. So happens I'm leaving here, too," she said.

"Running like a rabbit with her tail between her legs?" The corners of his lips turned up.

"No, like a greyhound that's just discovered there's a race on, and I'm in it."

"And where is this track you're running on?"

"Kearney, Nebraska. Aunt Iris and Uncle Leroy's. Turns out that Kearney has a college there. A *university*. It's too late to start this fall, but if I move down there now and backdate the time I got there, I can establish residency."

"What's that mean? Residency? If you're there, you live there."

"Not exactly. You have to live in the state for a year before you qualify to pay in-state tuition. It's cheaper," she said.

Sonny looked at her, his face pleased, his anger evaporated in a minute, like it always did with him.

"Does this mean we will have a college graduate in the family?"

"Yeah. Some day. I mean, I hope so," she said. "I'm leaving week after next. Right after the Red Birds play at Batesland."

They sipped their tea, both of them smiling.

"Does Clayton know you're leaving?" Sissy asked.

Sonny looked at his watch. "He'll know in about another hour when he gets home from work. I left a note on his door." Here he held up a hand to forestall her objections. "Yeah, yeah, yeah, I know. I'm a coward. But I called Rabbit to take my place playing bass. He's coming to practice tonight at Clayton's. You told him you're leaving?"

Sissy shook her head. "No. I'm going to tell him tonight."

Then together they both said, "Clayton's going to shit."

They were still laughing when Lily came back in, wet from being caught in the sprinkler.

* * *

When Rabbit showed up at the Red Bird practice session, Clayton was surprised but not as angry about Sonny leaving as he would have been. He even grudgingly admitted that maybe Sonny had been responsible because he got Rabbit to take his place.

Sissy said, "See that experience in the seminary did teach him something."

Clayton only grunted as he wrote up the playlist for the Batesland gig. Sissy decided it wasn't a good time to tell him she would be leaving, too. Instead, she got Darlene to sing a couple of the standards that the Red Birds always played. Darlene had a nice voice, maybe a bit on the little side, but that was probably insecurity. She'd get stronger with time and practice.

Halfway through the practice session, Speedy walked into the living room.

"I knocked," she said, "but you were playing so loud I figured you didn't hear me."

Clayton gave her a questioning look, but when Melvin jumped up and kissed her cheek, his eyes grew big. He shot a glance at Sissy, who waggled her eyebrows.

Speedy sat down quietly on the sofa by Darlene. She wasn't jumping up every few minutes, wasn't talking constantly like she used to do. Sissy noticed that Speedy had a little tummy, but if she didn't know better it could be just food bloat. At nine-thirty, Clayton shut them down.

"Tomorrow is a school day for Darrell and Darlene," he said. "I want them to get a good night's sleep."

As they were leaving, Speedy asked Sissy if she could spend the night with her.

"What? You aren't going to stay at Melvin's?"

Speedy looked down at her dirty tennis shoes.

"Melvin's kind of old-fashioned. He says he wants to do this right, so I won't move in until we get married."

"Really? So when are you getting married?" Sissy asked.

"That's what I want to talk to you about. We thought we'd just get married by the JP next Saturday before the Red Birds play in Batesland. Would you stand up with us?"

"Sure," Sissy said. "Sounds like you aren't planning anything fancy."

"No. The bride is wearing white. White tennis shoes, white blouse, blue jeans. Same for you, if that's okay."

"It's your wedding," Sissy said. "I never did understand women like Viola who think they have to spend an arm and a leg and their firstborn male child on a wedding. Oh, sorry."

Speedy giggled, skipping down the street ahead of Sissy like a little kid.

"I think Viola would be glad to sacrifice her firstborn male child," she said.

They walked past the Jackson Drug Store, closed. Dimly through the window they could see the soda fountain off to one side, the circular racks of paperbacks standing like watchers in the dark, the prescription counter way in the back with the pink neon mortar and pestle sign casting a rosy glow.

"Speedy," Sissy asked, "you were at Scenic on the Fourth of July, weren't you?"

Speedy didn't answer right away. They turned left off Main Street, walking under the awning over the door of Satterwhite's Insurance. Her back was turned.

"Speedy?"

"Yeah, I was there," she said at last. "Seems like ages ago. I can't even remember how I got there. I rode up with someone."

"That was a pretty crazy night," Sissy said. "I didn't know about Buffalo, though, until later. Did you know about it? I mean that night?"

"I can't remember."

"I remember Buffalo dancing with Zooey. Did you see that?"

"You know, I really do like Melvin," Speedy said. "He's a good guy. He's going to be a great dad." She skipped a step on two, stubbed her toe on an uneven patch in the sidewalk.

Sissy reached out and caught her shirttail, didn't let go.

"We need to talk," she said, pulling Speedy down on the curb at the corner of Main and First. Across the street to the south, the wind ruffled the Crosbys' lawn, rocking the sign over the add-on part of their house that was Frank Crosby's law practice.

"We could go to your house and watch TV or something. This curb is pretty hard on my butt," Speedy said with a grin, but she didn't put her tongue in cheek.

"What happened?" Sissy asked.

"What do you mean, 'what happened?' I don't know what you're talking about."

"You dated Melvin before, you said. But that was a couple of years ago, wasn't it?"

"Yeah, so what? We're together now, and that's all that matters."

"I know about a few of the guys you dated. But there's one I think you dated that you never told anybody about," Sissy said. "Buffalo Ames."

"Well, so what?" Speedy snapped. "Lots of women dated Buffalo Ames. I only went out with him a couple of times. It's not like we were engaged or anything."

"But he thought there was more to it than that. Didn't he?"

Speedy jumped up.

"I don't have to talk to you! I don't have to tell you anything. It's none of your business." She turned and ran down the street toward Sissy's house.

Sissy followed. About a block from her house, she heard Taffy barking furiously. He barked again when Sissy walked up the driveway and through the back door that Speedy had just unlocked. The kitchen was dark, but a faint light came down the stairwell. Sissy hesitated, then deliberately walked up the steps.

Speedy sat on the edge of the other bed in Sissy's room, sobbing.

"I told him I was pregnant, but I wasn't going to marry him," Speedy sobbed out. "He wouldn't let it alone. He kept telling me I had to marry him. Nobody tells me I have to do anything."

Sissy sat down beside her on the bed.

"What happened? I mean, what happened up there across the railroad tracks in Scenic?"

"I told him a couple of days before the Scenic rodeo," Speedy snuffled. "I told him, no, no, hell no, it was never going to happen. He wouldn't listen at first. Then he said okay, but he was going to be part of the baby's life. He was going to make sure I didn't—didn't—you know. Do away with it. Him. Her. He was going to make sure I took care of myself, you know, didn't drink when I was pregnant, all that. So, when he saw me at the rodeo, he pestered me again to marry him. I wasn't going to marry him! Sissy, you knew Buffalo!"

"Well, no, I knew who he was, but I didn't really know him. Since he died, though, a couple of people told me he was a decent guy. What was wrong with him? I mean, it can't be any worse than Melvin!" Sissy said.

Speedy stared at her. "Are you blind? Melvin isn't great looking, I know, but he's at least average looking. Buffalo—he looked like a *buffalo*. And he didn't have any real job. He said he was going to get a job with the tribe, but you know how that goes. Maybe he could, maybe not. And the next tribal president that comes in throws out everyone and starts over with his own relatives. How was he going to support us?"

"Okay, okay," Sissy said. "But what happened?"

Speedy swallowed, and then went on.

"Buffalo got mad. He just got mad and walked away. I saw him flirting with Zooey at the rodeo and dancing with her in the bar. I think he was trying to make me jealous. I went outside to get some air just before the band quit playing. I was starting to feel sick. I don't know, maybe I'd had too much to drink. Maybe it was the start of pregnant sick, you know? I walked over past the railroad tracks so no one would see me puking. I was just standing up when Buffalo came up behind me. He was mad and yelling at me for drinking. I pushed him. He was standing on the edge of the tracks there, where the bank slopes down. I pushed him. I didn't think—I don't think I pushed him very hard, but he was wearing those stupid high-heeled cowboy boots and he was drunk, and there was gravel there on the edge of the tracks. He just went over backward. There was a big rock there. His head smacked on it, and then he just lay still. Sissy, I was surprised!"

"What did you do?"

"For a minute I just stood there waiting for him to get up. But he didn't, did he? So, I thought, you know, maybe I should turn him over on his side, in case, in case he should puke or something. So, he wouldn't choke to death on it. He was making a funny sound. Like he couldn't breathe or something. And he was limp. I got him over on his side, and then he just stopped breathing. Or he stopped making that sound anyway. There was blood running out of the back of his head where he hit on the rock. I didn't kill him! I didn't mean for him to die; it was an accident, Sissy, I swear it."

She leaned over sobbing on Sissy's shoulder.

"All right, all right," Sissy said, patting her. All right, but what was she going to tell Tom Holm? Nothing, that's what. Nothing. She would be a witness for Speedy and Melvin's wedding, but she would not be a witness for an FBI investigation. She would play and sing for the last dance at Batesland, then she would pack her things and go and never see Tom Holm again.

A banner above the entrance to the Batesland Community Center read: Harvest Dance. Never mind that it was a black-on-white banner that no one would be able to read after dark because the outside of the building was poorly lit and the parking lot not at all. Speedy rode up with Melvin, sitting close to him in his pickup. Melvin had beamed at the short ceremony earlier before JP Nels Nelson; Speedy giggled and hugged Sissy, thanking her for being a witness. The JP's wife was the other witness, a plump middle-aged woman who looked disapproving through the short ceremony read from Nelson's much-thumbed book. Melvin had asked Clayton to be his witness, but Clayton said he wouldn't be a party to it.

As she walked from the parking lot to the building, Sissy noticed many more of those bumper stickers that she had first noticed on cars at Scenic on the Fourth of July: *Red Power*. When the band was setting up, she looked out at the audience. Most of them were Indians, something she expected at Scenic or Interior, but not at Batesland, which was on the edge of the rez, but a town of White residents with mostly White farms and ranches surrounding it.

Clayton gave a thumbs-up and the band started their usual opening riff.

"Good evening ladies and gentlemen and welcome to the Batesland Annual Harvest Dance." He remembered to get that part in. "There's no place anywhere near this place, so this must be the place. We *are* the Red Bird All-Indian Traveling Band, here to play tonight for your listening and dancing pleasure. Here on my right, on the bass guitar, is that paragon of earthly virtue, that thumping, humping, bumping seriously grrrreaatt musician hailing from Jackson town, who never ate a carrot in his life, Rrrrabbbbittt Richards!"

Rabbit bunny-hopped around the stage, wrapping the cord to his bass around his left foot, but just before he was about to yank himself down or pull the plug out of the amplifier on the other end, he stopped and took a bow.

"*Annnddd* hailing from Jackson town, the hash-slinging, face-slapping, best guitar picker and singer in the state of South Dakota, Sisssyyy Robberrrts!"

Clayton had to stop including Sonny in Sissy's introduction since Rabbit had taken Sonny's place, but she was grateful that he had stopped referring to her as the best *girl* guitar picker. Sissy took her bow. As they swung into the first song, Rabbit stumbled a bit on the bass line, caught it with a little grimace and went on. Nobody in the audience seemed to notice, but an air of discomfort, of sullenness hung over the crowd. Couples pushed each other around the dance floor mechanically, with little of the usual good-humored laughter; people avoided eye contact. The two men and one woman who worked the taps and mixed drinks in the triangular booth at the corner of the room did so with little enthusiasm and no smiles. They took the orders, took the money, and shoved the drinks across the bar as if they were angry at having a job. At the exits, the bouncers stood balanced on their toes like runners waiting for the starting gun.

When the first break came, Sissy walked through the lobby to the restroom among people standing in clots of two or three, muttering to themselves or not speaking at all. A silent rain had fallen during the first music set, so now the lobby floor held a small pool of water from the open door, perhaps from a leaking roof. As she followed the muddy tracks back to the toilets, she noticed that the people in the crowd were mostly Indians, not usual here where the majority of the local residents were White. She heard whispers but couldn't make sense of what people were saying, except for a rumor that the bartenders were charging Indians more than White people for the same drinks, and some Indians had been refused service at all, when they weren't drunk, weren't disorderly.

Clayton scrapped the playlist for the second set, throwing in the happiest songs he could think of, eliminating "Kaw-Liga," but the crowd moved like excited electrons bouncing off each other. Sissy saw Tom Holm with Speedy at a table in the front, not relaxed as he sipped his beer. He sat up straight and watchful. Speedy held a Coke bottle by the neck in her lap. At the second break, Clayton made a circling motion with his hand, tilting his head toward the door. Rabbit and Sissy followed him to the door as Melvin tried to reach Speedy through the milling crowd. Holm gave Melvin a nod over the heads, put an arm around Speedy, and pushed her ahead of him toward Melvin.

Outside in Clayton's car, Melvin and Speedy and Rabbit crammed into the backseat with Clayton, Sissy and Tom Holm elbow to elbow in the front. The evening had turned very chilly for early September, but first frost was likely by the twentieth, Sissy's dad's birthday and the first day of pheasant-hunting season. The windshield fogged with the warmth of their breath.

"This place is a powder keg," Holm said. "One lit match and the whole place will go up."

"God damn it, it's getting so we can't play anywhere without chicken wire around the bandstand. Shit, there goes that new amp I just bought," Clayton said.

"Anybody bring anything to drink?" Rabbit asked.

"There's beer in the cooler in my pickup," Melvin said.

"Oh, *beer*." Rabbit made a disgusted sound.

"You can always go back inside and order a drink if you don't like the beer," Melvin said as he got out and walked to his parked pickup at the side of the building, past groups of people standing around talking. He manhandled the cooler out of the pickup and had started back when a mass of people, tangled and shouting, poured out of the double doors of the building, shoving into another group and another until they bumped up against him. He turned his back, sheltering the cooler, got shoved from behind, stumbled, and righted himself, carrying the cooler in front of his body like an offering.

"Oh, damn it," Holm said, jumping out of the car. "Come on!"

The thickening crowd shoved each other, shouted obscenities as Rabbit followed Holm through the crush. Rabbit grabbed the cooler while Holm took Melvin's arm, and they ran for the car, Rabbit using the cooler like a wedge.

Speedy opened the car door and jumped out, but Sissy was right behind her, grabbing her and pulling her back.

"You idiot!" Sissy yelled over the crowd roar. "You're going to get yourself trampled, then where will you be?"

Clayton moaned, "Oh shit, oh shit, there goes my new amp!"

Melvin piled into the backseat, Holm in the front, slamming and locking the doors on the passenger side while Rabbit wrestled with the beer cooler, finally getting himself into the backseat on the right side with the cooler on his lap. Clayton got the doors shut and locked on the driver's side. Somebody started throwing beer bottles and cans, then rocks that rained down on the roofs and the hoods and the trunks of the cars. A bottle hit Clayton's window with a loud crack.

"Roll down the windows," he yelled. "Get them down!"

"Shit! Why? And get beaned with a bottle?" Holm said.

"They can break out my back glass and my windshield, but I can at least save all the side windows," Clayton yelled. "I own a body shop, and I tell you, window glasses are expensive even at my cost." He rolled down his window, just as a full can of beer came sailing at him, hit him a glancing blow, and bounced back outside. He rolled his window back up.

"Waste of good brew," Rabbit said, calming as he cracked a beer of his own. "Nothing like beer if you can't get the real stuff."

Speedy sobbed loudly against Melvin's chest.

"I thought you were going to be killed," she bawled, as Melvin patted her and smiled.

"Saturday night in South Dakota," Holm said thoughtfully. "Makes me wish I was back in Oklahoma with the civilized tribes."

"Shut up," Sissy said. "At least we plains people fought. You guys got your asses kicked and shipped all the way from the east coast to Oklahoma."

"Ah, intertribal rivalry," Holm said, as the fights ranged up and down the aisles between the cars, between pairs of people, groups of people, Indians and Indians, Whites and Whites, Indians and Whites, men and women, men and men, women and women. Somebody yelled "*Red Power!*" and then the fights began in earnest. Right in front of the car, a big White man wearing a gimme cap took a swing at a pair of Indians, who ducked in opposite directions. One of them looked like he went down while the other one drove for the White man's guts with a fist, then the White guy dropped like a felled oak with the Indian men on top of him. Seconds later, another White man threw himself on top of the pile. The Indians got up laughing and slapping each other on the back. The second White man helped the first one up, holding a hand to a nose spurting red. Another Indian hit one of the first two Indians in the back of the head with a bottle and ran, but one of the other Indians tripped him, and he went down. A body slammed backward against Clayton's door, rolled to his front, and pushed himself off, leaving a muddy, bloody handprint on the window. A crumpling sound came as someone leaped from the back of the adjoining pickup onto the roof of Clayton's car then onto the hood and turned around spiderlike, looking through the window. Loretta looked through the window at them, her hair loose and sticking to her face, her blouse torn and muddy, face twisted in a grimace that slowly faded to a grin.

"Hey, Sissy," she said loudly. "How're you doing?"

Sissy gave her a little wave.

Loretta jumped down from the hood and came to the passenger-side window. Tom Holm looked at Sissy, who nodded. He rolled the window down.

"Some night, huh?" Loretta said, leaning her arms on the open window frame.

"It's pretty crazy, all right," Sissy said. "You okay?"

"Yeah, sure. I'm just getting warmed up. Red Power, ennit? Say, you guys got any beer?"

Rabbit cracked another beer, handed it across the seat to Sissy, who handed it to Loretta.

She took a long drink, saluted them, said, "See you later," and walked off. She took another long drink, then lobbed the beer at a couple of fighters on the ground. "Fuck you, you sonsabitches!"

A light, cold rain had begun to fall again, then heavier.

"Jeezus, what a waste of beer," Rabbit mourned.

"Clayton," Sissy said, "I quit."

"What! What? Why? What do you mean, you quit? In the all the years you've been singing and playing with the Red Birds, this is the first time anything like this bad has ever happened. What the hell you quitting for now?"

"I'm not quitting because of this," she said, gesturing at the riot in front of them.

"Then why? Why?"

"I got a few things I want to do with my life," she said.

"Well, well, uh," Clayton sputtered. "What am I going to do for a singer and a rhythm player? You can't do this."

"You got a damned good singer who can learn rhythm pretty fast," Sissy said.

"Who, who?" Clayton hooted.

"Think about it," she said.

EPILOGUE

KEARNEY, NEBRASKA
SATURDAY, OCTOBER 25, 1969

I came home to Auntie Iris's house from working at a nice little café by the college. The work was familiar; I liked my fellow waitresses, even the little weasel of a cook who whined all the time about everything but was a softie at heart. I picked up the mail from the dining room table and thumbed through, looking for a letter from Mom that wasn't there but instead found a letter addressed to me in a neat rounded hand. I slit it open with a finger.

> *Dear Sissy,*
>
> *I hope you are well and that you find whatever you are looking for.*
>
> *The Buffalo Ames case is closed. I <u>know</u>. Thanks for all your help, even if you didn't meant to help. The FBI has a fund for such things.*
>
> *If you ever want to try a different school, the University of Oklahoma is pretty good. My wife and I have a spare bedroom. She's always been good about rescuing strays, and she already knows you aren't civilized. Good luck.*
>
> *Tom Holm*

Enclosed was a stiff blue government check with those little squares randomly punched in it. The amount was two thousand dollars. I started to tear it up, but instead I put it in the back of my dresser drawer. Two weeks later, I put it in my checking account. It paid for most of my first year's tuition and books. Tuition and books were not as expensive back in 1970 . . .

YEARS LATER

I love music. I love the way that it takes me to a different place, a better place where I can be anyone I want to be, where there are roads leading to other places just over the hill or around the bend, but that is my *special*, my refuge. I had sense enough to realize that if I did that for a living, that would diminish it, make it everyday and usual, and I would lose the wonder and the anticipation of greater things. I got a degree in sociology and became a counselor because people always talked to me, and I decided that if I had to listen to everyone's problems and help them figure out their lives, I might as well get paid for doing it.

They tell me bad things that sometimes make me uncomfortable to know, the meannesses they've done, the evil thoughts they've had, the times when they've lain awake at night afraid that someone will find out things they wouldn't even confess to their priest, and the things that evil people have done to them. They never realize that when they have told me, then someone does know the terrible things they did or thought or how little they felt and helpless when a terrible thing was done to them. Sometimes—it used to be usually—they're drunk when they tell me, but most times the people who confess their foibles are sitting in my blue-carpeted office, stone cold sober. I used to believe it's a curse I have, to be the listener, but it's a blessing, too, a gift that I see my own daughter has inherited. Her friends come to her to mediate their arguments, even over something as simple as to how to fairly divide one candy bar between them. I overheard a conversation where one of her friends told another whose grandmother had just died that she should go talk to my daughter. She never gives advice, but they all seem to leave feeling better about whatever was bothering them. They see her as something other than what she is. She hates it. She is a human wailing wall, a wall where people poke confessions into the crevices. Sometimes it helps.

On the rare weekend, I still play my guitar and sing, but no longer with the Red Bird All-Indian Traveling Band, and when I sing "House of the Rising Sun," I think, *Take* that, *Clayton!*